BRAZEN

Mo Shines

QBORO BOOKS
WWW.QBOROBOOKS.COM
"QBB – We write them hot books! You didn't know?"

Q-BORO BOOKS
Jamaica, Queens NY 11431
WWW.QBOROBOOKS.COM
(For store orders, author information and contact information Please Visit
Our Website for the most up to date listing)

ISBN 0-9753066-5-0
First Printing April 2005
Library of Congress Control Number: 2005902615

"Scripture taken from the HOLY BIBLE, NEW INTERNATIONAL
VERSION Copyright © 1973, 1978, 1984 International Bible Society.
Used by permission of Zondervan Bible Publishers."

*This is a work of fiction. It is not meant to depict, portray or represent
any particular real persons. All the characters, incidents and dialogues
are the products of the author's imagination and are not to be construed
as real. Any references or similarities to actual events, entities, real
people, living or dead, or to real locales are intended to give the novel a
sense of reality. Any similarity in other names, characters, entities, places
and incidents is entirely coincidental.*

Cover Photo & Art - Copyright © 2005 by Mo Shines - all rights reserved
Cover Concept - Mo Shines
Cover Photography – Charles A. Brown
Cover Design – Candace K. Cottrell
Editors – Shonell Bacon and Lissa Woodson

This book is dedicated to my father Kenneth Chavis and the rest of my family members who have passed: my grandfather Lawrence Chavis; my grandfather Walter Hardy; my stepbrother Jamal Fletcher; Merrianne "Mom" Fletcher; and James W. Fletcher.

I know God is using all of you as my guardian angels.

ACKNOWLEDGMENTS

First and foremost, I would like to thank GOD, the creator of Heaven and Earth, for this blessing. You are my rock, my fortress and my deliverer. Thanks for never forsaking me.

Thanks to my beautiful faithful wife and partner Jenny. You're my strength when I'm weak. Thanks for always believing in me. We've been together 12 years but this is just the beginning. We still have a long prosperous life ahead of us.

To my loving and caring mother Benita. You have always been there for me no matter what. Because of you I've always been rich in love. You are a strong beautiful black woman who always puts my happiness before your own and I salute you. To my stepfather Jeff thanks for the tough love growing up. It definitely made me stronger.

To my bright and beautiful sister Nicole, you are my heart. Keep dreaming and stay focused. God has so many wonderful things planned for your life. To my brother Lance (God is walking with you.) To my goddaughters, Ariana, Mya and my godson, Jeremiah.

To my publisher Mark Anthony (Thanks for believing in me!!! You're a man of ya word.) and the rest of my Q-boro family, Kiniesha Gayle, Anna J., Erick S. Gray, Nakea, Candace K. Cottrell, DeJon, Vonetta Pierce, Gerald Malcom.

To my grandmothers, Mary Hardy and Bessie Chavis. To my uncles, Walter Hardy and James Fletcher and his wife, aunt Dee. To my loving aunt Renee (you've done so much for me). To my cousins, Tishana (throwin' them bows), Thea (stop lookin' so mean), Bonnie, Bernard "Ultra"(NASCAR ain't ready for you!), Rosette, Susan and Barbara Randall, Araynia

(Keep shining bright) and Colin Fletcher (You're one talented cat.), Todd, LaDaz (I ain't forget about you couz'), Big Dee and Brent.

To the rest of my extended family in Arkansas (the Credit family), South Carolina (the Chavis, Watson, and Deidre family), North Carolina (the Hardy family), Atlanta and Virginia. To my godparents, "Papa" & "Mama" Lucas and my godsisters, Glenda and Bonnie.

To my mother-in-law Clara Faris (Thanks for always believing in me). My sister-in-law Dawn a.k.a Ms. Pink (Stay strong. God is with you.), Andy, Tito. To my father-in-law Jun and his beautiful wife Elba Pellot (We're forever grateful.), Andre, Edger and his wife.

To my Grits & Butter family, J-Hard (keep selling, playa!), Stephanie Pierce (you're a marketing genius!), T.C. (always ready to ride or die.), Candace (book cover/website designer), Charles Brown (Photographer), Shaun Mixon (Model on cover) and my editor Lissa Woodson (you're the best).

To my One Hood family, V-Nice (one of the illest holdin' a mic.), Temoe (you'se a smooth cat.) and Dale (my nigga!). It's our turn to shine. Let's get it!

Thanks to all my peoples, Vincent (my brother from another mother.), T.C. (my brother from another mother), Dre (you'll always be my nigga!), John "7TH Emp" (the industry still ain't ready for your gritty beats.) Rubin "Jun" and Tineisha, Lee "Lexus", Carl Slater, C.L. (the black cowboy), Tanell (Thanks for editing the script) and Lee Davis, Mookie (219th), Carl "Doe" Harrington, Karl Blackford, Kevin Dalton (Ya'll my niggaz fa life.), Swizz Beatz, Ricardo and Reggie, Black Mike, Ant, Eric Sapp (One of the hottest authors livin'.), Pat "Offbeat", Nicety (Roc-A-Fella), Aaron, Claudie-Bee (Roc-A-Fella), V-Lou, BaShaun, Dee-Low, Joe Wrecka, Big Will—NJ

(Keep shinin'), Reggie Scott and Jeff Friday—FilmLife (thanks for the opportunity.), Derrick Williams, Royce "My Block Films" (Holla at me!), Melissa (FilmLife), Johniee Walker (Nabfeme), T-Weapons, Logan Coles, Kev "Benz", K.B., Bailey, Mimms, Nelson, Craig (VZ), Kinnard, Jeff, Ron and Keith(Killa Queens), Brenda, O.C., Ebony (MindBodyHair Salon), Robbin (Creative Hair Designs), Chico, Wayne.

And to anybody I forgot to mention, my apologies.

"And because lawlessness will abound, the love of many will grow cold."

Matthew 24:12

PROLOGUE

A BNN newscaster gives a news update: "During a time when cops throughout New York City are trying to recover from a scarred image of over excessive brutality, along with out-right murder and unbridled corruption, one man has come forward, painting an enthralling and honest depiction of the war happening in the inner-city. His gritty, urban tale pulls you into the depths of police corruption within the so-called ghettos of New York revealing the deceit, violence, drugs and blood money hidden behind the blue wall of silence. This is the dark side of the force certain media outlets refuse to show you. It'll leave you wondering who you really need protection from the cops or the drug dealers. It's all coming up in our following segment after these messages."

CHAPTER 1

"Watch the gate!" The correction officer shouted as the heavy-duty steel bars slammed shut, echoing off the concrete walls of Marion Federal Prison. This hellhole happened to be a top-level maximum-security facility where only the most notorious and violent prone criminals, murderers and predators from across the nation were warehoused in the massive federal system. At one point in time even The Godfather, extradited from his mafia crew in New York, had the unwanted privilege of residing here a few years back.

Now that the hardened criminals were behind the five layers of electric fence, three layers of brick walls, and over four miles of inside wiring and alarms, most of the people in suburban America could sleep comfortably, if not peacefully. But unknown to them, sometimes the criminals and the police were one and the same. And the dirty cops managed to stay outside of these walls.   Well, at least most of them. Unfortunately the folks in urban America know this first hand.

The uptight beefy white CO sporting dark shades and a military crew cut was manning the gate from a control room that sat three feet off to the side.   Reinforced shatterproof glass encased the booth giving him a panoramic view of the hallway.   Sweat dripped from his wrinkled brow due to the sweltering heat as a little fan clamped onto the metal desk struggled to create a breeze on this particularly hot July day. Chewing on a toothpick poking out the corner of his mouth, he turned the key to the OFF position on the control panel.

Past the steel bars sat a long, dimly lit, main corridor. An orderly group of convicts rocking prison issued greens strolled down the east end toward one of the many awaiting cellblocks. A few white boys were sprinkled here and there, but mostly Black and Hispanic brothers dominated the incarcerated pack.   Not unusual in the American judicial system. A system designed by America's founding fathers— the same thieving bastards that slaughtered, raped and almost wiped out the entire Indian population in order to conquer their precious land and profit off their natural resources. Now the natural resources were prisoners, men of all walks of life who had come to the end of the road, or at least to a place where they would spend the rest of their natural lives.

The inmates shuffled along in two lines, shoulder to shoulder, fifteen men deep almost like a military formation while weary eyed, COs with potbellies and cocky attitudes, watched and controlled their movements.

The guards were so comfortable in their control, so comfortable in the rhythm of the place that they caught up on things as they walked the row.

"Hey, did you catch the game?" The chunky CO asked in his Puerto Rican accent.

"Nah…I was too busy waxin' some ass last night," The muscular CO replied with a huge cheesy grin spreading across his caramel face.

"I been married over twelve years and don't even get to smell it anymore." The other CO chuckled. "I might as well be locked up with the rest of these pricks."

They held everyday conversation that convicts were reluctant to hear about. The kind of normal activity that had once been a part of their lives, but they were now reluctant to voice. Actually, the grim faced cons hardly spoke to one another and the few who did, spoke in hushed whispers. No talking during movement happened to be one of the facilities many strict, yet petty rules and regulations prisoners had to deal with. If the COs wanted to be assholes, they could take away a disruptive inmate's phone privileges and shut down the packages they were allowed to receive from the outside world in retaliation.

Then, of course, there was always "the hole." It's the ultimate seclusion from the rest of the prison world, a place where loneliness reigned supreme and dark nights tend to be unbearable. A man couldn't get any closer to hell.

In cellblock "F," a dark narrow corridor cut through the housing area with ragged cramped cells running down both sides. Locked in cell-3 was an inmate cropped up on a worn cot tucked in the darkness, pulling on half a Newport. A shaft of light crept through the gated slit of a so-called window into the gloomy, confined, eight-by-ten concrete box. The stale air stood still since no breeze circulated due to the sealed off windows.

This hardened convict was Sean Coleman, twenty-eight and ruggedly good-looking. His chiseled medium-sized structure was draped in prison greens. He stood, stretched his five-foot, eleven-inch, 190-pound frame, then crossed to the iron gate, stepping from the shadows into a beam of light that cut across the gloomy cell. Stress lines etched in his caramel-colored face made him appear slightly older than his true years. His jet-black hair was cropped into a low-cut wavy Caesar, which blended perfectly into his five o'clock shadow.

Gripping the cold cell bars with his sweaty palms, he stared past them, and blew a cloud of blackish-gray smoke through his nostrils. His toughened yet sad, dark brown eyes told the story of a man with a troubled past weighing heavy on his broad shoulders. A dirty mouse scurried along the shiny shellacked floor into one of the cells on the other side of the tier where a stocky white male with a baldhead and a shit load of tattoos was grinding out a set of push-ups.

The continuous and often deafening, piercing whistles and cat-calls being shouted back and forth from cell to cell by many of the restless inmates echoed throughout the entire tier. Loud noise was just one of those things Sean had to deal with in prison. And the sickening smells of sweat, urine and feces? Forget about it.

"Hey, Sean, let a playa beg a smoke," an inmate asked from the next cell over, his tattooed forearms hanging out of the bars.

"Here," Sean said, passing the lit cigarette through the bars.

The inmate grabbed the cancer stick. "Good lookin', playa."

Suddenly the steel door to the security bubble cracked open and a CO with the looks and size of Arnold Schwarzenegger stepped into the cellblock. As soon as the CO's steel toe boots hit the concrete, all the loud talking quickly dropped about twenty decimals. The CO's heavy footsteps echoed off the ground as he made his way down the corridor toward Sean's cell. As he continued past numerous cells, the low whispers of conversation carried through the tier where a few hours later its unwilling residents would fall into either a dreamless or nightmarish sleep.

The CO stopped right in front of Sean's cell. Sean tossed him a respectful nod, but didn't say a word.

"You got mail," the CO informed him slipping an envelope through the bars. The CO's piercing icy blue eye's scanned his cell for a moment.

"Thanks," Sean replied, taking the mail. He glanced at the name: *Lisa Coleman*, then tossed it onto the cot. It was from his wife. They hadn't spoken in months—not because she didn't want to. The decision was Sean's alone.

The CO headed back up the tier and disappeared out of sight as the steel door that separated him from the inmate housing area slammed shut behind him.

Scanning the dark corridor, Sean's mind drifted. A man could take two roads in life—one narrow, one broad. As a police officer, he took an oath to serve and protect. But somehow the lines between right and wrong became fuzzy. Somewhere along his journey to "serve and protect" he lost his path, not to mention his soul. Before facing the ultimate betrayal and ending up behind bars, Sean was an undercover cop with over three long years in NYPD, dedicated to upholding the law and putting a stop to police corruption.

Pushed to the limit by jealousy and blinded by the rage engulfing his broken heart, he finally exploded and in that same instance, he flushed what was left of his fucked up life down the drain. All for the bittersweet taste of revenge.

Six months prior to his downfall, Sean had been recruited by an old friend and partner of his deceased stepfather from Internal Affairs and sent in undercover to bring down a couple of corrupt narcs from the Bronx ripping off local drug dealers. And that was the beginning of his end.

CHAPTER 2

Six months earlier, in January, on a late and chilly evening in Saint Mary's City Park, tucked into the corner of 149th Street and St. Ann's in the South Bronx, the dark green Jeep Cherokee with jet-black tints cruised the area slowly. Over the years it had become a bare shell of the "great park" it once was. The city just let the place slowly wither away from the lush landscape, flourishing oak trees and brand new playgrounds, into a mess of cracked cement pathways and pothole stricken basketball courts with bent rims and missing nets to the filthy broken water fountain that the derelicts pissed on. St. Mary's was now a haven for the zombie-like junkies that lurked in the shadows shooting up and getting high on dope.

Even a day-old corpse wouldn't want to be caught around these parts after sundown. Unfortunately too many lifeless bodies were found here, either riddled with bullet holes or stab wounds. This part of town was treacherous and it had a deadly past due mostly to the Wild Cowboys, a group of murderous drug dealers that use to control the hood by any means necessary. By now most of them were either dead, strung out or in prison for life.

Near the splintered wooden benches at the center of the park, a group of rowdy looking knuckleheaded teens, all rocking the standard street gear and various styles of Timberland boots, huddled together in a semi-circle, watching two kids go at each other's throat in a heated freestyle battle. The immediate area surrounding the noisy gathering was darker than the rest of the park due to a broken lamppost overhead and the fact that winter nights seem to come earlier each day. After every couple of hot bars spat by the two dueling MC's, a couple of spectators in the bunch barked, "oohhs!" and "aahhs!" The leaves rustled in the various trees scattered throughout the park as a cold breeze danced back and forth through the area.

Bobby, a chubby, nineteen year old Puerto Rican wannabe thug, sporting a backwards navy blue and red "NY" fitted cap, urged on the skinny dark-skin kid who was spitting some ferocious lyrics in the other rapper's screwed up face. He was totally oblivious to the trouble awaiting him.

Bobby had definitely eaten one too many cheeseburgers in his short lifetime and the big round belly protruding through his red G-Unit shirt showed every extra pound. He was the mini-me version of his older sibling José, St. Ann's HNIC—Head Nigga in Charge.

The Cherokee rolled up the weathered asphalt roadway only authorized departmental vehicles were supposed to use. The brakes squeaked slightly as it jerked to a stop. Suddenly the high beams popped on, illuminating the group of teens. Their eyes quickly shrunk to squints under the intensity of the blaring lights hitting their pupils.

The two teens in the very center stopped their heated battle as both doors cracked open and two plainclothes narcs exited the Cherokee.

"Fuck these pigs want?" a big-nosed Arab looking kid spoke, the words carrying across the concrete to the alert ears of one of the cops.

Detective Jay Robinson, in his early forties with a muscular build, dark brown skin and chiseled good looks stepped out, popping an Altoid mint in his mouth. His deep-set, ice-cold brown eyes scanned the teens along with the rest of the perimeter. He stood a little over six feet and weighed about just over two hundred pounds; his dark skin and baldhead glowed beneath the only working streetlight. He focused his gaze, relishing that his search for one boy in particular would now pay off.

Jay spotted Bobby in the rear of the group and headed for the teens, gliding with the confidence only a man with a badge affords. Not to mention the .40 caliber Smith & Wesson tucked in the black leather holster strapped to his waist, hidden behind the aged, all-black, camouflage jacket.

Warren, his ex-partner and fellow detective, followed right behind him, wearing a scruffy beard and long cropped thick blonde hair that brushed the shoulders of his worn out leather coat that looked like it was from the early 80's. Nearing forty, and a little over 170 pounds, his somewhat vacant blue beady eyes revealed a troubled soul lurking beneath. The silent but deadly type, he was all business—and the perfect partner in crime.

Their Captain had split them up a few months prior due to all the complaints and media attention they were generating at one point in time. But the duo still managed to work together unofficially when it was time to handle their business in the streets.

A few of the teens caught a quick glimpse of the stainless steel .38 tucked into Warren's leather shoulder holster as he adjusted his coat and flipped up the weathered collar to ward off the bitter cold nipping at his exposed neck.

Jay, a twenty-year veteran of the narcotics division, knew the streets like the back of his hand. Thanks to the city's low pay scale his optimism had been chipped away after spending years watching drug dealers make tons of fast cash while he and fellow officers struggled to make ends meet. Presently, he was riding a thin line between justice and the seedier side of life. Deeply entrenched in murders and extortion, there was truly no turning back. At this point it was all or nothing. And Jay happened to be playing to win.

"Shit, rap's definitely headed down da fuckin' tubes," Jay said sarcastically, half-glancing at Warren as they approached the awaiting group. "Nowadays, every snot-nosed drop-out swears he's Rakim. Back in da days MCs were literate."

Finding humor in the stale remark, Warren shot him a sly little smirk in agreement.

Jay headed straight for Bobby. "Let's talk," he demanded, locking eyes with the frightened boy. "The rest of you pricks get lost." He turned, scanning the other teens lingering around. "Go read a book or somethin'."

Warren stood off to the side, covering Jay's ass, just in case one of the teens decided to get stupid. One hand on his gun, he was ready to take action.

Warren's story was exactly the same as Jay's, except he only had twelve years in. And as far as Jay knew, Warren had been in and out of rehab three times within the last two years for sucking on that plastic dick—smoking crack took a front seat to everything else. Not to mention, he also had a hard-on for booze and snorting coke. But as a partner, and especially with the kind of shit Jay was into, he couldn't have asked for a better *partner in crime*. Warren was game for whatever as long as it involved making cash.

The teens stared at the two officers for only a few seconds. This kind of police harassment was normal. The group quickly split up and hurried off in different directions not wanting any more trouble with the renegade cops. Bobby ran trembling fingers through his curly hair sticking out from under his cap as he watched his friends scurry out of the park and into the night without him. Sudden beads of sweat broke out on his forehead. One of his homeboys, Slim, who got the nickname because he was practically skin and bones, was a loyal friend and stayed behind, hesitant to leave Bobby's side.

"Hard of hearin', li'l fuck?" Jay inquired, coldly eyeing Slim.

Slim's dark brown eyes darted to his crisp white Nike airs, as he shook his head and hurriedly bopped away. Jay's gaze traveled over Bobby a few moments without saying a word. This technique usually unnerved every fronting ass thug before interrogation. That icy glare of Jay's seemed to peer into the depths of Bobby's soul and the painfully long silence that went along with it soon had Bobby wiping his sweaty palms on the back of his baggy jeans. He thought about running, but it wouldn't do him any good. With the white cop standing so close behind him, he didn't have a chance of getting away.

The brisk breeze whipping through the park sent two empty soda bottles rolling around on the concrete just as the blaring music coming from a silver Camry with two hoodlums slumped way back in their seats zoomed pass drowning out the silence briefly. If things went as planned, by the time Jay started tossing question after question in his lap, the boy's nerves would be a total fucking wreck.

"You know me don't ya, Bobby?" Jay asked abruptly in a sinister tone that made Bobby wince, his frosted breath expelling into the air as he looked into the cops haunting eyes.

With a knot of fear growing deep in the pit of his stomach, Bobby quickly nodded and spat out, "You dat *detective*." He inched back, his eyes widening with panic.

Obviously, he definitely knew the cop with the crazed look in his eyes. This was the same crazy narc that tried to extort money from his big brother José a few weeks ago. He had a real bad rep in the hood. Rumor on the street had it that Jay was a bloodthirsty corrupt pig who left at least four niggers on ice within the past year alone. Murder was definitely the case.

"Good," Jay said flatly. "Then we can skip the intro." Jay leaned in close. "Be upfront wit' me and you straight. Lie, it won't be a good thang." He jabbed his index finger into Bobby's heaving chest. "We understand each other?"

Bobby nodded so hard his head almost popped off his husky shoulders.

Just then both of their police walkie-talkies crackled to life, "Car fifty-one, respond to 161st street and Grand Concourse. Reports of shots fired."

Within a matter of seconds, "Copy that, car fifty-one responding," an officer replied over the airwaves. Then the police radios went silent again.

"Good. Where ya brotha José hidin'?" Jay asked, his penetrating stare burning holes through Bobby's corneas.

"I. . . I don't know." Bobby stuttered lying, shifting nervously back and forth on his heels. Jay followed the boy's gaze, which was locked on Slim who had just hurried across the street and disappeared into the night. There wasn't another soul anywhere in sight along the deserted block or in the rest of the gloomy park. Only Bobby and the two-hardball narcs stood out in the freezing weather. His dark brown eyes quickly dotted back to Jay's intimidating glare.

Sizing Bobby up, Jay knew he had the kid totally shaken from his jerky body language and the sweat trickling down his cheeks on one of the coldest nights that week.

"Come on. I just wanna talk to him." Jay urged inching even closer until his nose was almost pressed to Bobby's broad snout. So close that Bobby got hit with a whiff of hot, cigarette breath and the smell of the beer Jay and Warren had downed prior to pulling up.

"I told you, I don't know," Bobby said, edging back slightly. Watery eyes dropped to his cream and broccoli

Timberland Chukkas as he tried to avoid making more eye contact with Jay.

"Ya brother hasn't been payin' taxes," Jay informed him, slightly irritated by the kid's blatant lies. He stepped back a little, reached into his jacket pocket, pulled out a syringe containing a brownish liquid.

Bobby gasped, taking in a long, slow breath. Warren scanned left, then right, but held his ground just behind the frightened boy so he couldn't run without getting caught.

Sliding off the plastic cap covering the tip, Jay gave the needle a few taps with his index finger.

"This poison he's pushin' has fiends droppin' left and right," Jay said, gazing at the swirling concoction inside the plastic tube.

Suddenly, Jay reached out, clutching Bobby's shaking hand in one of his huge palms. He immediately gave it a forceful twist upward and held Bobby's limb crab-locked in an excruciating position.

A whimpering sound escaped Bobby's thick lips.

Jay knew from experience that the grip would send immense pain shooting straight up Bobby's left arm, right up into the shoulder blades.

Instinctively, Bobby tried to pull out of Jay's vice grip. Warren stepped in to help out his partner by wrapping his huge arm around Bobby's neck, applying the illegal chokehold cops were forced to stop using a few years back.

"Cool down, kid," Warren snarled as he applied even more pressure to Bobby's already compressed throat, only adding to the debilitating pain already pulsating throughout his body.

The wind kicked up suddenly making Jay's coat flap open somewhat as he watched Bobby begin struggling to breathe.

Reluctantly, Bobby stopped resisting, gasping for much needed air. He knew he only had two choices: give in or choke to death. And Bobby loved living so he chose life. Or so he thought.

The boy's body relaxed as he quit struggling. Warren eased up a little on the headlock so the kid could catch his breath. Bobby sucked in as much oxygen as his weed-damaged lungs could possibly handle. At that second, he was just relieved to finally be breathing.

"The good book says, lyin' is a sin." Taking advantage of the moment, Jay jabbed the sharp needle into Bobby's twisted arm. "And ya know, Bobby, sin only leads to death."

"Yo, what'cha doin'?" Bobby winced, his voice cracking from the sting of the sharp needle piercing his skin.

"Sendin' a message, Bobby," Jay replied, and with a press of his thumb flushed the heroin into the boy's bloodstream. "Sendin' a message."

Within seconds the dope took effect and Bobby was lost in the high. Disoriented, his legs wobbled and folded. Jay and Warren quickly propped Bobby up on one of the empty benches.

Deep down inside, Jay had grown weary of this kind of shit. There were times when even he couldn't stand the horrible monster he had become. But whenever the thoughts popped into his mind, he quickly shrugged it off and stayed focused on the bigger picture—money. He wanted to retire and put his treacherous double life in the streets behind him. The only problem was he still needed a little more time to fatten his nest egg. Besides the $250,000 already stashed away, he planned on making his exit with at least seven hundred and fifty grand.

Jay also had to worry about the bigwig downtown. He was short-changing him on the payoffs and hoped that he wouldn't find out and expose Jay's corrupted ways. Since Jay felt it was next to impossible for the pencil-pushing higher-up who sat behind a desk all day in a cozy office to know exactly how much cash he took in on each and every shakedown, Jay assumed he could get away with stiffing him on most of it. Bad decision. Payback is always a bitch. And if the suit wearing peckerwood was already hip to Jay's bullshit scheme, he'd take Jay down faster than a whore changes panties.

"The kid's cooked," Warren stated flatly, eyeing Jay. "Let's get outta here."

"Would you relax, snowflake," Jay replied with a sinister chuckle while his eyes scanned the surrounding area making sure there were no witnesses around. "You scared of ya own shadow."

"Kiss my pale ass," Warren joked. "I enjoy my freedom."

At that particular moment, Warren was just itching for another hit of that rock but couldn't let Jay catch wind. Last time Jay went ballistic and as far as he knew Warren was still clean. Jay hoped he planned on keeping it that way. No matter how many times he tried to kick the habit, the rush just kept calling him back. Fuck it. Warren had already accepted the fact that he was a stone-cold addict. Besides, a hit here and there helped him escape the harsh realities of being a failed father, husband and corrupt cop with way too much blood on his hands. Unfortunately, there was nothing that Jay could use, smoke, drink or take that would help him escape the same.

Bobby's eyes rolled into the back of his head. The empty needle still stuck in his vein.

Bobby's drug infested body began to convulse. The cold air fanned back and forth with every wave of his numb hands. After a few more violent jerks he went limp and fell over, crashing onto the cold hard pavement. Drool rolled from the corner of his mouth, down his chin and trickled onto the cement. His lifeless eyes watched as Jay and Warren calmly strutted back to the idling Cherokee, climbed in and coasted off down the hill.

CHAPTER 3

The same night on Simpson Avenue in the South Bronx, the Right Look clothing store sat tucked in the midst of a busy shopping stretch. The mannequins in the picture windows were dipped from head to toe in the latest fashions from Roc-A-Wear, Sean John and other hot designers. Mom and pop stores that sold everything from 99-cent goods to electronic equipment and jewelry lined the crowded commercial block.

A few customers browsed through the aisles of Right Look, tried on clothes under the watchful eyes of security, and made purchases at the main counter. Rap music pulsated through the store as a young African kid sporting a New York Mets baseball hat pulled low over his eyes sold mix-CDs from a glass-top counter near the front entrance.

Suddenly an argument near the dressing rooms broke the peaceful tranquility.

"Bitch, you betta put dat dress right back down where I left it!" The skinny Puerto Rican chic hollered at the slim black girl holding the denim dress she had left on the chair outside of her changing booth.

"Who you calling a bitch, hoe!" The black girl barked, still clutching the dress. "Come make me!" Closing in on each other, they both were ready to go toe to toe.

Behind the huge, clear-coated cherry wood counter at the rear of the store, José, a three hundred pound Puerto Rican gangster in his early-thirties, quickly interrupted them both.

"Easy, easy ladies, ya'll too sexy to be scraping," he injected, defusing the heated situation. "I have another dress that size in the back. And if ya'll behave, I'll give ya'll ten percent off."

He turned to his young, cute sassy female employee, Tishana, as she rung up a flashy black male customer.

"When you finish," he said, "get her the dress."

She acknowledged him with a sly smirk.

José could have been Fat Joe's twin with his golden skin, wide smile, huge frame and all. A diamond encrusted chain and medallion with the word *Crack* flooded with even more ice, swung from his monstrous neck with the name "José" tattooed in black script letters, glistening beneath the ceiling lights. As the neighborhood kingpin, whenever any serious hustlers from outside his circle needed grams, pounds or keys of weed, coke, crack or heroin, they came to him cause he had the best prices in town.

When it came to José's violently controlled territory, his team, and *only* his team supplied all the low-level dealers within his well-established borders. Copping weight from outsiders was a major no-no. Anyone caught breaking that number one rule was dealt with brutally by one of José's many and willing heartless soldiers.

But at the moment, his mind wasn't on his mainstream line of business. Nicole had just strolled through the glass door as if she owned the joint.

"Keep it up," José bellowed. "One day I'ma stop playin' and fire ya late ass."

"You always poppin' in late," she replied, rolling her eyes, then tossing her hands on her slim hips, knowing full well she had struck a nerve.

"I can do dat, ma, it's *my* store," José retorted playfully and before he could say another word she flipped him the bird.

"I'ma spank dat ass, girl. Keep that shit up."

"As long as you spank it with—"

"Hey," he said, holding his finger to her lips. "Keep that shit down. I don't want everybody after the good shit."

She laughed, tossing her braided hair over her shoulders as she walked away.

With Nicole behind the cash register, José strolled to the window. His eyes scanned the dark street, the busy mall and the customers headed for his store. A cocksure grin spread across his face as he mentally calculated the purchases the two women in the fitting room would make. Life was good.

José's prosperous kingdom ran north to south stretching from 134th street to damn near 174th street. From east to west, it ran from the edge of the Harlem River into the depths of the Sound View area. Taking over the area took balls, a lot of dead bodies and regular payoffs to the cops.

Maintaining control of his prime real estate wasn't a game. There were no discussions or debates when it came to settling disagreements or disputes, just bloodshed. Democracy held no place in the streets of the Bronx. It was a total dictatorship.

José's mind flashed back to a misfortune run-in with one of his last competitors.

It happened last March on a cool afternoon on Webster Avenue. A rowdy bunch of noisy eight-graders made their way past a tall, rail-thin, dark skinned Dread with his thick matted locks tucked under a red, yellow and green knitted cap who was leaned up against a poor excuse for a grocery store, which was really a front for a new smoke spot. The rusty weathered awning-hanging overhead could use replacing along with the graffiti sprawled windows in front of the store.

A chilly gush of wind whipped through the block, rustling the Dread's acid wash jean jacket. He lit up a pregnant joint and inhaled deeply. Holding the smoke in for what seemed like an eternity, he blew the grayish-white smoke through his dark lips. His eyes were blood shot from all the weed he was blazing.

A sexy coco-brown sister with short curly braids exited the smoke spot with her pearly whites showing.

"Tell ya boy stop tripping." She laughed jokingly. "He know he can't handle this." Her blue jeans hugged her juicy thighs like spandex. Her 34-28-38 frame was stacked like three extra thick buttermilk pancakes and her angelic sculptured face was the strawberry topping. Her wide hypnotizing hips swayed with every step she took.

"But me sure can, sexy," Dread replied scanning her from head to toe. Without breaking stride, she crossed to her cherry red Ford Expedition and climbed in. A fly red-bone chick was in the passenger seat, grooving to a rap song on the radio. Turning up the music full blast, she pulled off, blending in with the flow of traffic.

A few seconds later, a mineral gray BMW 745i outfitted with twenty-inch Antera rims wrapped in Pirelli low profile tires sped up and slowed to a screeching stop in front of the store. José and Chico hopped out with a sense of urgency, quickly closing in on Dread. Stopping within a few feet of the Jamaican, José stared at him a few seconds before speaking. From the menacing expression etched on his mug, Dread was going to have a big problem. If he was nervous, he damn sure didn't show it, continuing to tote on his steadily decreasing joint.

"What up, Dread," José snapped with a sinister sneer. One of his eyebrows cocked as he stood there with a sly smirk. His fitted cap was pulled low over his eyes, and he was dressed in black army pants, hoodie and gloves. His expensive jewelry was suspiciously absent. Chico held down José's rear, surveying the people and different stores on the block.

The Dread's bloodshot eyes locked on the big angry looking Puerto Rican and his muscular sidekick who was sporting all black like his boss. "Wha' ta go on?"

José gave the store a good once over.

"This a nice little spot ya got here," José said, taking notice of the light-brown Jamaican cat with the build of a linebacker eyeing the three of them from behind the bulletproof glass partition that enclosed the counter and cut off the rest of the rear from the front of the store. It made it next to impossible to rob the spot unless someone was lucky enough to catch them slipping with the bulletproof door open.

Still toting on the joint, the Dread continued to eye him down, blowing a trail of smoke through his broad nostrils. His lips crawled into a taunting leer.

"I guess I wasn't taken serious," José said, clapping his palms together, "when I told ya'll all this was mines." José finished, pointing up and down the block.

"Boy, wha' ya chat bout?" Dread snickered, sucking his teeth. Tossing his joint to the concrete, he crushed it under the sole of his brown British Knights.

"What I chat 'bout, nigga?" José barked. In a blink of an eye, his black .45 was staring Dread square in the face. "Fuck that Jamaican shit, you in America now, nigga."

Remaining calmer than Bill Clinton during the Monica Lewinsky scandal, Dread replied, "Do wha' ya gon' do," without so much as batting an eye. His dark lips curled into a devilish smirk, taunting José.

Not wanting to disappoint him, José fired. The first slug shattered Dread's left eye as the second bullet chewed through the flesh of his jaw. Blood and brain matter spattered the storefront window behind his head while the rest of the carnage rained down onto the concrete sidewalk. Dread's soul had departed before his face smashed into the ground. Screams could be heard up and down the block as everyone in the immediate vicinity scrambled to safety. This kind of shit was normal in the hood, where its residents survive off fast reflexes.

Grinning from ear to ear, José leaned over and spat on him. "Wha' ya say now, star?" he said in a fake Jamaican accent. The overwhelming smell of gunpowder still clouded the chilly air.

Chico's stainless steel .9 mm was already firing as the big Jamaican dude came charging out the store with a long sharp rusty machete held high. The slug snapped his huge head back as it lodged into his brain. His corpse hit the concrete with a sickening thud. Blood ran from the entranceway of the store onto the concrete mixing with the collecting pool of his partner's blood. The wail of police sirens could be heard off in the far distance as the two killers dashed back to the BMW.

Suddenly, José paused as he was about to hop back into the car, "Yo, go get the weed!"

"What about the cops?" Chico replied, with a worried look on his face.

José tossed his hands up with a menacing sneer. "Fuck the cops. Go get the fucking weed." Chico did as he was told.

The loud conversation taking place between two of his employees working behind the counter of the clothing store welcomed José back to reality.

"Did you see busted ass Mike in the club last night?" Nicole asked Tishana with a smirk. She couldn't hide the contempt in her voice.

"Girl, you think I didn't." Tishana laughed as she scanned a pair of jeans. "He was tore up from the floor up."

"You got dat right. He should've never broke up with me," Nicole finished with a chuckle. As usual the phone started ringing off the hook. Nicole took her time getting to the telephone hanging on the wall behind the counter.

Every inch of José's treasured domain had been annexed through bloody street wars. He emerged the victor every time, nearly quadrupling his product on the streets of the Bronx. He was a calculating, short-tempered and ruthless hustler determined to never relinquish his throne, which happened to be a murderous mix in the hood. If José wanted a cat dead, the poor mark wouldn't know it until a slug tore through the back of his cranium. But in the same breath he was the type of cat to hold the door for old ladies and feed the hungry. The kids in the community loved him because he made sure they had money in their pockets and bought them all new bikes every Christmas.

Answering the phone, Nicole listened a moment. "Hey Ma..." she replied with a Colgate smile, recognizing the voice on the other end. She called out to José. "Your mom's on da line!"

José tore his gaze away from the window and walked to the counter. He grabbed the cordless receiver.

"What's up, Ma?" As he listened, he eyed the 27-inch flat screen hanging from a support beam in the middle of the store. The basketball game was on. The New York Knicks was beating the Chicago Bulls, fifty-six to thirty-two as usual.

"Bobby hasn't come home yet," she informed him in a worried tone.

Glancing at the clock on the wall, José wasn't the slightest bit concerned. It was only seven-thirty at night.

"Stop worrying, Ma, he's probably with some girl," he assured her. "If he's not home in another hour call me back and I'll find him. Okay?"

"Okay, I just hope he's alright," she continued fretting.

"He's fine, Ma," José said. "Just relax and get some rest. Love you."

His ailing mother, a devoted Catholic, had instilled certain values in him at a young age, but over the years the bitter streets had stripped most of them away. Only the most cold-blooded ruthless motherfuckers stayed on top. It had everything to do with power, and the powerful ruled by absolute and brutal force. This kind of life wasn't for the weak and the squeamish.   Niggers with merciful hearts didn't survive long in the belly of the beast. Fortunately, this was a side of life his brother Bobby didn't have to deal with.

As José hung up the phone, Slim burst through the door in a disgruntled state almost knocking over an exiting customer and yelled, "José, dey killed Bobby!" He was sobbing hysterically. "Da. . . da cops killed ya brother!"

In that instance, José's whole world was completely shattered as he turned to acknowledge Slim. With Slim's words still echoing in his ears, the walls started spinning and he became lightheaded. Everyone behind the counter froze. A few customers nearby stared openly at José. People in the back of the store moved between the aisles checking the next set of racks, oblivious to the pain flowing into the big man's body. Even Nicole covered her red lips with a shaking hand.

Suddenly, breathing became a hard thing to do as tears swelled up in his eyes. Losing control, José grabbed Slim's distraught ass by the collar, practically snatching him off his feet and barked, "You fuckin' lyin' to me!"

José didn't want to believe it as he searched Slim's eyes for the truth. All he found in them was complete and utter sadness. Strength drained from his arms faster than a premature ejaculation. He released his grasp on Slim.

The truth smacked José like a sack of nickels and his mind ran wild. No, no…his baby brother, Bobby couldn't be dead. Nah. Not him. Not Bobby. No fucking way. He had promised his mother that he would always look out for Bobby.

Oh shit! What if Slim had told the truth and Bobby was really dead?

Somebody would have hell to pay. He didn't care if they *were* cops. They could bleed just like everybody else.

CHAPTER 4

Across town in a well-kept brownstone in the North Bronx, Sean and his wife, Lisa, were in the midst of a romantic dinner in their second floor apartment.

Just about every piece of their tastefully modern furniture came from one place and that's Seaman's Furniture. From the metal framed, glass-top dinner table to Sean's black leather recliner sitting in the middle of the living room directly in front of the thirty-inch Sony TV with a surround sound speaker system. A few pieces of African art hung on the cream colored walls. "Whenever" by Maxwell played on the stereo system.

The buttered broccoli practically melted in Sean's mouth. "Damn, girl, you did your thing on this," he stated savoring every bite. The delicious smell of lemon smothered salmon filled the air as steam rose from the homemade mashed potatoes with the skins.

"Make sure you leave room for me," Lisa replied with a devilish grin.

Lisa, a beautiful chocolate honey in her late twenties with clear skin and silky jet-black wavy locks flowing down to the beginning of her back, also had a plump round ass a quarter could bounce off twice before hitting the floor. Her 34-25-37 measurements filled out the skin-tight jeans, which fit her like a glove, and complimented her thick, toned thighs. Confidence oozed from her.

The four nights she spent working out every week at Bally's definitely came in handy. And when she looked at a man with those deep brown seductive eyes, he risked falling in love instantly if he wasn't careful. Sean didn't want to be careful. He loved her with all of his heart and had since the first time he saw her in high school.

Sean, flashing all pearly whites, raised his glass of champagne and proposed a toast. "To our third wedding anniversary," he said, staring deeply into her sparkling eyes.

"Cheers." Lisa lifted her glass unable to contain the smile spreading across her red lips as she eyed him back.

The crystal glasses clinked with the first touch, and then they sipped a little bubbly and shared a quick kiss on the lips.

"Love you," Sean said, completely sincere, leaning back to look deeply in her eyes, which welled with unshed tears. "I don't always show it but—"

Suddenly, Lisa grabbed Sean's sweatshirt and pulled him closer, shutting him up with a deep sensual tongue kiss.

"I can't wait for dinner to end," she said softly as her fingers trailed the length of his thighs. "I'm craving dessert. And the only thing I want is this long, thick chocolate bar."

A flush of pleasure shot through Sean as his mind started to wonder off. Her fingers teased and tortured him as he had a quick flashback of one of their past sexual escapades. Lisa was face down and ass up on a plush love seat as Sean feverishly pounded her soaked, throbbing kitty, while shoving his thumb deep up her tight, hungry ass as she moaned in pure pleasure.

Seconds later, as Lisa led him by the hand into the bedroom and they discarded their clothes, Sean's vision became a reality. Completely lost in ecstasy, sweat poured off their naked bodies as Sean slipped into her moist, creamy center with long loving strokes, making sure he tapped her G-spot with the head of his penis every time he went in deeply. Juices flowing from her center built up on the base of his thick shaft, turning him on. He drilled away harder with each thrust, suckling her hardened nipples until she screamed in sheer pleasure.

The musky scent of sex slowly overcame the last scent of dinner. They fell into a smooth, workable rhythm, one that was as old as time itself. Her body tensed, then trembled and tensed again as she released for the very first time in months. The orgasm was like none other he had ever experienced, and made coming together that much sweeter. Her soft touch on his chest, and a quick stroke across his nipples electrified his entire body from the tips of his toes to every last hair follicle. *Damn*, he thought as he regained focus.

"I missed this," she said sincerely, mirroring Sean's thoughts exactly. "I missed you."

A couple of months ago, neither one of them thought they'd be celebrating their anniversary. Even though this was their third year as a married couple, they were high school sweethearts and had been dating for over ten years. At first their relationship was all good.

Their relationship began deteriorating soon after Sean graduated from the police academy and hit the streets. The lack of communication was the key to it all. Plus the fact that neither one of them had learned to truly compromise. Over time the stress of the job caused him to start drinking more and more, when neither of them had taken to the bottle before. He became impatient, withdrawn and short-tempered. They were constantly arguing and fighting. Lying there in bed with sweat still dripping off his body, Sean thought back to the final argument that caused the short separation.

In the dimly lit kitchen, Sean had poured himself a shot of Hennessy. Raising the glass to his lips, he downed it all in one gulp. Feeling a pair of eyes on him, he turned around to find Lisa standing there with her arms folded, giving him the evil eye.

"I'm sick of you drinking all the time, Sean." Lisa shouted. "Look at you. You're turning into an alcoholic."

"I ain't no alcoholic," Sean slurred, not wanting to hear the truth. Exiting the kitchen, he headed into the living room. He stumbled over to the leather easy chair and collapsed into a drunken heap.

"The liquors reeking out of your pores, Sean," Lisa said, wrinkling up her button nose. "What the hell are you doing to yourself? You're so much better than this."

He just stared at her with a blank look in his sad eyes.

"I don't know what's happening with us, Sean," Lisa continued, choosing her words carefully. "But until you do something about your drinking, maybe we shouldn't live together."

"What?" Sean snapped, creasing up his already screwed up face. "How you gonna put me out? I pay half the fuckin' rent."

Tapping her foot on the floor, Lisa stood there, shaking her head. "I...I can't live like this, Sean. Please just go."

"You act like I don't have no place to go," Sean replied, trying to hide his broken pride. "If this is what you want, fuck it! Don't be askin' me back."

Sean rose from the chair with his feelings crushed, grabbed his jacket out of the hallway closet and stormed out of the apartment, slamming the door behind him. He came back a few days later to get most of his clothes and other necessities. A few days turned into two long months.

Lisa kept the apartment and was stuck paying the bills. Sean finally moved back in three weeks ago after they decided to try to work things out. Maybe he should have asked what happened in her life in those two months they were separated. Maybe he should have asked how she, a normally hot natured woman, handled those particular urges. But something, he didn't know what, had kept him from asking and by the time he mustered up the courage, the time for questions had passed. But a nagging thought would creep up in his mind every now and then. The uncertainty was killing him.

About thirty minutes later, Sean lounged on their king-size bed with his right hand down his boxers and the remote in his left palm, watching the 10 o'clock News. The BNN news reporter gave the latest update, "Tonight, a disturbing find on the city's south side. Two elementary school children found the body of a nineteen year-old Hispanic male, which turned up in St. Mary's park in the South Bronx. Police said it appears he died of an apparent drug overdose."

Sean shut off the TV in frustration just as Lisa emerged from the bathroom, lingerie clinging to her wet voluptuous curves. Her sheer top was wide open in the front exposing her hard cinnamon colored nipples. Hot, horny and ready to be worked over again, the naughty look on her face, and the flash of her dark brown eyes showed she craved another much-needed orgasm.

"Why'd you turn it off?" she asked, seductively swaying her thick luscious hips side to side like a runway model as she sashayed over to the foot of the goose-down covered bed.

"Kids killin' kids, kids overdosin'," Sean answered sounding slightly defeated as he just shook his head, barely noticing the little erotic show Lisa was putting on for him. "I see this shit at work. I don't need it followin' me home."

It depressed him to see young kids dying in the streets everyday. The hood was practically a killing field and with each day that passed, it only seemed to get worse and worse. Nothing ever seemed to change. The most screwed up part about it was the politicians and lawmakers truly didn't care as long as it stayed confined to the ghetto.

"Forget work," Lisa replied, crawling onto the bed like a sex kitten and slowly mounting Sean. She planted wet kisses on his chest working her way up to his full lips. Still somewhat distracted, he turned his face away, caught in deep thought. Sometimes turning "off" the lust was a major problem for Lisa. Feeling rejected as usual, Lisa angrily withdrew but stayed saddled on top of him. Just before they separated, it had gotten to the point where they hardly had sex anymore, maybe once or twice a month if she was lucky. So getting it twice tonight was like striking pure gold.

"Talk to me, Sean." She huffed, showing her annoyance and frustration.

Sean didn't respond. He was lost in a world of his own. She just stared at him a moment before loudly proclaiming, "You don't talk to me anymore."

The harsh tone in her voice immediately snapped him out of his trance.

"What you talkin' 'bout?" Sean asked slightly irritated. He turned to look at her. "We always talk." He tossed his palms up in a "what?" gesture. "We're talkin' now, aren't we?"

"Not about work," Lisa replied, her eyes widening.

"What happens on the job stays there," Sean replied, becoming more irritated. "You *know* that."

"You promised that you would change, you promised."

Steam whistled out of the cranking radiator working overtime to heat the spacious room. The high temperature had the windows sweating.

"I know, baby, but some things are better left unsaid," Sean reasoned. "Let's not argue."

He had made it a point never to tell Lisa anything about work. He felt it was unnecessary to burden her with his troubles. She didn't know Internal Affairs had recruited him over six months ago. She still thought he was just a regular plainclothes cop in the narcotics division. But he was the one who had been naïve. He thought the stress of being a regular officer dealing with the criminal element day-after-day and watching kid after kid either die in the streets or go to prison with no end in sight had finally done him in. He switched paths and the lines became even blurrier.

In the chaotic streets of New York City, all kinds of drugs were sold twenty-four hours a day, seven days a week, 365 days a year—rain, sleet or snow. There was a war being waged within its borders to bring an end to this murderous drug trade destroying the inner city ghettos. Sworn to uphold the law, cops were fighting drug dealers determined to continue their prosperous enterprise by any means necessary. Sean knew from experience that on a daily basis, both sides won and both sides lost. And the war kept going on like the world kept spinning.

When Sean switched to internal affairs, he began to see that some of the men the city entrusted with the responsibility of enforcing the law had completely crossed that line and never looked back. Some of them were more heartless than the drug dealers and crooks.

Criminals don't play by the same rules cops have to abide by, which can get a good cop killed in the streets. So, in order to win the battle some cops ride the line between legality and corruption. Everyday narcotics officers face temptations, which could poison the soul and corrupt the mind of any honest underpaid and overworked officer of the law. Sean, under the guise of being a fellow officer who could be just as corrupt, had become a person who could be killed if the fact that he was undercover got out. But more than that, every illusion of morality had been shattered. And there was no turning back.

"You keep holding it in," Lisa said, eyeing Sean cautiously. The stress had taken a toll and a look in the mirror had shown trouble all in his face.

"Look at you, it's eating you up."

Sean didn't respond. He knew she was right. Lisa slid off him, and rolled over onto her side, giving him her back. She stared at the wall in silence, and a glance in the wall length mirror showed him that her eyes had watered, this time in pain. All she wanted was for Sean to communicate with her more and to show her the amount of affection she needed. Raised by an abusive stepfather, Sean had become a master at hiding his feelings. Working in Internal Affairs, he had become a master at befriending people who could be betrayed with a single word from his mouth or a report from his pen. Sean had these two issues warring within him every single moment. He had enough trouble just staying sane.

Lisa took a long, slow breath. "I've genuinely tried everything in my power to help you," she said, "but you just won't open up." She pulled the cover around her bare shoulders. "I don't know whether it's because you don't want to or if you just don't know how."

She reached over, switching the alarm radio on to a soft jazz station. A soothing instrumental filled the room as she turned back to Sean.

"Your job makes you withdraw even more. I want my old Sean back. The man I fell in love with in high school. Ever since you became a cop, that man has disappeared. I wonder if I'll ever see him again." She rolled back onto her side and pulled the sheet up to her neck.

Sean watched her through the mirror for a moment, then gently caressed her shoulder. "Lisa, hold me. I just need you close."

Lisa turned over, a slow smile spreading across her lips, that didn't quite reach her tear-filled eyes. Sean planted a soft kiss on her lips and embraced her in his arms for a moment, then just as suddenly as he reached out, he released her. He rolled onto his back and stared up at the ceiling, hoping that she would be satisfied with his genuine show of affection.

Unwilling to give even a bit of ground, Lisa reached out, tightened her grip on his shoulder, forced him to turn and face her. She raised her arms and embraced him, pulling him to her breasts. Sean tensed as her fingers slowly stroked his back. She caressed him, loved him, and stroked him.

Breathing in the scent of her sweet fragrance, his hands trembled as they reached out, then rested on her full hips. Lisa shut her eyes, slowly drifted off, but her eyes fluttered as she started thinking about the social studies lesson she would teach her fourth grade class tomorrow.

She had been teaching for a little over six-years now and truly enjoyed working with kids. Plus she was good at it and actually cared about their future. Being a teacher had sparked her desire to have children but she knew that Sean didn't really want to have any kids. Especially with the craziness in the world he saw everyday. Deep in her heart she felt she could eventually convince him otherwise.

Sean continued staring off into the darkness, thinking, *Why can't she understand there are times when a man just doesn't want sex. Shit, it's rare, but it happens.*

His unwillingness to talk about important things had eaten away at his core and hers. Each day the job tightened his lips and closed his heart. He would have to change. He had promised that he would. Unfortunately, he didn't know where to start. Hopefully Lisa wouldn't give up on him.

CHAPTER 5

Later that night, in the sub-level of the city morgue, José, totally drained and slightly distraught, viewed Bobby's pale corpse laid out on a cold metal slab. A white sheet draped over his lifeless body from his chest to his ankles. A bright green tag hung from the big toe on his right foot as though the color alone could replace the breath of life that had been taken away so suddenly.

A cute Russian doctor with the body of a sex goddess stood a short distance away near her desk observing the depressing sight. Normally, José would at least try to holler. The lift of her penciled eyebrow signaled that the body lay out before him had become all too common for her as an increasing amount of young kids and teens were dying from senseless violence.

Suddenly José looked up at her and asked, "Did they find out what was in the needle?"

"A deadly dose of heroin," she replied, moving closer to him. "Was he a user?"

"Hell no, I made sure he stayed clean," José snapped offensively. "Do you know if he felt any pain?" Tears rolled down his cheeks, falling onto the cold tile floor.

"More than likely not," she said, trying to be comforting. "He was probably too high to feel anything."

José stared at her, wanting to give her a good smack for making such a dump ass comment but now wasn't the time or place. Plus he knew she was only trying to make him feel better even though it only made him feel worst. The woman inched away from the rage in his eyes, walking briskly back to her paperwork covered desk.

On the other side of the room, two more linen-covered corpses were laid out on gurneys awaiting autopsies, or for family members to come and face the grim reality of death face-to-face.

Tears streamed down José's pain-etched face as he tried to hold it together and thought about breaking the bad news to his cancer-stricken mother and his hotheaded sister, ReRe. He knew his mother would be completely devastated and ReRe would definitely be aiming to kill somebody. And it might not be the right somebody.

José had never felt this much rage and sadness bundled up in his heart at one time. Vengeance was the only thing flashing through his brain as the blood boiled in his icy veins. Those fucking pigs had crossed the point of no return when they murdered his baby brother. Now death was the only thing promised them. And he didn't give a fuck if it cost him his own life in the process. He wouldn't rest until they were dead and stinking.

Deep down, José knew those pigs were serious about their paper but never in his wildest dreams had he imagined it would come to this. His thoughts quickly reflected back to the last confrontation he had with the two crooked narcs on one of his drug blocks.

"How ya'll just gonna up the price like that?" José had asked. "We already had an agreement."

"This ain't no fuckin' negotiation," Jay shot back, lighting up a smoke. "Next time we collect that spread betta be tight." With that said, Jay and Warren strutted back to the idling Cherokee, leaving José standing there on the sidewalk with a serious chip on his shoulder.

During the previous few weeks the reoccurring thought to just swallow his pride and pay off them dirty squares had been weighing heavily on his mind. He just kept pushing it away. Being the kind of cat José was, he refused to be shaken down by bitch ass niggers even if they had badges.

Not the type of cops to take no for an answer, Jay and Warren began applying pressure on his operation, busting some of his most profitable spots, back-to-back for the past four weeks in a row.

José couldn't help but to remember the story Hector told him about the last shake down, a shake down that practically forced Jose to go into hiding.

The Cherokee pulled up in front of a medium sized, two-story warehouse with an old dirty sign that read: Wholesale Beer and Soda. The decrepit looking brick building needed a serious facelift. The brown paint was peeling off the walls and the huge metal gate in the loading dock was rusted in certain spots. The place appeared to be closed. The windows were blacked out and gated. Two dirty white delivery box trucks covered with graffiti sat parked out front in the wide driveway sparingly littered with beer bottles and garbage.

Jay exited the jeep followed by Warren and Sean. They headed to the closed entrance. Pounding on the thick metal door, Jay lit up a cigarette and waited for an answer.

"Pass me a smoke, I left mines in the jeep," Sean said, still patting his empty coat pockets. Jay pulled a cancer stick from his pack and handed it to him.

Sean flicked his lighter on, lit up and took a pull.

After a few moments the door opened, revealing a short but stocky stone-faced Mexican with a black revolver tucked into his waistband. His golden tanned hand gripped the rubber handle, ready to draw the weapon if necessary. Adding to his tough-guy appearance was a shaggy goatee. He nodded once he saw who it was.

Jay stepped in. "Where's Hector?"

"His office. Wait here, I'll get him," the Mexican replied walking down a dark narrow hallway leading to an office. Opening the door he disappeared inside.

A few seconds later the Mexican returned followed by Hector a huge Dominican, sporting an expensive jogging suit that did little to hide his bulging gut with a thin gold chain and Lazarus medallion lying on his hairy chest. An expensive pair of square framed glasses accented his chubby hairless baby face. This was no young boy. He had to be at least thirty-five. His thick curly hair was cut into a smooth fade that happened to be thinning on top.

"Hey, my favorite, pork chop," Hector said, sporting a fake smile. "Who are your friends?"

"Partners," Jay replied. "We need to talk."

Hector offered all three men a hearty handshake. "This way."

They trailed Hector back to his rear office. Crossing to his oak desk, he slumped down into his plush leather chair.

A slim but tough looking Hispanic male with a patch over one of his eyes and jet-black slicked back hair, stood off to the side, observing the three cops with a stone grill and a cold gleam in his eye.

Making himself right at home, Jay sat in the chair

situated in front of the desk. Sean and Warren remained standing.

Hector grabbed a cigar from a custom wooden cigar box sitting by the telephone on his desktop. "You guys want a stogie? They're Cuban." He lit up the fresh hand rolled tobacco.

The three men shook their heads. They were there for one thing only and that was business.

"Let's skip the fuckin' small talk," Jay snapped sitting up straight. He was dead serious as his eyes locked on Hector. "Ya boss José's been missin' in action."

"We're two different people, my friend," Hector replied, tapping the ashes into a marble ashtray. "He does his thing, I do mine." Hector glanced from Jay's menacing glare to the other two cops standing in the background.

"Well, he's behind on taxes and the interest is buildin' by the day."

"So what that gotta do wit' me?"

"It has everything to do with you, bein' your establishment here stores most of José's supply," Jay replied.

Hector's eyes widened. He started fidgeting with the cigar.

"Oh, yeah motherfucker we know. So the way I figure it, you gonna cover his piece."

"So now you leaning on me? That's bullshit and you know it," Hector snapped, trying to maintain his cool. "There's nothing more to discuss. You guys know your way out."

Warren pulled his gun, "Fuck you, you cocky motherfucker!"

Almost simultaneously, Slick leveled his nickel-plated automatic at Warren's head as Sean reacted, quickly training his gun on Slick.

Jay stood up, refereeing the situation evenly. "Calm down. Put that shit away."

All the while Hector remained cool as a fan.

Warren reluctantly holstered the firearm, still glaring at Hector.

Hector signaled for Slick to put his tool away. Hesitantly, Slick obliged. No sooner than Slick's hand left the handle of the gun, a bullet tore through his skull.

Slick never saw it coming. Jay was too fast for him. Hector sat there with his jaw dropped open, frozen in place. Sean couldn't believe how quick Jay had pulled his gun and put a slug in Slick.

"What's wrong Hector?" Jay asked, still clutching the .40 caliber. "You look a little jumpy."

Hector continued staring at Slick's corpse collected into a heap on the floor, his blood draining out onto the concrete.

"You lucky I like you, Hector," Jay said, eyeing the stunned man. "I don't know why but I do. So here's what you're gonna do. You're gonna open up that safe of yours and fill up this bag with money. If not, you're gonna join ya friend and we gonna burn this motherfucker down."

That was all Hector needed to hear, he quickly snapped out of his daze and crossed to the mini-refrigerator sitting on the other side of the room. Opening the door, he exposed a safe hidden inside. He was shaking so bad it took him a moment to get the combination right. After struggling with it a few seconds, he finally got the safe open. Inside were at least twelve stacks of large faced bills and a few legal documents. He quickly tossed every stack into the bag and tossed it on the desk in front of Jay.

Jay couldn't help but reveal a wicked smile as he eyed the cash bulging out the open bag.

"Make sure to tell José he can run but he can't hide forever," he said.

That was the last straw. After that, José switched gears and went underground. His team reversed the way they operated. Old spots were shut down. New spots surfaced on the low. The cash was still flowing and the pigs didn't know about his clothing store, so José figured things were all good. Little did he know he was dead wrong.

"Doctor Monroe to room 210" came the sexy voice of a female nurse over the hospital's intercom, snapping José out of his mind for a minute. His steady flow of tears bounced off the sheet covering Bobby and ran onto the floor as he touched his brother's cold hands. Trembling, he pulled his own hand away not wanting to remember how Bobby's cool scaly skin felt. The stench of death hovered in the stale air.

Now, José's thickheaded stubbornness had finally come back to bite him in the ass. Bobby didn't deserve the hand he had been dealt. Sure, he was a knucklehead kid, but growing up in a cutthroat environment like Third Avenue forced many kids to be. Toughness was only a front used by misguided teens trying to survive in the streets of the ghetto.

Bobby didn't have anything to do with José's drug trade. José made sure his little brother kept his nose clean and went to school. He wanted him to graduate and be the first one in the family to go to college. He hoped Bobby would experience all the positive things he was never exposed to growing up.

José's vision had entailed a better life for Bobby. Now that dream had faded away along with his brother's short life. It hurt knowing he couldn't bring him back. If José could have switched places with Bobby, he would have but unfortunately that was no longer an option.

A few minutes later José stormed out the morgue's front exit into the brisk night air. He quickly crossed the street to the idling BMW. Chico, José's most-trusted henchman waited, slumped in the driver's seat. He was one of them pretty boy Puerto Rican cats that spent about fifteen minutes in the mirror every morning combing holding gel through his slicked back hair. It was something José considered a weakness. In their line of business, pretty didn't mean shit. But overall, he happened to be one of the Bronx's most stone-cold killers.

Chico's muscular 5'11" frame gave him the appearance of a boxer ready for battle. The all black .45 planted on his lap attested to his belief in letting the cannon talk first and avoiding the murder charge later. They grew up right across the hall from each other and knew one another since they were five years old. They were more like brothers than friends. And Chico was completely devoted and loyal to José.

José hopped in the passenger side, and the BMW sped off down the block with the rims glistening beneath the streetlight. For the first time in ages, the music had been turned off, allowing José to think. To plan. To fester.

As they passed 149th street, a police car with its sirens blaring flew past headed in the opposite direction, spurring José to action. He whipped out his cell and dialed. A second later, another henchman answered.

"Those faggots killed my little brother," José barked into the phone becoming more determined by the minute to revenge his brother's death.

On the other end, Wise stated the need for caution.

"Nigga, I could give a fuck if they cops! They outta here! You hear me, Wise? I want every nigga wit' a ratchet in the BX gunnin' at those fuckin' pigs. I'm droppin' fifty grand a head!"

Chico glanced warily at José, then focused on keeping the beautiful piece of machinery just under the speed limit as they cruised through the hood on their way back to the spot.

"Fifty grand! Spread da word!" José yelled before hitting END.

CHAPTER 6

The Cherokee sat parked by the curb at the beginning of a deserted pier in Manhattan near 96th Street. The FDR expressway loomed overhead in the background. The continuous buzz of traffic traveled to the two men's ears. Jay and Warren downed beers at the edge of the weathered dock. From where they stood, a lit up view of Queens and the Triborough Bridge sat over in the distance. The smell of rotten fish and dirty water hung heavy in the air as waves broke against the weathered concrete retainer wall along the river. They usually met up at this spot to drink, split up cash or discuss their various schemes.

"You sure this kid's ready?" Warren asked, tossing his empty can into the choppy dirty black waters of the East River. The container quickly disappeared beneath the uneven surface. His sad eyes followed a piece of jagged wood floating by in the forceful current.

"Definitely," Jay said, taking a sip of beer. "With the debt he's in, he needs this."

"The fucker better not freeze up."

"We've been workin' the streets six months now," Jay replied and then crumpled up his empty can and flung it into the river. "He's good."

"Can we trust him?" Warren asked, his blue eyes furrowed with concern. The cold air flushed his normally pale skin a bright pink. He lit up a Winston and took a long anxious pull.

Jay locked eyes with his old partner and asked, "Have I ever fucked you?"

"Have you?" Warren asked jokingly as he stared at Jay a moment before breaking the ice. "Last time me and you got drunk I woke up with a loose ass."

"Shit. You wish," Jay replied, laughing at the unthinkable. Then his grin widened. "Ya know what they say, once you had black you never go back, baby." He gave Warren a gentle smack on the ass. "And you know ya my bitch."

"Fuck you, dirt bag." Warren half-chuckled. Noticing the cigarette was out, he relit the cancer stick again. He took a deep, slow drag, allowing time to pass. "Okay the kid's in but don't you two *homeboys* start that *it's a black thing* crap trying to leave my white ass outta the loop." He forced a cloud of smoke through the corner of his thin ashy lips.

"Never." Jay laughed, glancing at his wristwatch. "We have too much history, baby. You know ya my favorite Caucasian."

The stench of garbage hit their noses as a tugboat pushed a weathered barge with a huge load of trash from the Sanitation department up the river. Its horn sounded as it passed by in the distance. Warren glanced at the overworking boat as it disappeared into the night.

"How much cash you have stacked?" Warren asked, turning to look at Jay.

"Not enough," Jay replied evasively.

"Come on, after all the money we've gotten our hands on? You should have enough to buy the Brooklyn Bridge."

"What about you, nosey, how much paper you sittin' on?" Jay asked, eyeing Warren as his talkative partner suddenly became quiet.

"I got a little bit put up," Warren replied, observing Jay's questioning look. "I got a bit."

"Just like I thought."

"What's that supposed to mean?" Warren asked.

"Nothin', forget I said it."

Minutes later, Jay passed out in the passenger seat of the Cherokee and started dreaming of better times in his distant past:

In the living room of a small quaint house near the edge of Queens and Long Island, wedding pictures of Jay and a beautiful bright-eyed, young bride Dawn rested next to a picture of a younger Jay in his police uniform on top of the mantle over a brick fireplace. Across the room, Jay and Dawn sat snuggled up on the sofa watching a scary movie. Jay hugged her even tighter after she jumped during a real scary part, planting a wet kiss on her cheek. Blushing, she turned all smiles as he rubbed her swollen belly, which was about the size of a basketball. Dawn was eight months pregnant with their first child.

With their son now seven years old, Jay chased after his giggling little boy who was running after a rolling baseball in the back yard of their house. Back down to her normal size, Dawn stood off to the side smiling at the sight of the both of them.

After a few years, the good times became a distant memory as Jay and his wife Dawn started arguing more and more. He pointed angrily to the gas, phone and credit card bills piled on the kitchen table. The vision of his wife's pained face, the bills landing on the floor with a sweep of his hand, faded away.

Suddenly Jay found himself in a cramped corner office with a picture box view of the Manhattan skyline scribbling his John Hancock beside the X on a legal document. The old oak desk and the commercial grade carpeted floor were cluttered with law books and files.

When Jay finished signing along the dotted line, he shook the middle-aged Jewish lawyer's outstretched hand and made his exit, shutting the door behind him. The metal sign on the door read: DIVORCE LAWYER.

Jay then found himself entering a dreary studio apartment with a few pieces of mail in hand. Glancing through the stack, he tossed all the unwanted bills in the trashcan and tossed the remaining mail onto the kitchen counter. His bachelor's pad was depressing, dim and sparsely furnished. A twin-sized metal fold up cot sat in an upright position off in a corner and a thirty-seven-inch Panasonic rested on twin orange milk crates pushed up against the wall.

The loud wail of a passing car's horn jarred Jay from his dream and out of his drunken slumber in the passenger seat of the Cherokee. How could he care about killing José's brother Bobby? How could he care about how he came about all of his money these days? Nothing in life seemed to matter much anymore since he didn't have his wife and son to go home to anymore.

Gaining his bearings, he peered out the window and spotted Warren breaking another law by urinating at the end of the dark pier. Needing to relieve his bladder, Jay hopped out the Cherokee and took up the spot right next to Warren. Deep down, Jay wished his marriage could have worked out but it was no use crying over spilt milk. Life goes on.

CHAPTER 7

The next morning was very uneventful for Sean. Feeling drained, he spent most of the passing day sleeping off the stress of life. He didn't climb out of the bed until it was almost time for work. Practically sleepwalking he made his way into the bathroom and turned on the shower. Humming his favorite tune, he pulled his t-shirt over his unkempt head and slipped out of his boxers, stepping under the running water. The warm water felt good over his dry skin.

That evening it was cloudy and windy as a thunderstorm approached. A few noisy kids zipped up and down the sidewalk playing tag along the well-kept, tree-lined block Sean called home. One kid dashed to home base just as the kid who was "it" almost tagged him. Happy to be safe, the excited boy spun around and did a victory dance while the "it" kid ran off to try to tag the rest of the scrambling players.

Sean emerged from his brownstone with a whole lot on the brain, pausing for a moment to exhale before maneuvering past the rowdy children to his silver Acura parked mid-way up the block. The whole time he wondered where his marriage would end up further down the road.

The cold breeze nipped at his ears as he pulled his wool hat down over them.

Sean truly loved Lisa with every fiber of his soul and only wanted to see her happy. There were no real words that could accurately express his inner most feelings. In his heart they were forever one. He would lay his life down for her in a heartbeat. And nothing like her beautiful smile could brighten up his day. But whenever it came time to express that love, Sean would just clam up and shut down.

Growing up in an abusive household, he began hiding his emotions at a young age. That way he didn't give his sadistic stepfather the privilege of witnessing him shed a tear whenever the big man decided to exercise his demons on the youngster. His step-pop enjoyed mentally and physically abusing him whenever his nurturing mother wasn't around. She didn't have a clue. And the threat of death kept Sean's mouth shut.

Sean let the cold, sluggish sounding engine warm up a few moments before pulling out of his parking space into the thin traffic.

The abuse finally stopped once Sean got old enough to handle his own and decided enough was enough. Confronting his stepfather in a complete rage, Sean finally saw fear in the cold-hearted son of a bitch's eyes as he cowered behind Sean's mother dialing 911 like the scared little coward he had actually been all along.

But by now, keeping everything close to the chest had become second nature to Sean. It was his shield against the heartbreaks and evils of the cruel world.

A few minutes later, the wipers feverishly worked the windshield, beating back the drizzling rain as Sean drove, grooving to a hot joint on the radio. Billy Ocean's "Caribbean Queen" had him reminiscing about the few good times he experienced growing up in the eighties when his real father was still alive.

Sean's real old man had been a hustler from Brooklyn. Even though he pushed dope, he was still a good brother with a good heart who never put his hands on Sean. One problem—Sean's pops had violated the first rule of the game. Never get high on your own supply. The end result was his drug-addicted father being murdered in a pissy project hallway on Avenue D in lower Manhattan. His father's death was an unwanted birthday present. Sean had just turned nine.

The blaring horn of a car idling behind him at the traffic light, which was now green, brought Sean back to reality. Glancing in the rearview mirror, he ignored the angry white man giving him the bird. He stepped on the gas and proceeded through the intersection.

****

Later that night during a heavy downpour, near 169th Street and Park Avenue in the South Bronx, a soaked young woman darted into Webster projects with her two children trailing right behind her. Due to the bad weather, most people stayed inside avoiding the unforgiving rain. A bunch of towering projects, abandoned buildings and bodegas made up the surrounding landscape.

On Park Avenue, across the street from the looming projects, the Cherokee sat idling by the curbside. Jay was behind the wheel, surveying the surroundings. Sean puffed on a cigarette in the passenger seat. They were observing the 21-story red brick building adjacent to them. The relentless rain beating against the glass blurred his vision.

"You miss me last night?" Sean asked jokingly as he glanced over at the older man.

"Like a head cold," Jay responded, his eyes still on the prowl. "How'd the anniversary go?"

"Okay I guess. . ." Sean said shrugging. "No arguin'."

"You definitely have a diamond," Jay informed Sean, eyeing him for a second. Sean nodded though he didn't need another man to tell him.

"Truthfully, I'm just happy we're back together. Bein' separated for two months was hell," Sean said, opening up a little, before quickly drifting off in thought.

Jay lit up a Camel, and the flickering flame revealed the black-on-stainless automatic perched in his lap. He shook the flame out before it reached his dark fingers.

"To this day I regret the way that shit went down with Lisa," Sean said, shifting around in the leather seat. "I shouldn't have walked-"

"Look, young-blood, that kinda shit happens," Jay cut in smoothly, patting him on the shoulder. "What matters now is it worked out."

Sean peered at Jay for a moment. "I appreciate you watchin' out for Lisa the way you did."

"Don't even speak on it," Jay replied nonchalantly, blowing a trail of gray-bluish smoke through his nostrils. A long pause unfolded between them and Sean felt that Jay had tensed, but just as quickly composed himself.

Finally, Sean broke the silence and asked, "You heard about that poor kid overdosin' in St. Mary's last night?"

"Nah," Jay replied evenly. "How old was he?"

"Nineteen, I think."

"It's a shame, fiends are gettin' younger and younger." Jay smirked. The police radio crackled in and out.

Jay reached over, turning the volume down. "There's Black," he announced in an excited tone, pointing towards the target.

Black, a tall, slim black male in his early thirties hopped out of a white Yukon with the 24-inch rims still spinning and dashed toward the project building. He got the nickname "Black" when he was a young kid because his skin was the same color as tar. Back then he hated it, but now, he wore the name like a badge of honor. Now, on a cold night in the middle of January his dark skin nearly rendered him invisible as he bopped up the concrete path into the lobby. Still visible through the lobby's window, he crossed to the elevator, hit the button and waited.

"*He's* king of the hill?" Sean asked as he glanced over at Jay.

Jay nodded.

Black had the projects and the surrounding area on lock and anybody who objected was found decaying in an alley or dumpster somewhere. The only person Black might have feared was José, who just happened to be his supplier and the brother of his main girl, ReRe.

"That truck's at least forty grand." Sean looked over the Yukon. "Not to mention the rims cost 'bout twelve a set." He turned back just in time to see Black disappear into the elevator.

"See that's what the hell I mean," Jay grumbled, unable to hide his envy. "I'm up to my neck in alimony and child support. Payin' mortgage on a fuckin' house I don't even sleep in. Tell me life ain't a bitch." He tucked the weapon in its holster.

Sean glanced at Jay, actually feeling his pain. Both of them sat in silence, thinking about the hand life had dealt them.

Finally Jay broke the silence, "Once I retire, I'm coppin' a few acres out in the middle of Arizona somewhere." He closed his eyes and began visualizing it. "One or two horses. . ."

"And a few women," Sean said, injecting his dreams into Jay's plans for the future.

"*Lots* of women," Jay quickly corrected with a harsh laugh.

A black unmarked Chevy Impala with dark tints pulled up across the street from the Cherokee. A cloud of smoke escaped from the slightly cracked driver's window. The window rolled up to a close just before the motor died.

Jay threw one jean-clad leg up on the dash and checked the small revolver he kept strapped to his ankle. "Let's rock," he announced, killing the engine.

Exiting the Cherokee, Jay and Sean crossed to the unmarked car as Warren stepped out, flicking his Winston butt into the debris-filled gutter. Droplets of rain glistened off of Jay's shiny head as the streetlight hit it. Sean and Jay tossed Warren nods, never losing stride as they hurried up the concrete walkway toward Black's building. Warren fell right in step, bringing up the rear.

Sean entered the unkempt lobby; Chinese restaurant flyers were scattered around the tiled floor. All three men were drenched from the rain. Sean shook the water of his black waterproof Northface jacket. Crossing to the elevator, Jay pressed the metal button repeatedly. The down arrow over the elevator doors glowed red.

Warren lit up another cigarette. "How's it looking?"

"Black rolled up solo," Jay responded, shaking off some of the rain. "It's his lady's crib, so be on point."

Eagle eyed and focused, Jay and Warren were clearly in their element. Sean shifted back and forth on his feet, wishing he were at home with Lisa. Tonight would be his first time running up in a drug spot with them. He swore both of them could hear his heart practically pounding through his chest. Jay eyed Sean, warily.

"Second thoughts?" Jay asked Sean.

"Nah," Sean replied, faking a confident smirk as he made eye contact with Jay. "I'm good."

"Then get ya game face on, young blood," Jay stated flatly.

Just then the elevator doors slid open, and a voluptuous young lady with Afro puffs and a slamming body wrapped in a designer velour sweat suit, emerged and smiled at them as she brushed past. They stepped in the tiny elevator making sure to avoid the pool of piss collected in the corner.

Jay's lustful eyes were still glued to the girl's plump round ass as the elevator doors shut. If they didn't have business to handle, Jay would've been all over her. He had a serious reputation throughout the department for being a ladies' man. The funny thing was he usually got any woman he wanted. And most of them ended up falling head over heels for him while he only lost interest in them.

But there was something about the new broad he happened to be screwing lately that was different. He hadn't felt this way since meeting his first wife. Well actually his second wife. Either way, he couldn't believe he was actually getting strung out and it wasn't just the pussy that had him. She actually was a classy woman with a head on her shoulders. Not to mention she was a nasty girl in the bedroom.

Inside the elevator, the stench of urine and cigarette smoke mixed, hanging heavy in the cramped rising box. Stepping on his recently discarded butt, Warren pulled his .38 from his shoulder holster and cocked it. "Let's get this over with."

Jay eyed him with one eyebrow cocked. "Just be easy on that trigger. We don't need any mistakes." Then he glanced over at Sean.

Already clutching his weapon, Sean definitely had his game face on. His slanted dark brown eyes of steel were focused like a well-trained soldier prepared to go to battle.

"I see you ready now," Jay said with a sinister tone and confident smirk. "Keep ya shit tight, Young-blood."

Sean nodded.

The elevators slid open and the three narcs quietly slipped out into the dim narrow hallway with firearms in hand. For the projects, the hallway on this floor was surprisingly clean except for a couple of names tagged in red marker along the walls. Jay pointed to apartment 6-B sitting at the end of the hall as he headed toward it, Warren and Sean trailing him.

Jay pressed his ear to the door. "Sounds like he's on the phone."

"Just make sure ya drop off dat package tonight," Black said. "Hit me when it's done."

Just then, the loud crash of a metal door giving way resounded in the hallway.

Slumped on the burgundy leather couch in his girlfriend's living room, with a Bob Marley sized blunt between his dark lips, Black almost jumped completely out his blue Sean Johns.

The front door hung halfway off the hinges, still rattling from the force of being kicked in. Jay charged in with Sean and Warren hot on his heels. Police shields swung from their necks as they proceeded down the tight hall.

"Police, don't fuckin' move!" Jay yelled at the top of his lungs as they rushed into the living room, cannons aimed right at Black.

One of P-Diddy's flashy dance videos played on the big-flat screen. For it to be the projects, his girl's crib was seriously decked out like it fell right out one of the pages in the Robb Report. A bulky black Tec-9 with electrical tape wrapped around the handle rested on the end table.

Stifling his shock, Black yelled, "What the fuck?" He stood and reached for the Tec-9.

A loud boom sounded as the Jay fired a warning shot with his .40. The shell blew the gun right out of Black's clammy grip, almost ripping off his fingers.

"Ahhh... shit!" Black screamed like a bitch, snatching his hand back.

"Nigga, you two seconds from a body bag," Jay yelled, gripping his gun even tighter until the veins popped out along his brown knuckles, ready to let another round fly. "Now get ya fuckin' hands in the air!"

"All right, all right" Black tossed his hands up, praying to God the narc wouldn't pop him. "Fuck y'all doin' in my cri—"

That was all Black had a chance to say before Jay rushed over and butted him upside the head with his gun. The blow sent Black crashing to the linoleum floor. A nasty gash appeared over his left eye.

Black clutched his wounded brow in his palms. Blood oozed through his fingers, dripping down the length of his forearm onto the oatmeal colored linoleum tile.

"You really shouldn't play wit' guns, Dickhead," Jay barked sarcastically, towering over him with a sly grin and the gun stuck in his grill. Black glanced up, catching a too close for comfort, personal view of the slug waiting impatiently at the opposite end of the chamber.

Sean kept a tight grip on his glock, taking everything in from the sidelines. The tense filled situation had the vein in his forehead throbbing as a line of sweat trickled down his temple.

"Get me to a fuckin' hospital," Black winced, glancing at the blood soaking his palms.

"Move ya fuckin' hands," Jay snapped, examining the wound briefly. "Man, it barely broke skin. If I was you, I'd be worried about my freedom. Possession of a firearm, that's one-to-three. "

"Attempted murder of three cops," Warren injected, exaggerating the charges for the trio's benefit.

"That's another twenty-five," Jay finished. "But some cooperation will get shit overlooked."

"I look like a fuckin' snitch," Black snapped, glaring up at Jay.

"That's not what the fuck I meant, dickhead," Jay growled. He believed in getting right down to business. Fuck the small talk. He leaned in until his face was only a few inches from Black. "I'm talkin' overlook shit money. You stay operatin' money. Shit clickin' yet?"

Black nodded.

"Good, now, where's the fuckin' stash?" Jay asked sharply, notching Black's rib cage with the barrel.

Black remained silent. Seconds passed like kidney stones.

"I don't like repeatin' myself." Jay groaned through clenched teeth, pressing Black's face to the floor with the heel of his construction boot. He didn't have the patience to play waiting games.

"Ah. . . ah. . . all right, all right," Black squealed. "The. . .the bedroom closet."

Jay motioned for Warren to retrieve the stash.

Catching the hint, Warren rushed to the bedroom at the end of a dim hallway. He kicked open the closed bedroom door and entered cautiously. Panning the area, he was ready to shoot anything that moved. Piercing blue eyes scanned the room. The king sized bed was unmade and a half empty Hennessy bottle sit on a nightstand. In the corner of the room some sort of weird metal and leather contraption hung from the ceiling by heavy-duty chains. Other than that, it was clear.

As Warren's eyes focused in on the apparatus, he realized it was one of those slings used for fucking. A smile broke across his pale sunken face as he nodded. "Shit. I could use one of those."

Getting back to business, he spotted his target, crossed to the closet and ripped open the closed door.

In the closet, the twin barrels of a black-on-black sawed-off stared back at him. A frightened Puerto Rican broad, no older than twenty-one, aimed it at Warren's head, shaking uncontrollably as sweat dripped from her brow.

Besides the fear ridden all in her wide dark brown eyes and shaky breath, she was beautiful with the kind of luscious lips that were perfect for sucking. A flash of memory helped him to recall that she was José's sister.

She raised the gun.

"Whoa, whoa. . . NYPD, lady," Warren said, completely shocked, keeping his gun on her as he tried not to shit his pants. "You kill me, you fry and nobody wants that."

"Fuck you," ReRe replied, gripping the sawed-off even tighter.

"Easy, easy," Warren said, switching gears. "Don't do something you'll regret. Hand me the gun. I won't hurt you." He had to fight to keep from shaking. It wasn't in his best interest to let her know he was shook up.

Time stood still as she held her ground. Warren didn't like the feeling of helplessness and fear he felt staring down the two barrels she had shoved in his grill.

"I won't hurt you, I promise," Warren lied; trying to sound sincere as he slowly holstered his gun. "Just hand me the gun."

After hesitating a few moments, she finally gave in, slowly lowered the sawed-off and handed it over to him.

Warren calmly un-cocked the sawed-off, tossed it on the bed, then snatched her by the neck out of the closet. He pressed the gun to her temple. Now, his hands were the ones shaking. Damn his nerves were shot. Having a saw-off stuck in ya grill will do that to anybody.

Warren took a real good look at ReRe. Her size twenty-seven-inch waist led to thirty-six-inch hips, which lead to her pretty suckable toes with French tips wrapped in some open toe Manolo shoes with six-inch heels.

"Now, you're gonna blow me, bitch," Warren growled, unzipping his rusty black denim. Seizing a handful of silky, black hair with his free hand, he forced her down on her knees. He eyed her tear-soaked face a second, but saw a flash of defiance in her eyes. This bitch would probably bite his shit off.

"Fuck it. You ain't worth it."

He released his grip, smashing the butt of the gun down on her skull.

She crumbled to the floor on impact, out cold.

"I can't stand whimpering bitches." Warren sneered, then started ransacking the closet. Clothes flew off the hangers, designer shoes hit the wall as he invaded what looked to be, the woman's bedroom. As he ruffled through the stack of sneaker boxes lined up along the floor, three fell over. At least twenty different bundles of cash wrapped in rubber bands lay at his feet, along with some loose bills and about fifteen zip-loc bags filled with bundles of crack vials and vanilla packets packed with cocaine.

"Jackpot!" Warren practically shouted, a broad smile crossing his thin pink lips. He grabbed an empty duffle bag from the closet floor, filling it with the greenbacks, tossing the drugs to the side. As he got up to leave, he froze as reality hit him—he had forgot to take some dope for himself. He ripped open one of the zip-loc bags, grabbed a few crack vials and some vanilla packets, tucking them in the pocket of his jeans and left. Jay would never know.

A quick glance at the woman on the floor showed that ReRe was still unconscious. It didn't look like she'd be coming around anytime soon.

Jay and Sean stood guard over Black as Warren returned with the duffle bag draped over his shoulder.

Jay cast a cautious gaze over at Warren.

Warren winked, motioning to the bag clutched in his pale hands. "There's a few grams back there." He grinned. "And I'm not talking crackers."

"That ain't good," Jay replied smoothly, turning his attention back to Black, squatting next to the heavy breathing man. "You'll be sixty still in prison greens unless you pay to play, baby. And that's fifteen hundred a week. No shorts, no excuses."

"What kinda shit is that?" Black growled, his tar-colored skin turning a shade darker.

"Taxes, baby, everybody pays taxes," Jay responded, nudging him in the ribs with the gun. "I don't give a fuck what hood ya claim. Bottom line, we own these fuckin' streets. The choice is simple," he said, pointing to the bag of money. "Tossin' salad upstate or freedom."

Black didn't respond. His eyes darted around the room as though he still thought he had options.

"Times up," Jay stated coldly, having run out of patience. He had a real short fuse.

"A'ight. . . you'll get your paper," Black replied, knowing he really didn't have a choice if he wanted to stay out on the streets.

"Good pick." Jay smiled, and stood up. "Tell José he can run but he can't hide forever." He walked to the door, signaling for Sean and Warren to follow. Sean exited last, slamming the door behind him.

Minutes later, on a dead end street, the Cherokee and unmarked car sat idling in the middle of a cul-de-sac. Jay and Warren stood beside the vehicles, sharing a smoke. The white tendrils of air curled around them like snakes. The rain had stopped but the ground was still wet. Single and two-family homes ran up and down both sides of the block. Only a few adventurous souls came out to struggle in the gloomy weather.

In the front seat of the Cherokee, Sean counted the money from the duffle bag. Three stacks of cash sat on the seat next to him as he added Jacksons and Grants to each appropriate pile in clock-wise order as though dealing a hand of spades.

"That bitch scared me to death," Warren said, puffing on the last bit of his cigarette. "My fucking heart almost stopped."

A quick smile crept across Jay's lips as he watched Warren flick away the cigarette butt.

"How we looking, kid?" Warren asked Sean, rubbing his hands together.

"A little over eight grand." Sean inhaled sharply. "That's twenty-six a piece."

Warren smiled. "Not bad for twenty minutes, huh?"

"I don't make this in a month," Sean responded, grinning from ear to ear.

Actually, there was a time when he first got married, when he didn't make this much all year. He climbed out of the jeep and handed each man a fat wad of cash.

Sean separated himself from the other two cops and placed a quick call to Lisa. Standing a few feet away, Warren and Jay continued cracking nasty jokes.

"Hey, sexy, what you up to?" Sean asked when Lisa answered.

"Nothing, lying in bed watching a repeat of Martin." Lisa replied.

"Remember the Apple PowerBook you been wanting?"

"Yeah."

"Well, now you can get it," he said.

"You know we can't afford that."

"Yes, we can. With all the overtime I been puttin' in, we have the money. Trust me."

"You coming home?" Lisa asked.

Sean quickly glanced at his Diesel watch. "Yeah, in a little bit." They still had another thirty-five minutes before their tour ended.

"Okay, I love you."

"Love you too," Sean said. Something about the sincerity in her voice touched him deeply. Hanging up, his mind drifted off back into time when he first met Lisa…

The one-day that would change his life happened the beginning of his senior year in Dewitt Clinton High School. Anybody who was somebody usually lined up along the four-foot stone retainer wall near the student parking lot and the school's entrance.

Sean, the starting quarterback on the varsity football team, occupied his favorite spot mid-point along the wall with his boys, Morris and TC. They were laughing and joking about the events of the night before.

"I still can believe you pissed on his carpet," Morris said, laughing.

TC couldn't hide the wide grin that inched across his face. "Yo, my bad, kid, I shouldn't mix liquors. I'll pay for it."

"Yeah aight, just wait to you get a rug," Sean joked, finding the whole incident hilarious. "As soon as it's tacked down I splashing it."

Suddenly, Sean stopped laughing. His mouth opened so wide, his jaw damn near popped as he spotted a sexy honey headed his way. She was sucking on an apple flavored blow-pop like there was no tomorrow. Feeling a slight twitch in his jeans, he zeroed in on her luscious gloss-covered lips as they went to work all over the hard candy shell.

This mouth-watering treat was Lisa. With the sun glistening off her radiant cheeks, her long permed locks bounced and her juicy hips swayed with each step. Her cute, chubby but mean-eyed best friend, Ebony was right by her side as they headed for the entranceway.

Instantly, Sean threw on the sexy grill, which he practiced in almost every bathroom mirror he ran across. Lisa and Sean locked eyes as she and her playa-hating friend strutted past the gawking trio of boys. She flashed him a bright Colgate smile. He returned her inviting beam with a quick wink and a half nod, all the while trying his hardest not to blush. Catching the slightest whiff of her sweet fragrance, he smiled.

Soon as she was out of earshot, Morris and TC immediately started clowning him.

"Damn, son, she got his nose wide-open," TC joked.

Morris laughed, patting Sean on the back, "You ain't ready fa dat."

Breaking into a broad kool-aid grin, Sean just said whatever and brushed them off. But there was one thing for sure his boys were right about: Lisa had him stuck on stupid. No denying.

A few classes later, Lisa rummaged through her locker in the school hallway. Someone whispered in her ear, "Call me" and tucked a folded note in the front pocket of her tight denim jeans. She turned to see whom the voice belonged to.

Standing there posted up in his best gangster lean was Sean, basking with confidence. The moment he had been waiting for all day had arrived. Ever since spotting her earlier, he couldn't shake the girl from his thoughts. When he ran into Lisa at the lockers, his heart jumped into his throat rendering him speechless, but somehow he mustered up the courage to actually go over and speak to her. Now here they were, face to face and he was fronting like "the man" as she flashed him her pearly whites, batting her long, curly eyelashes.

The celebration-taking place in his mind was short lived when she flatly replied, "I'll think about it," and slammed closed the locker, strutting off down the hall without so much as a backwards glance.

Later that night, Sean felt his heart start pounding uncontrollably as his personal line finally rang. He had been sitting near the phone in his room playing Donkey Kong on Super Nintendo for the past three hours waiting for her call. Calming himself down, he took a deep breath and picked up the phone, trying to act like he didn't know who was on the other end.

"Hello," he said in the sexiest voice possible like he wasn't even aware it was Lisa on the other end.

"Hi Sean," Lisa replied. They talked for over two and a half hours that night, about everything from school to sports and how she loved to shop in Macy's on 34th Street.

Over the next four months they were inseparable, going everywhere together from bowling to late night walks along the FDR drive. Lisa met Sean's parents and Sean only met Lisa's mother since her parents were divorced and her father lived down in Miami.

The only thing they hadn't done after that was make love. It wasn't like either one of them were virgins. Lisa didn't believe in giving herself to every cute guy she dated. She had only slept with one guy. The boys she dated had to be very special. Sean, on the other hand, was just playing it cool 'til he could hit it. And boy did he want to hit it.

It happened on a Friday two weeks before the school year ended. The last class had let out and all the rowdy teenagers were filing out of the building for the weekend. Lisa approached her locker, eyes widening as she focused on the single red rose taped to it. She plucked the rose off and held it to her delicate nose.

She whipped around to find Sean standing right behind her. She pulled him close and hugged him. He kissed her neck gently, slowly making his way up to her luscious lips. Sean instantly felt a hardening between his thighs as chills swept the length of his body. The soft scent of her pleasant perfume filled the air.

The short denim skirt Lisa wore had Sean turned on. All he could think about was how sweet she must taste. He couldn't wait until he was on his knees, biting on her inner thighs and sucking her pretty toes.

At that moment, Lisa's nipples were poking through her blouse. Taking notice, Sean backed up and said, "I have the place all to myself." He caressed her chin with his finger, realizing right then and there he had to have her.

Grabbing Lisa by the hand, Sean led her into the boy's locker room. They didn't have to worry about being spotted since school was over and they were the only two people left in the entire building.

With Sean being on the football team the coach had given him a spare key to the locker room and he knew they wouldn't get caught because Paul the head janitor was always home at least two hours before the last class ended. And the principal and all the teachers headed straight to their cars soon as the bell rung. They were just concerned with getting out of the hood before darkness fell.

Most of the locker room was dimly lit except for the last row, which was illuminated by the flicking flame of a candle. Whatever surprise Sean had set up was out of her view hidden behind the chain of lockers. Mary J. Blige's "You Remind Me" bumped from the same direction as the dancing light. Sean guided her over to the last row. A thin narrow wooden bench in the middle of the floor ran the length of the lockers.

One-third of a melted candle burned on top of a small boom box that vibrated every time the bass boomed. His eyes dotted to the rose tucked in her locks on the side of her beautiful face. A smile spread across his lips as she stood there blushing like a shy virgin.

They embraced and immediately started tonguing each other down without saying a word. Lisa felt Sean's cock start to stiffen and grow as he trailed his tongue down her neck and then gently bit her partly exposed collarbone. Shivers danced up her spine as one of his fingers found its way past her panties and rubbed her swollen clit. The short skirt she had on gave him easy access.

Moving her panties to the side, Lisa straddled him as he stood with his back pressed to the warped metal lockers and wrapped her juicy legs around his trim waist. Slowly she slid down his rock hard pipe with her wet, tight hot kitty gripping him every inch of the way as he penetrated her love box for the first time. He could still hear her moaning "Aye," loudly in his ear as he stood on the dead-end street daydreaming. When Sean finally snapped back to the real world, Jay and Warren were still talking shit.

"The union isn't worth shit. They in cahoots with the department." Warren said.

Jay blew a trail of grayish smoke pass his lips, "That's why I look out for number one cause those bastards ain't gonna do it." He looked over at Sean. "Let's get outta here and go grab some drinks."

CHAPTER 8

Over ten miles away in upstate Yonkers, New York, the basement level of a rundown parking garage was filled with darkness and the faint chatter of a huge crowd. The wild barking of dogs sounded off in the distance. A long narrow hallway led to a room that resembled a bomb-shelter with the concrete poured floor and the thick grayish-stained concrete walls. One bare light bulb hung by a wire from the ceiling. Standing beneath the light a rowdy mixture of hustlers and thugs milled around, catching up on good times and bad. As the minutes ticked away, their senseless chatter grew louder.

Razor, a Mexican biker and hit man, covered with tats and the war scars to prove it rolled up sitting on a chromed out Harley chopper. Leaning the hog on its kickstand, Razor moved into position almost directly below the dim glow of the light. Some of his face and body was still partially hidden in the shadows. But his voice, thunderous and raspy would nearly wake the dead.

"You motherfuckers ready? It's a dog-eat-dog world!" he shouted at the top of his lungs.

Instantly the crowd went bananas, yelling and screaming like they were insane. Everyone moved forward, spreading out around Razor and forming a huge circle. The spot beneath the light bulb became center stage. Murmurs ran through the crowd. Hearts pounded as the crowd held their breath, waiting, watching.

Just at the point Razor opened his mouth to address the crowd, his cell rang. Tossing a single hand in the air, he flipped it open. His commanding force swept through the room and the chatter died instantly except for a couple of quick coughs and the sound of feet shuffling.

"Speak," Razor snapped with a snarl to go right along with his bullish attitude.

"It's José," the voice on the other end replied. "We need to talk."

"Now's no good," Razor shot back, his gaze sweeping the area. "I'm busy, homes."

"Hey-" was all José managed to say before the dial tone buzzed in his ears.

It was back to business as Razor tucked the cell back in his black jeans and stepped back out of the center. A chubby, shirtless, brown skinned thug covered with sweat clutched the leather collar of a vicious red-nose pit at his side. He inched forward trying to maintain control of the dog as he stepped into the center. A goateed white boy, dressed in baggy jeans and an oversized red sweat shirt, held the chain end of a spiked collar attached to a murderous blue-gray pit on a heavy-duty chain.

As soon as both were in position, yelling and screaming started up again as the crowd grew excited.

The two men circled each other as the pits, barked and growled, desperately trying to lunge at one another. Drool flew from one dog's gaping mouth as the other exposed his sharp, jagged teeth.

Their owners jerked forward, sneakers dragging on the ground as they struggled to hold them back, allowing the excitement to build and more money to change hands. Finally, with the crowd's anticipation now at its peak, the owners released the collars. The two bloodthirsty pits sprang forward, leaping off the ground and landing in the center.

The shouts and screams became deafening as the two ferocious dogs viciously tore at each other's flesh. The crowd roared itself into frenzy with every bite.

Suddenly the noise died down. The yells trickled to almost a complete halt. The dogs settled down from growls to piercing whines. A golden skin man with a round build entered the area. The crowd parted like the Red Sea. His golden link chain rankled with every step. Two henchmen, one a menacing-looking brother, the other a deadly Puerto Rican, flanked his sides.

The owners pulled once more on the dog's chains. They ceased the urge to fight, somehow sensing that they were no longer the center of attention.

Money disappeared into baggy pockets as hands lowered, their owners realizing that this dogfight was now a lost cause.

"Fuck's wrong with you," José snapped, his wide frame barreling down on Razor.

"Nothing personal, homes," Razor said, shrugging. "There's a lot of money changing hands here."

José stepped into the center of the circle. The dogs were pulled away as he scanned the various faces of the crowd. "Who da fuck wanna make some real paper?" He continued scanning the group. "I'm lookin' fa real niggas."

The group lunged forward, like vultures circling dead prey.

José gave a brief story of Bobby's death. Two boys came forward sharing the little bit of information they knew about the two narcs.

"That's good. That's all good," José said, flipping them a cool hundred each. Then he counted out more money and held it up. "Ten grand to da motherfucker who bodies them."

A roar went up from the crowd as José turned his back, walking out of the circle. Razor followed. The dogfight resumed, but even more of a heated frenzy had come over the crowd.

A few minutes later, in the kennel area of the garage the sound of barking dogs was deafening. All types of pits lined the numerous cramped cages.

Plugging an extension cord into an electrical socket with exposed wires showing at the other end, a young black worker placed the wire at the base of the skull, electrocuting the wounded red-nosed pit lying on the ground in front of him. As the electricity shot through the dog's body, it convulsed a few times, then went limp. He tossed the fried corpse into a black plastic garbage bag, tied it up and flung it over in a corner to be discarded at a later time.

Razor rubbed the huge head of a vicious looking Rottweiler with a white patch over its eye and then placed him back into the tight raggedy kennel.

José waited patiently until the door closed tight. He grabbed Razor by the edges of his collar. "Don't ever pull dat shit again. If I call, there's a reason."

Razor nodded.

José released his hold, straightening the man's clothes as though he hadn't just threatened the man's life for something as small as hanging up on him.

"First they kill my baby brother now they fuckin' wit' my sister. It ends now!" José shouted.

"Just give me the four w's, homes," Razor replied in a tone that was dead serious.

José lit up the fat blunt he was holding and said, "I'll holla at ya tomorrow wit' the info'." He took a deep pull. "Make sure it's painful."

CHAPTER 9

Back in the Hunt's Point section of the Bronx, Sean, Jay and Warren downed glass after glass of alcohol in a seedy strip club filled with blue-collar workers who drank booze and talked loudly. The place provided the perfect celebration point for the trio. Topless dancers with big boobs and perky nipples worked the main stage as one voluptuous stripper gyrated on the pole. She slowly pulled her thong down to her ankles.

"Watch your spending habits and don't get flashy," Jay said, downing the rest of his rum and coke.

Sean nodded, and glanced over at the lounge area. More strippers were busy drinking, flirting and giving lap dances to overzealous drunken patrons with sticky hands and bankrolls of cash to spend.

Warren sipped his beer, watching as one of the dark-skinned strippers wiggled and made her ass cheeks clap together. She glanced over at him and grinned. He motioned her over and she strutted toward him like a lioness stalking her prey. A few jealous eyes followed her path over to Warren.

"How about a lap dance?" Warren asked, lightly smacking her fat ass.

"Twenty dollars, honey," she replied coolly and stood wide legged in front of him. Her lustrous mound of dark curls peeked out of her thong.

"Here's a hundred." Warren's devilish grin appeared as he slipped a crisp Franklin in her palm. "Make it special."

"Honey, you get VIP. Follow me." She turned and switched off, her voluptuous ass jiggling with every step.

Warren quickly stood, trailing behind her like a lamb to slaughter. Sean watched them disappear into a back room, then turned to Jay.

"We could've made a killin' if we would've grabbed the product," he said.

A brief moment of silence passed before Jay said, "You forget rule one?" He eyed Sean closely. "We never touch the drugs."

"Now we follow rules," Sean replied, mashing out his cigarette in the glass ashtray. "Give me a fuckin' break." He glanced at a thick creamy brown stripper strutting along the stage shaking her plump ass to a crunk beat. A few men hollered catcalls at her.

"Shake down a few fuckin' corners, now you an expert and shit, huh?" Jay asked, clenching his jaw muscles, but he didn't blow his cool.

"Maybe," Sean replied unable to hide the contempt in his voice. He lit up another smoke.

"You're thinkin' wit' emotion." Jay didn't look at Sean as he sipped the cool brew.

"*I'm* thinkin' wit' emotion?" Sean repeated laughing so hard he had to hold his sides.

Jay chugged his beer. "You like jail?"

Sean sobered up. A mere mention of that word could put fear in even the cleanest cop's heart. He didn't even have a chance to answer as Jay continued on.

"'Cause that's where emotional niggas like you end up, wonderin' how the fuck they got there." Jay shoved the empty beer bottle to the side.

Sean nodded solemnly, wondering if Jay knew how close to him his words had hit.

"Weigh the risks of movin' product on the streets," Jay continued, "Too many eyes, people talk."

A voluptuous stripper with honey colored skin strutted by in only a thong that got lost in the crack of her huge ass. She gave Jay a seductive rub on the back. She winked at him as he glanced her way. Her sweet scent mixed with the smell of tobacco and beer.

"You're right," Sean admitted in a low murmur. Besides it was his job to sit back, play the humble role and let Jay lead. Not being able to voice his real opinions and put Jay in check whenever he got the urge was the hardest part about being undercover. That's where the real stress and frustration came into play. But for now he just had to suck it up and play his position. He'd be able to get everything off his chest once it was finally time to bring Jay and Warren's dirty asses down.

"Shit, even I gotta pay taxes to keep the bigwig downtown off our asses," Jay uttered absently, sipping his drink. "But we pocket the lion's share of the pot."

"You serious?" Sean asked, leaning in. Hell, if he could find out which top dog Jay was paying off, he'd blow this case wide open. That would definitely earn him a detective's shield. A lot of the upper brass knew about the corruption running rampant in the department, but most chose to ignore it and a few crooked ones even demanded a cut of the blood money to keep it quiet. With all the connections and power they had in the city, Internal Affairs had to fish them out carefully.

Jay nodded.

"Who?" Sean asked trying to sound nonchalant, really hoping he'd spit out a name.

"Now *that* I can't say," Jay responded then took a long swallow of beer. He made it his business not to tell people more than they needed to know. "This job used to matter. Now it's 'bout grabbin' all you can before gettin' out."

"So bring me up to speed on this drug dealer José. Why you gunnin' for him so hard?" Sean asked, lighting up a cigarette. He eyed the stage as a white stripper with the body of a black girl gave some lucky customer a blowjob. The black guy receiving the oral treat was grinning from ear to ear.

"Last summer he killed a kid that happened to be one of my best informants," Jay answered as he told Sean the details of the murder.

Eagerly buying all sorts of cold ice cream treats, a bunch of little kids crowded around the Mister Softee ice cream truck with the usual happy go lucky tune that was music to any child's ears blasting from its speakers on the sweltering summer afternoon on 141st street near Cypress Avenue. The foul stench of hot rotting garbage coming from the huge pile of black and white plastic garbage bags stacked by the curbside hung in the already highly polluted air.

A couple of feet away, holding court on the corner, Julio was posted up against a street sign sweet talking a sexy Puerto Rican chic with a honey coated complexion, hazel eyes and a 34C-24-38 frame that would put J-Lo to shame. Her honey blond straight hair hit the middle of her back.

Standing about five-feet nine and weighing a little over one hundred and thirty pounds, Julio's plain crispy white wife beater clung to his chest and midsection. His torso was cut up like a lightweight boxer in training. He had tattoos covering almost every inch of skin up and down both his well-toned arms. The red bandana wrapped around his forehead covered his eyebrows only leaving his light brown eyes exposed.

"When you gonna let me suck them pretty toes, mami?" Julio asked, glancing down at her perfectly manicured feet wrapped in a pair open toe Jimmy Choo sandals with four-inch heels. His lustful eyes traveled back up the length of her body until he reconnected with her beautiful bright stare.

"Julio, why you so nasty?" she asked with a giggle.

"You know you like that."

Julio was so busy running his mouth that he didn't notice José approaching it was too late. Spotting the sawed-off 12-gauge clutched in the dangerous man's burly hand, Julio's smile quickly faded replaced by pure terror and he took off running for his life.

Julio only made it a few steps before the blast from the shotgun chewed up his entire back and the upper part of his legs. People screamed for their lives as they scattered, running for cover. The pellets left his flesh with more holes than Swiss cheese turning his white wife beater T-shirt completely red. Julio hit the ground hard, skidding on the concrete asphalt.

"Aah, it burns, it burns!" Julio cried out in pain. Sprawled out facedown on the hot concrete, his body twitched and jerked as his blood ran into the gutter, disappearing into the metal sewer drain. Standing over him with the twin barrels still smoking José racked two more shells into the double chambers. Julio slowly rolled over onto his back and found himself staring into the black lifeless eyes of death. He struggled to speak, but no words were found as he started choking on his own blood.

"Look what you made me do, Julio," José said, shaking his head in disgust. "You were one of my best workers. You never should have crossed me!"

With that said and done, José squeezed the trigger. Both slugs left Julio's face looking like an over flowing plate of spaghetti and meatballs. Anyone that didn't know him wouldn't be able to tell if he was male or female. None of his facial features were recognizable. His eyes, his nose and his mouth were gone. The only thing left was a bloody heap of flesh and shattered bone.

José turned on his heels and calmly strutted over to the black Cadillac Escalade waiting for him at the curb. He opened the back door and tossed the shotgun into the backseat then climbed into the front passenger seat. Soon as he slammed the door shut, the idling truck busted a quick u-turn and peeled off down the block.

Two local hoods rushed to Julio's aid. "Call police, call police!" the tall skinny black one cried out. He happened to be one of the cats from the block that didn't care too much for José. He cradled what was left of Julio's bloody head in his arms as they waited for the cops and an ambulance to come.

As the speeding Cadillac made its getaway, the eagle-eyed driver glanced over as José sniffed a small amount of coke out of his palm. "Not to pry in ya business and all, but what did the kid do?"

With traces of white powder still visible on his nose, José looked over at the driver a moment.

"The fuck was snitching me out to them pigs like I wasn't gonna find out about it," José replied. "Now shut the fuck up and drive."

Back on the block, the police pulled up about five minutes later and started processing the crime scene, moving people back. They covered the dead man with a white sheet. His blood quickly saturated the sheet turning parts of it bright red.

At least twenty minutes had past before the ambulance finally arrived. But by then it was way too late. Julio's spirit had already returned to the Creator the moment both slugs tore his face completely off.

"After Jose killed my informant, he went into hidin' and stopped payin' us off," Jay said, polishing the rest of his beer off. "That's like spittin' in my face. You let one cat get away with it, ten others are gonna try."

* * *

Meanwhile in the dark back room, Warren leaned back on the couch, enjoying one of the best blowjobs of his life as the stripper's head greedily bopped up and down, leaving trails of saliva along his shaft. Her round juicy ass clapped as she rocked back and forth on her knees, snaking her hot wet tongue over his short piece of wood. Warren slid one of the vanilla packets from his coat pocket and carefully unfolded it revealing a small amount of cocaine. His hands trembled slightly as he anticipated the coming high and the approaching orgasm. He poured some of the snow into his palm and took a hit. Purple hills and puffy white clouds unfolded before him as his eyes rolled back, and he sunk deeper in the plush cushions.

In the small cramped men's room of the strip club, a hoodlum decked out in a tan Dickie outfit with a long john shirt peeking from underneath, puffed on a fat blunt as Jay entered and made eye contact.

"Fuckin' problem wit' ya eyes, pops?" the high hoodlum snapped harshly, obviously not realizing whom he was talking to. Standing there posted up against the graffiti scrawled wall, the thug was too hard for his own good.

In a flash of lightning, Jay grabbed him by the throat almost crushing his Adam's apple and pressed his gun up under the boy's unshaved chin.

"Actually, my doctor says I need glasses," he replied, glaring into the frightened hoodlum's eyes. "What you think?"

Scared shitless, a yellow stream of urine quickly pooled around the hoodlum's new black, shell topped Adidas. Jay looked down following the sound of piss. Spotting the yellowish pool on the dirty white tiled floor, he cracked a devilish grin, releasing his crippling grip on the boy's neck. The shaken and embarrassed hoodlum scrambled out the exit nearly trampling over Sean as he entered the men's room.

Sean glanced back at the fleeing thug then looked at Jay, puzzled.

Jay shrugged. "It's a shame when a man can't even take a leak in peace."

Sean just laughed, crossing to an unoccupied urinal.

"Listen, I was serious when I said, we gotta watch how we spend money." Jay said, taking the empty urinal right next to Sean. "Don't make any big purchases that's gonna draw attention to you. We don't need the wrong motherfuckas takin' notice."

"I got you." Sean assured him.

CHAPTER 10

The next evening, Sean sat behind the wheel of his Acura, questioning Lisa over the speakerphone while trying to control his anger. "Where the hell were you last night, Lisa?"

"Stephanie had problems with Rick. She needed to talk," Lisa responded softly, her heart pounding uncontrollably. She knew good and well she was lying.

"So you don't call?"

"I'm sorry. I fell asleep."

As Sean approached an intersection, the traffic light changed from yellow to red.

"Whatever," he snapped before shutting off the cell and slowing down at the crosswalk. Deep in his gut, he had an ill feeling she was fucking around on him, but he couldn't prove it. Scanning the dark street ahead of him, he shook the thought off, unwilling to imagine the woman he loved and married giving herself to another man. That shit would definitely send him over the edge.

Lurking in the nearby shadows, Slim and two menacing goons eyed Sean's Acura idling at the crosswalk. Razor, one the goons, pulled an all black .357 from the small of his back. The other shifty-eyed goon, spat out a glob of tobacco.

"Dat him?" Razor asked sharply with ice in his veins, ready to ambush the Acura.

"No," Slim responded. Actually, he was kind of relieved it wasn't the right cop 'cause he didn't want any part in killing no pig. But he didn't have a choice. José expected him to point out the two narcs that iced Bobby.

"You sure?" Razor snapped, his finger stroked the trigger, itching to put it to use.

Slim nodded and Razor reluctantly tucked the gun back in his waistband, pissed that he didn't get a chance to quench his thirst for bloodshed.

The traffic light turned green and the Acura sped across the intersection. Sean didn't realize just how close he had been to danger. The taillights disappeared into the dark night.

A few minutes later he pulled up at the precinct tucked on the south end of Randall's Island and strolled into the worn three-story brick building. Police officers and civilians worked at their desks while other employees moved about. Typical precinct chatter filled the stale air as Jay emerged from a rear office and crossed to Sean who was getting a drink of water at the fountain. The two men knocked fist and headed for the staircase.

Their captain, an older white male, rough around the edges, sporting a stuffy suit jacket headed up the steps as Jay and Sean advanced in the opposite direction. From his enormous potbelly, you knew he never skipped a meal or late-night snack.

"What's up, Capt'?" Jay inquired, pausing on the steps. Sean barely managed not to bump into his partner.

"You two my office now!" Captain Hardy demanded, his gray steely eyes hardening. His fire laced tone clearly signaled he was not happy with the two of them.

He stormed straight for his office with his salt and pepper hair flapping in the breeze.

Jay and Sean exchanged "what the fuck" glances as they lagged behind. Sitting a few desks over, a burly red-haired cop in a tight fitting green polo shirt flipped the Captain the bird behind his back while winking at the two passing narcs. Jay threw him a quick smile. Sean just nodded.

The Captain stomped into his office with Jay right on his tail and immediately barked, "Close my freaking door!"

Since Sean was the last man in, he quickly shut the door.

"What's the problem, Capt'?" Jay asked, trying to sound concerned, but the look on his face revealed he really didn't give a fuck as he pulled up a seat.

Tensed up and tight-lipped, Sean remained standing, trying to read the grumpy old man. He wondered how the poor fuck didn't realize he had two of the dirtiest narcs running loose in his squad.

The Captain pulled out a cigar, lit it up and sat back in his plush chair. He eyeballed the two sorry ass cops a moment and then spoke, "Stiffs are popping up all over town from bad dope. The media's having a freaking field day."

"You know I'm workin' it, Capt'," Jay replied, his demeanor cooler than the other side of the pillow. He scooped up some peanuts from the plastic bowl sitting on the Captain's fairly neat desk. "Just give me some time."

"Action speaks louder than words, Detective," the Captain said sharply, puffing on the cigar, curls of smoke rising. "I want the assholes pushing that poison behind bars within the next two weeks."

"We on it, Capt." Jay assured him.

"Good, now get out there and get me some numbers."

Jay and Sean quickly left the office and headed straight out of the precinct exit to the Cherokee parked on the premise. The two men sat silent as Jay pulled the Cherokee out of the parking lot, sped up the street and disappeared around a bend.

* * *

Minutes later, standing in front of a rundown tenement building, Howie, a junkie in his late thirties, argued with his baby's mama as their infant daughter slept peacefully in the stroller. Drugs had definitely taken their toll on him from the blotches and pockmarks covering his aged face to his crusty, chapped lips. The few rotted teeth he had left were stained a brownish yellow. He barely weighed one-fifty soaking wet. He was the average neighborhood fiend, but he did have some redeeming qualities as a part-time snitch.

"Since, ya ain't doin' right by ya baby, I'm takin' ya cheap ass ta court," she barked, throwing a hand on her fleshy hip.

"Can't make a loaf of bread outta crumbs." Howie patted his empty pockets for emphasis.

She looked him up and down, disgust flashing in her dark brown eyes as she snapped, "Maybe you'd have money if ya wasn't wastin' it on dope."

"I stopped usin'," Howie replied defensively. Glancing past her, he spotted the approaching Cherokee and quickly took off, strolling down the block in the opposite direction.

"Where da hell ya goin'?" she yelled at him. Howie didn't break his stride as he kept walking like he didn't hear her.

The Cherokee pulled up along side Howie, keeping his pace. The driver's window dropped and Jay leaned into view. "You in a hurry, Howie?"

Howie stopped dead in his tracks and pointedly turned to Jay. "Hey, I didn't even see ya." His eyes darted to his worn boots.

Jay threw the Cherokee in park, motioning for Howie to approach. Sean observed from the passenger seat as Howie shuffled over to the jeep.

"You been duckin' me?" Jay asked as Howie stopped and stood at the driver's window.

"Nah," Howie said, fidgeting with his shirt. "I wouldn't do dat."

"Get in," Jay snapped, his ice-cold eyes flashing with anger. "I'm tired of this bullshit."

"I gotta be somewhere," Howie lied trying to weasel his way out the situation.

"Get the fuck in, Howie!" Jay's face scrawled into a tight snarl.

Howie reluctantly hopped in the back of the Cherokee and Jay pulled off.

Across the street, a beefy figure tucked in the shadows watching Howie roll away in the Cherokee with the two narcs. He stepped into the light under the street lamp and watched the Cherokee disappear up the block. His dreadlocks hid part of his pockmarked face.

Dipped in a Roc-A-Wear denim outfit with a pair of fresh Nike airs, Mel was a hustler from around the way. He was one of those paranoid cats that stuck to the shadows. If there were a hole in the wall, he'd find it. He turned, slithered off down the nearly empty block, making a mental note to holler at Black.

Jay glanced at Howie through the rearview as the Cherokee shot up the street, "Ya lose my number?"

"Verizon cut off my jack," Howie replied shakily.

"Just stop while you're ahead," Jay warned, tossing a wad of cash into the seat next to Howie. "Here. That's courtesy of Black."

Howie's eyes flashed with greed as he snatched up the stack of bills, flipping through it with a great big kool-aid smile.

"I see my tip paid off," he said without taking his beady pupils off the cash. He planned on shooting it all up his rail thin arm tonight and busting out a nasty hooker over in Hunt's Point. One of those dirty bitches was definitely getting fucked in her shit-box later on.

"That it did," Jay bragged, pulling the Cherokee over on an isolated block. He turned to Howie. "Ya got what I need?"

"I'm workin' on it," Howie responded uneasily, barely able to keep eye contact with Jay.

"Workin' on it?" Jay glared at Howie. "I just threw ya a bone and you fuckin' wit' me already, Howie."

Howie's face emptied of all guise as he said, "Nah, I wouldn't do you like—"

Jay, cut him off before turning to Sean, "Isn't there a warrant on this clown?"

Sean nodded, playing along. Jay reached over the seat, grabbed Howie's frail arm, flashing a pair of cuffs.

"Don't please," Howie pleaded. "Tomorrow. . . I'll have it *tomorrow*."

Jay released Howie's wrist, still glaring at him. Howie's gaze dropped to his lap.

"Freedom costs," Jay informed, him eyeing the bankroll in Howie's palm.

Noticing Jay beaming at his greenbacks, Howie tensed, curling his slender fingers tightly around the cash. "Come on. Don't do me dis way. I need dis bread, man."

"And I gotta hit my arrest quota," Jay stated, harshly with a devilish grin. "You fuck me, I fuck you."

Reluctantly, Howie slid the wad back into Jay's outstretched palm.

"You know a narc is only as good as his snitches and right now you got me lookin' like a fuckin' ass," Jay said.

"It ain't even like that."

"Get out," Jay demanded, as he tucked the bills in his pocket.

"Here?" Howie asked, his eyes widening in disbelief. They had to be at least fifteen blocks from his hood.

The look Jay shot him said it all. Howie hopped out without any further hesitation. The Cherokee sped off down the block and from the side view mirrors Sean saw Howie flip them the finger.

Black's white Yukon flew up the block and slowed, pulling over to the curb in front of a rundown pool hall. Packed with lowlifes, knuckleheads and hard rocks from the hood, this definitely wasn't a spot for the cowardly hearted. ReRe reclined in the passenger seat clutching an all black revolver in her small palm resting on her lap.

"Fuck is dis nigga, man?" Black complained, starting to get irritated. "I told his ass to be outside."

Just then, Mel slid out of a pitch-black alleyway a couple of stores up from the spot. Glancing in the side view mirror, Black spotted Mel and shook his head, laughing to himself. It always bugged him out how Mel shunned the light like a fucking vampire or something.

Mel strolled up to the passenger window and asked, "What's crackin', my nigga? What up, ReRe?" He was way too animated as usual.

ReRe tossed him a half nod. She never got too friendly with niggas out of respect for her man and her brother José.

"Ain't shit," Black replied, still grinning.

"What da fuck so funny?"

"You, ya shadow creepin' motherfucker," Black shot back, laughing even harder.

"Laugh if ya wanna. Dat's why I see it all, baby. Matta fact, dat's exactly why I hit ya," Mel exclaimed.

Black sobered instantly. He slouched back in the plush leather seat and listened.

"I saw dat crackhead nigga who be washin' ya truck hollerin' at dem boys dat ran up in ya spot."

"You talkin' 'bout Howie?" Black asked, cocking his bushy eyebrows.

"Fuck, I don't know da cat name. But I know fa sure it's dat nigga who be scrubbin' down dis bitch," Mel said tapping on the side of the Yukon.

Black just shook his head. As everything began to click, he was finally able to put two and two together. So, that's how the pigs knew where ReRe's spot was.

"Good lookin' out, Mel. I'ma bless ya fa dis," Black assured him, stretching across ReRe to knock fist with Mel. "Just hit me tomorrow."

"No doubt," Mel replied, giving a slow nod before ditty-bopping back into the darkness.

The Yukon pulled back into the flow of traffic. They rode in total silence as Black contemplated his next move and ReRe stewed in her own vengeful thoughts. Her blood boiled as she thought about making that snitch pay for dropping a dime on them. She was a ride or die type chick. Always had been, growing up with an older brother who was a notoriously murderous drug dealer. And she definitely didn't stand for anybody crossing her man. She was determined to put Howie under the next time she crossed his path.

And just like that fate intervened as the Yukon pulled up to a red light. ReRe glanced over at the corner bodega. Howie emerged from the store, tapping on a box of Salems. He didn't even notice the truck idling at the intersection. Busy popping another CD in the radio, Black hadn't noticed Howie either.

Like a bolt of lightning, ReRe leaped from the truck dashing at top speed toward Howie with the gun in her outstretched palm. Black whipped around just in time to see Howie. Howie turned and noticed ReRe closing in on him. Two rapid shots rang out. Both slugs slammed into his narrow frame. Howie dropped right there on the very same spot were he stood. Sprawled out, face down, on the cold concrete, blood gushed from his gaping mouth. ReRe stood over him, pumping another slug into the back of his skull. Just for grins.

Everything had happened in slow motion for Black, who still held a single CD in his thick fingers. With his jaws wide open, he sat motionless, not believing what his own eyes were seeing. Now he definitely knew ReRe was a down ass bitch, but *damn*! She was a crazy ass thoroughbred.

The loud wail of approaching police sirens immediately brought Black back to reality. ReRe spun around, dashing back to the truck as Black waited, ready to floor it. He glanced in the rearview just in time to see a police cruiser speeding up the block toward him while another cruiser shot out of the cross street at the intersection and cut him off from the front. By this time, ReRe was already in the truck, but they were blocked in with nowhere to go. Shit. He couldn't let ReRe take the rap for this shit.

"Give me da gun," Black demanded.

"Nah, fuck dat," ReRe shot back. "I did it. I'll hold mine!"

"No, da fuck you ain't," Black barked, snatching the pistol from her grasp just as one of the four cops ran up and stuck his Beretta through the open, driver side window and yelled, "Freeze!"

"She ain't have nothin' to do wit' dis," Black replied dropping the revolver onto his lap as he lifted his hands in the air. "I'm ya man." In his mind, thanks to Jay and Warren, Black already had his "get out of jail free" card.

* * *

An all black Range Rover idled in front of the 40th police station on Bergen Avenue near the corner of 149th street. One of the pitch-black windows that hid the features of the two occupants inside was half way down and a stringy cloud of cigarette drifted out into the brisk night air.

After a few moments, ReRe emerged from the precinct with her clothes a bit ruffled and her hair fuzzy. A slight smile spread across her otherwise solemn grill when the window lowered all the way down and José poked his big head in the frame.

"Hey there sweet thing. You need a ride?" José said, exposing a full dose of his pearly whites.

"Shut up, stupid," ReRe said, giving way to a quick giggle. She grabbed the door handle. "Move over."

"Is that anyway to treat the man who just bailed you out?"

***

Three days later on a Friday morning at St. Raymond's Cemetery on the Cross Bronx Expressway access road and Randall Avenue, various expensive cars and sports utility vehicles crammed the narrow roadway cutting through the massive cemetery leading to the burial site. Tombstones stretched beyond eye view in almost every angle. A huge crowd of mourners surrounded a newly dug grave as a cold breeze whipped through their ranks. The smell of freshly unearthed soil hung in the air. The bare tree branches shook in the jagged breeze whipping through the cemetery. The sounds of traffic lingered off in the distance.

While holding his hysterical mother in his bulky arms, José scanned all the teary eyed faces in the crowd that were present to pay his brother their last respects. Usually he wouldn't be caught dead in a suit but due to the circumstances it was the only thing appropriate. He hated to see his mother in so much pain. This happened to be one situation he couldn't make better with money or an expensive gift.

"He's in a better place now, Ma," José said, trying to ease the hurt. His frail mother only cried harder, collapsing into his chest. Her pale cheeks were flooded with tears.

Car horns and the noisy flow of traffic could be heard in the distance. Seated on the first row, draped in a full-length white mink was ReRe. Her eyes were hidden behind a pair of dark shades as she cried her heart out in Chico's comforting embrace. His beady pupils were blood shot red from crying.

The expensive metal gray coffin adorned with brass handles rested on the heavy-duty straps of a dolly ready to be lowered into the six-foot grave. A beautiful flower spread was draped over the closed casket.

As the cemetery crew carefully lowered the coffin into the ground, grieving family members and friends tossed long single stemmed red roses onto the coffin. One by one people started returning to their vehicles. José supported his ailing mother all the way back to his BMW.

CHAPTER 11

One week later inside the security bubble of housing area 4-lower, in the C-73 building on Riker's Island, an overweight female correction officer sporting a Mohawk and broad, flat chest and thick side burns, sat at a metal desk thumbing through the Daily News newspaper. It was still somewhat cold since February had just rolled in. Through the Plexiglas separating her from the housing area, she had a view of the inmates roaming around the day room and the cells that ran up and down the narrow corridor.

Black bopped up to the bubble and pressed his broad nose to the Plexiglas. "Excuse me, CO!"

She ignored him, not even bothering to look up as she continued reading the cartoon section.

"Yo, CO," Black shouted, starting to get upset.

Taking her sweet time, she finally looked up from the page with a silly ass smirk on her face and barked, "What?"

"Let me get soap."

Reaching down beside her, she grabbed two half-bars of soap from a bucket on the floor and tossed them through the slot in the Plexiglas at Black. "Here. Don't ask for more," she snapped.

He snatched up both pieces of soap from the hole and bopped back down the corridor toward his cell.

The heat from the radiators only made the stench that hung in the stale air that much stronger. Most of the inmates watching Jerry Springer shared a laugh as a couple on the show fought.

Moments later, inside his cell Black feverishly scrubbed a white T-shirt with soap and water over a small metal basin as an inmate stepped in. "Yo, what up, Black?"

Black looked up, recognizing the inmate from his hood. A smile quickly crept across his face. "What da deal, fam?" He stopped washing the shirt and quickly shook the water from his palms. "I thought you was upstate?" he inquired as they exchanged pounds.

"Da D.A. brought me down on a new charge," the inmate said as he stood back and took a good long look at Black. "What da hell you doin' here?"

"Bullshit murda rap," Black replied, shrugging as if he didn't have a care in the world.

"Look like ya gon' be keepin' me company awhile," the inmate implied jokingly.

"Fuck dat, I got otha plans," Black assured him. He was dead serious. He knew exactly how he planned on getting his charge reduced. *Just wait and see*, he thought. His determination to get back at them pigs for what they did to his girl ReRe and the money they took from him, only strengthened every day he spent behind bars.

"So what's up wit' ReRe?"

"She good, actually dis her time I'm holdin'."

"You'se one honorable ma'fucka 'cause a nigga like me couldn't do it," the inmate replied, shaking his head. "Not for no pussy."

"First off she's wifey," Black snapped. "She ain't just a piece of ass."

"Pardon me, fam," the inmate said apologetic. "I ain't mean no disrespect."

"None taken," Black replied.

****

The Cherokee barreled down the Westside highway towards Manhattan. The highway held a light flow of traffic. Across the Hudson River's murky choppy waters, New Jersey's shoreline lit up the foggy night.

Minutes later in Washington Heights, the windy streets were empty, almost ghost like, and sidewalks were void of hardly a soul. The Cherokee lurked along Broadway Avenue with Jay driving and Sean riding shotgun.

Approaching 135th Street and Broadway, Jay slowed down at the corner. On 135th Street, a group of guys hung out, boisterously drinking on a nearby stoop. Jay looked them over as the Cherokee rounded the corner.

He knew they weren't even worth frisking. At best they probably had a couple of nickel bags between them, which wasn't worth shit to him but another bullshit misdemeanor arrest. What he needed was some cold-hard cash, *quick.*

The now, dead quiet group stared at the passing Cherokee. Sean gawked right back at them, but his mind was really elsewhere. He wanted to know more about Warren as the Cherokee headed up 135th Street towards Riverside Drive.

"I heard Warren's been to da farm a few times," Sean said, as his curiosity finally got the best of him. "So that's why I ended up being your partner?"

Jay shrugged. "That. . . and the bad press we generated."

The two men fell silent for a few moments.

"We all fight demons," Jay stated evenly as he whipped the Cherokee down Riverside drive. "We're not warrin' with flesh and blood, but against principalities, against the rulers of the darkness of this world. The only real question is, who's gonna win?"

"Isn't that from the bible?"

Jay nodded.

"When did you become so religious?"

"I don't believe in God anymore," Jay replied.

"You serious?" Sean asked, staring at Jay.

"As a heart attack. I stopped believin' a long time ago. If he existed, why is the world so fucked up?"

Sean shrugged. "Well, I don't have the answer to that, but I do know he's real."

"Yeah, then where was he when my mother's punk ass man shot her in cold blood and left her to die in my arms?" Jay asked, drifting back to the day his mother was killed.

"I'm sorry to hear that," Sean said, with pain in his eyes. "I can definitely relate. I lost my real pops when I was nine."

Once again both men fell silent. Sean eyed Jay. The older detective seemed to finally be showing his feelings. The solemn look etched on his face revealed a man who had been hurt deeply. Sean decided to break the quietness.

"So, who won?"

"Who won, what?" Jay replied absent-mindedly.

"I'm talkin' about Warren."

"Oh, far as I know, he been clean 'bout…ten months," Jay said, lighting up a cigarette.

On 144th street, a black Navigator sat at the curb with its rear hatch open revealing detergent bottles inside. Standing at the backside was its owner, Carlos also known as "the Dominican Connect" keeping a constant eye out for anything that looked suspicious. He seemed real edgy. Double parked next to the Navigator was a souped up red Honda Accord with eighteen-inch alloy racing rims. Ricky, Puerto Rican, late twenties, popped the trunk.

Carlos grabbed two big detergent bottles from the Navigator, quickly passing them to Ricky. Ricky tossed them in the empty trunk as Carlos slid him two more bottles then closed the hatch.

"Dat's it, Papi. Pure, no flake," Carlos said, his eyes dotted to a yellow cab that passed by. "Where's my cash?"

"Easy," Ricky piped, throwing up his palms. "It's in da ride." He slammed the trunk shut as Carlos glanced up the street. The Cherokee had just turned onto the block.

"5-0!" Carlos yelled to Ricky as he dipped into the shadows covering the sidewalk and slid off out of sight.

Ricky's eyes almost popped out of their sockets when he spotted the Cherokee roaring towards him. He quickly stepped into the Honda acting like he didn't see the jeep approaching.

The Cherokee's spotlight popped on, illuminating the Honda as Jay threw the gearshift in park. "Twenty dollars says, he's dirty," Jay said, glancing over at Sean.

"That's one bet I ain't takin'," Sean said before stepping out the Cherokee, followed by Jay. With his eyes locked on target, Jay cautiously approached the driver's side and tapped on the glass with his gun trained on Ricky. Sean covered the passenger side and swept a flashlight over the interior. Nothing suspicious could be seen from the door.

Ricky lowered the window. "Problem, officer?"

"Step out," Jay ordered bluntly. Taking a deep breath, Ricky swung the car door open and soon stood only two feet away from the intimidating cop. "What ya doin' out here so late?" Jay asked, scanning him suspiciously from head to toe.

"Waitin' fa my lady," Ricky said boldly obviously trying to play it cool. "Dat no crime, right?" He asked, flashing a fake friendly smile, but his nervousness still showed through as he repeatedly bit his lower lip.

"Okay, Dickhead, spread'em on da hood," Jay demanded, giving him a quick shove on the back. Ricky moved to the front of the car and stretched out eagle style across the hot sheet metal. "Search him," Jay told Sean. Leaning into the Honda, he popped the trunk.

Sean crossed over to Ricky, pressing him down even further against the scorching hood with one hand. As the heat hit him, Ricky put up slight resistance and Sean twisted his arm behind his back. "Don't be stupid," Sean snapped, applying even more pressure.

With splintering pain shooting into his shoulder, Ricky quickly settled down. "Okay, okay, Papi," he replied, his face etched in pain.

Releasing his arm, Sean roughly patted him down and found a roll of bills in his coat pocket. Quickly slipping the knot into his own pocket, Sean continued searching him down to his ankles. Sometimes cats kept work tucked just inside their socks or foot ware. The smarter ones kept it hidden in their boxers because the cops tend not to search the crotch area too often.

Jay twisted open one of the detergent bottles in the trunk and poured out a white powdery substance. Dipping his finger in, he gave it a taste. His eyes lit up once he realized it was cocaine. "I guess this makes ya whites brighter?" he asked sarcastically, glancing up at Ricky.

"Dat no mine. De ride no mine," Ricky said, lying through his teeth. "I borrow."

"Okay, okay," Jay replied, shaking his head with a half grin. "So, you didn't know 'bout da coke in da trunk, huh?"

Ricky didn't respond, knowing he was up shit's creek minus the paddle. He closed his eyes and stood there praying to God, wishing he had never started slinging drugs.

"Where you hidin' da paper?" Jay asked bluntly, then said, "Where there's coke, there's sure to be cash."

Tightlipped and lock-jawed, Ricky remained silent so Sean pressed the glock to his temple with a dangerous gleam in his eye.

Not willing to test the quiet cop with the serious attitude and cannon poked at his skull, Ricky quickly ended his tough guy stance. "Back seat."

Shaking his head at how quick the man switched up, Sean lowered the gun.

Searching around, Jay found a bulky duffle bag stashed behind the passenger seat. Unzipping it, he glanced inside and a grin widened across his otherwise steel-hardened face. He zipped it back up and continued searching the rest of the interior, finding a nickel-plated .45 under the driver's seat.

"This could really hurt somebody," Jay said as he held up the shiny gun.

Ricky glanced up at Jay and spotted the firearm in his hand. His head dropped back down, knowing he was definitely going to jail for along time.

Jay tucked the gun in his waistband, clutched the bag tightly and crossed over to Ricky. "The sky just opened up and shined down on ya," he announced with a sly smirk.

"What?" Ricky asked, his face drawing a complete blank.

"Don't talk, listen," Jay barked. "This ya lucky night. Insteada sittin' up in sum sweatbox waitin' to be processed, you get to go home and fuck ya old lady. But we meet like this again you'll be fuckin' some sweet ass upstate."

"Ya...ya serious?" Ricky practically stuttered, standing there, eyes wide. His knees buckled as though he was about to drop to his knees and start hailing Mary for having a son like Jesus watching over him. Because that was the only way he had gotten out of this jam tonight. If it had been some legit cops making the bust he'd be taping pictures to his cell wall by this time tomorrow. Luckily for him he happened to be dealing with one of the most corrupt cops in the entire city.

"Clock's tickin'," Jay responded coldly.

Ricky made the sign of the crucifix across his chest and said, "Thank you, thank you" as he backed up towards the driver's door.

"Don't thank me, thank God," Jay snarled.

Ricky hopped in the Honda and sped off down the block. Jay and Sean shared a good laugh as they watched the speeding car weaved twice before disappearing around a corner at the next cross street.

Climbing into the Cherokee, Jay tossed the heavy duffle bag on Sean's lap. "We struck oil, young blood."

Sean looked down at the bag and unzipped it. His eyes widened as Jacksons and Grants practically spilled out. "It has to be over twenty grand here," he said, thumbing through some of the cash in his lap.

Jay hunched back in the driver's seat with a prideful tone filling his voice. "Do I know how to pick'em?"

He threw the jeep in drive and pulled off.

In an alleyway a short distance away, tucked in the darkness hiding behind a rusted six-foot iron gate and some thirty-gallon trashcans, Carlos had just witnessed everything. Now, he watched the Cherokee roll away with his money. Exploding in anger, he kicked over the trash cans, cursing the dirty pigs in Spanish. The pitbull in the neighboring yard barked in response.

CHAPTER 12

Later that night, Jay strolled toward his thirty-year-old, fourteen-story, brick co-op building, clutching the duffle bag at his side. A suspicious stranger waited inside the vestibule, yapping away on a cell phone. Something about him just didn't sit right with Jay as he entered the lobby. They made eye contact and the stranger tossed him a nod, acting nonchalant. Crossing to the elevator, Jay pressed the button, keeping an eye on the man the whole time.

The metal door to the staircase quietly swung open and Razor, crept out of the exit with a .44 bulldog aimed at the back of Jay's unsuspecting head. With the feel of a sudden presence of someone standing behind him, Jay spun around and found the weapon stuck in his grill. His facial expression didn't change one bit. His eyes maintained the same cold steely glaze of a soldier who had been in the trenches far too long to be worried about death now. The only thing he feared was fear itself.

This kind of shit was nothing new to Razor. He was one of the hood's many hired guns. Whether it came to doing a bid up north or sticking a barrel down a nigga's throat, he was at home. But the way this pig remained so fucking calm kind of rattled him a little.

"Up da piece, ma'fucka!" Razor demanded, his lips trembling as a line of sweat trickled down his scarred cheek. The barrel stood ready to let a few slugs fly Jay's way if he so much as made a move.

"Easy, playa, I'm a cop," Jay stated calmly. His mind raced as he pondered his limited options. "So ya don't want my blood on ya hands." He knew no matter what went down, he couldn't afford to let this cat get off a clean shot. As narrow as this fucking hallway was, he was sure to get lit up like 42nd Street if he didn't take the gun away.

Watching the scene unfold from the vestibule, the now hyper stranger kept an eye out for witnesses.

"Well, cop, look like ya fucked up," Razor stressed, pressing the gun to Jay's chest. A spray of spit showered Jay's face and he didn't even so much as blink as the droplets hit him. "Someone wants ya dead. Now, slide me da fuckin' piece slowly an' don't try shit!"

Slowly, Jay reached for his gun. Suddenly, he knocked the gun away from his body instead and pounced on Razor, catching him by surprise. The struggle over the gun turned fierce as Jay clutched Razor's gun wrist in one palm and threw haymakers with the other. The skin under Razor's eye split open on impact. The force shattered his cheekbone.

A child screamed, whining at being disturbed from a peaceful sleep. An elderly man peeked out, then suddenly ducked back into his apartment.

As they continued to scuffle, the gun fired wildly. Bullets ricocheted off the concrete floor and walls, leaving chunks of debris around them.

The stranger dashed out the entrance just as a slug slammed into the wall where he had been standing.

Gaining control of the gun, Jay shoved Razor backwards, blasting him in the chest. The bright flash of orange-red flames spit out of the dark barrel heralding his death. Jay squeezed the trigger again.

The first hollow-tip caught Razor right below the heart and he staggered back slamming against the concrete wall. The second slug went through the juggler vein in his neck. Mortally wounded, Razor slid down to the floor, leaving a trail of blood in his path.

Jay grabbed him by the collar, eyeing the blood pouring from his mouth and stated flatly, "Guess dis one job ya should've turned down, prick." But speaking was only a waste of words. Razor was no longer present in spirit.

* * *

Later that night, Jay spoke with Captain Hardy in front of the entrance to his apartment building, which was now crawling with detectives and uniformed cops. "You trying to give me a freaking aneurysm?" the captain asked, lighting up a cigar. "Cause that's what the hell you're doing."

"But it was *his* gun!" Jay replied, lighting his own brand of smoke. "Capt', if I didn't lay him, he would've laid me."

"Oh, you freaking psychic now, huh?" the Captain snapped sarcastically. He shook his head, cocked one of his eyes and took another puff.

Jay spread his hands out wide. "I saw it in his eyes."

Toting on his cigarette, Jay then remained silent and locked eyes with the Captain. After all he had been through tonight night, he definitely didn't want to listen to this bullshit. An uncomfortable silence hung in the air between them as curls of smoke rose into the air.

The captain spoke first, finally breaking the lingering tension. "You need a few days off?" he asked, easing up a little bit.

"Nah, I'm fine." Jay blew the grayish smoke through his nostrils. "I just don't know if I'm cut out for this anymore." Little did the Captain know Jay was just playing off his emotions. He planted that seed in the captain's heart so it wouldn't come as a surprise when he announced his early retirement.

As far as Jay knew, the only thing his captain could tell anyone was that Jay Robinson was a good cop with a lot of good collars under his belt, and that he had hit a dry spell lately. His arrest rate had been steadily declining lately since he just wasn't bringing the scum in like he used to.

"Maybe you've finally lost the thrill of the chase," Captain Hardy said somberly. "I understand because the same thing happened to me. That's why I'm behind a desk now instead of working the streets. A good cop has to know when to give up the streets and start climbing the bureaucratic ladder."

The captain had Jay figured all wrong.

The real reason Jay stopped bringing in dealers like he used to was he just didn't give a fuck about ridding the streets of hustlers and criminals anymore. That sense of public duty had long since faded away, replaced with envy and growing greed. All he cared about now was cold hard cash. Instead of locking up hustlers, he just robbed them right under Captain Hardy's not so watchful eyes.

"Nah, I'm fine. See ya at roll call tomorrow," Jay responded flatly. Flicking his cigarette butt to the pavement, he turned on his heels and headed into the lobby.

CHAPTER 13

Across town fifteen miles away, in a stock room in the basement of Right Look clothing store, José surveyed his workers like a lion scanning the lush rolling plains of Africa. Wearing jumpsuits with no pockets, the workers bottled up a couple bricks of crack at two different long metal tables as Chico supervised the operation.

"I want all this shit bottled up and on the street tonight," José barked at Chico.

Chico turned, acknowledging his boss with a quick nod before something behind José caught his attention.

"Look who's here," Chico said, his eyes locking in on the person.

José turned around. The stranger from Jay's vestibule stood waiting next to a pile of boxes. His leg was shaking.

José motioned for him to approach. "Where's ya partner-in-crime?"

"Dead," the stranger responded jumpy as hell.

"Dead?" José asked, slightly taken back, but other than that, he felt no pity for the dead goon. "How?"

"The cop you wanted axed."

José his temper started to rise. "Don't tell me that fuckin' pig's still breathing?"

After a brief moment, the edgy stranger nodded. He never saw the hit coming as José backslapped him with a hard right across his greasy face.

Sweat flew off the startled stranger's skin as he staggered back from the impact, clutching the side of his bruised cheek, more shook than ever.

"Now get the fuck outta my face before I feed you to the dogs out back!" José barked.

The man immediately hightailed it out of the basement. José looked at Chico and shook his head in disgust.

***

Night turned to day over the borough of Queens.

At Riker's Island in housing area 4-Lower, an electronic iron gate slid open. Behind it sat a long narrow corridor cutting through the middle of a dreary cellblock with cells running down both sides.

"Option, option!" the CO yelled, as all the cell doors suddenly slid open simultaneously. Inmates emerged from various cells, stretching and talking shit.

The CO patrolled the corridor, peering into each cell he passed, all business and uptight like the uniform he happened to stuff his two hundred and fifty pounds into.

The corridor soon became cluttered with inmates talking shit and profiling. Reaching the end of the cellblock, the CO made a u-turn heading back toward the other crowded end.

"Clear this corridor, fellas!" he ordered, flexing his weight with a "don't fuck with me" attitude.

Slowly, but surely, the convicts started making their way to the dayroom, pulling up the hard plastic chairs in front of the nineteen-inch TV as they laid claim to their usual spots.

Covering his mouth with his fist as he yawned, Black emerged from the concrete box and headed for the unoccupied phones. He picked up the receiver and dialed the number on a business card he held.

"Internal Affairs," a detective answered on the other end.

"I need Lieutenant Fitz," Black said in a low tone, concealing his lips with three of his fingers as he spoke.

"Hold."

Right then a frail fiendish looking inmate shuffled over, attempting to use the other jack hanging on the wall next to Black.

"Nigga, you see me talkin'?" Black asked. "Give me some fuckin' privacy." He eyed him down with a menacing snarl, ready to bitch slap his timid ass if necessary.

"A'ight," the inmate conceded not wanting any trouble. He immediately slithered back into the dayroom like a frightened pup with his tail tucked between his legs. He blended in with the rest of the inmates watching Jerry Springer.

"Fitz here," the man piped on the other end of the line. He was a Puerto Rican male in his early fifties, but he wasn't the average older man stuffed into a polyester suit. He had style. His jet-black hair peppered here and there with a few white strands was slicked back and cropped low around the sides. The two-piece suit he had on was pretty expensive. The metal desk in his office was a mess. Forms and files were stacked everywhere. "Who's speaking?"

"It's Black. I'm in Rikers."

"What happened this time?" Fitz said, with a weary sigh as Black explained the situation.

In the comfort of his chair, he kicked his leather square-toed shoes up on the desktop and listened. After about two minutes of non-stop rambling, Black had finally brought Fitz up to speed from the murder charge to the three cops that were digging in his pockets.

Something like this could normally get him killed, but Black didn't consider it snitching since he would never give up another cat from the streets even if they were sworn enemies. This shit here was different, so he jumped at the opportunity to rat out them dirty ass fucking pigs. He considered this payback for the way they busted up his girl ReRe and for all the paper they were extorting from him.

"So you telling me some *cops* jacked you. You better not be pulling my chain-What building you in?" On a wrinkled notepad, Fitz scribbled: C-73. "Okay. Don't worry, everything's confidential."

Mike, a short and pudgy detective in his mid-forties entered the room, munching on a foot-long hero loaded with everything. He had a few strands of hair combed over the spot where bare skin was winning the war. The happy go lucky type of guy with a wife and three kids, he didn't care much about staying fit. And it showed. He was your average Irish kilt wearing, potbellied, beer-swigging brute.

"All right, bud. I'll be in touch." Fitz hung the receiver on its cradle.

"That a hot tip or what?" Mike asked, with a mouth full of food as a piece of lettuce fell from his lips onto Fitz's desk.

"Yeah, but Sean's already inside," Fitz said almost instantly plucking the bit of foliage, dropping it into the trash pail.

"Oh the Bronx case?"

Fitz glanced up at his partner and nodded.

"Can't wait to nail those bastards," Mike said around another mouthful.

"You ain't the only one." Fitz sat back in his chair. A smile snuck across his slim face as he thought about bringing down Jay and Warren. Those two had definitely made enemies.

CHAPTER 14

The following morning, with the sun shining brightly, Sean's Acura pulled into the driveway of the single-family home his mother owned in the North Bronx. He parked behind her black Honda Accord. Sean waved back to the next-door neighbor as he stepped out of the car. Heading up the narrow concrete walkway, he climbed the steps leading to the front door and pressed the bell.

A few moments later, the front door swung open and his younger sister Michelle stood there with a wide grin on her pretty face. "What you doing here, knucklehead?"

"Who you callin' a knucklehead, knucklehead?" Sean replied with a chuckle as he stepped into the hallway. His sister was sixteen going on thirty and she always had on the latest urban fashion. The inviting smell of scrambled eggs and turkey bacon coming from the kitchen hit his nostrils. He followed his slim sister to the kitchen where his mother Gail was fixing breakfast.

"Hey, sweetie," she said with a smile, spotting Sean. Pushing fifty she didn't look a day over forty. He had one of those mothers that didn't gain a whole lot of weight the older she got. She had always worked out and jogged religiously for as long as Sean could remember, which she still did when time permitted.

"What's up, Ma?" Sean said, planting a kiss on her cheek. He and his mother were like best friends. No matter what happened between him and his stepfather, she was always there for him and made sure he felt loved.

"You want some breakfast?"

"Nah, I'm fine. I ate before I got here," he replied, walking into the living room. "So what's wrong with the computer now?" He headed straight for the Dell desktop occupying the mahogany computer desk in the corner of the room.

"Every time I use the computer, it freezes while I'm typing." Michelle said, busy making a phone call.

"You mean, every time you're in one of those chat rooms it freezes," Sean joked.

"Whatever." Michelle smirked, brushing pass him as she left the living room.

"I told her about that," Gail interjected from the kitchen.

Sean pulled out the swivel chair, sat down and turned on the computer. "Do you ever defragment the hard drive?" The computer took its slow time loading up.

"Defragment what?" Gail asked entering the living room with a steaming plate of food. "You know I don't know anything about those computers."

By the time Sean finished defragmenting the hard drive, his mother had already polished off her breakfast and was back in the kitchen washing the dishes.

Drawing quiet, Sean stared at the picture of his deceased stepfather hanging on the wall with the rest of the family pictures. His mother approached.

Gail placed a hand on his shoulder and said, "I'm sorry I was so caught up with work that I didn't realize what was going on."

Sean stood up and turned around to face her. "It wasn't your fault. You didn't know. I should have told you."

"Still, I should've caught on," she said, her eyes starting to water.

"Ah, Ma, don't cry." Sean pulled her close and hugged her tightly. "That's in the past, let's focus on the future."

Pulling away, she wiped her tears and said, "But—"

"But nothing," Sean cut her off. "It only made me stronger. Actually I feel sorry for him. He never really knew how to love or appreciate the loving family he had. It was his lost. The really sad thing is he had actually started changing for the better before he died."

"I love you, Sean."

"I love you too, Ma," he replied hugging her again. He wouldn't trade his mother for anything in the world.

****

Later that evening in the weight room of the precinct, Sean bench-pressed, struggling under the heavy weight as Jay gave him a spot. There were three forty-five pound plates on both ends.

"That's light weight, baby. Get that shit up," Jay shouted encouragingly.

Sean forced the cumbersome barbell up with every last ounce of strength in his body and racked it. Breathing heavily, he sat up grabbing his water bottle sitting on the floor. He twisted off the cap and took a big swig.

"They don't build ya young bucks like they used to," Jay joked with a grin as he watched Sean gulp down the water like a man who had been wandering through the hot desert for a couple of days.

"I was trying to boost your ego," Sean said, panting.

Jay laughed. "Well, it definitely *worked*." Crossing to his locker, he popped it open and grabbed a shirt. Photographs of naked women were taped to the inside of the narrow metal door. These were just a few of the many ladies Jay had run through over the years. But definitely not like the hot young black chick he was screwing. Now she was some class ass.

Warren's head appeared in the doorway and announced, "Time to hit the streets, fellas."

"Coming, father." Jay replied, not without turning around.

"Ya' mother finally sat you down and told you, huh, son?" Warren shot back.

They all laughed on the way out.

****

Hours later on a side block near the Cross Bronx Expressway, Jay, Sean and Warren, all wearing plainclothes, and a small team of officers in uniform wearing vests with "police" written on the front and back, stood in listening to Sergeant Frank. He was a white male in his late forties with a stocky build and a bald, egg shaped head. He almost looked like a cowboy without the hat as he stood there in his worn Levi's and dusty leather boots.

"Just because past transactions have gone smoothly doesn't mean it holds true today," Frank stated, popping an orange tic-tac in his mouth. "I want everybody alert. Now, let's take these perps off the street safely."

With that said, the group split up. Sean hopped in a black Infiniti coupe and, Jay and Warren climbed in the Cherokee. The rest of the team jumped in various unmarked police vehicles.

The parking lot of the Whitestone movie theater was full of couples and families parking their vehicles and making their way into the building for weekend entertainment.

The Infiniti snaked through the parking lot as Sean searched the area. After a moment, he spotted his target.

Two black guys stood beside a white Audi A6, eyeing the Infiniti headed their way. Rob, the leader of the two, tossed a nod to Sean while Boogie, the backup, just eyed him suspiciously.

Trim and muscular, Rob was a chameleon, who could definitely blend in on any drug-infested street corner. His medium-sized curly fro was lined up tighter than Steve Harvey's.

Boogie was 5'10", rough around the edges with boxed braids covered with a black du-rag. As soon as he spotted the black cat behind the wheel, he tensed.

Sean pulled the Infiniti into an empty spot right next to the Audi and hopped out.

"What's good?" he said, greeting them with an extended fist.

"Waitin' on you, playa," Rob responded as they knocked knuckles.

"Let's handle this business," Sean said, noticing Boogie still eyeing him down. He grinned and continued, "Two fa forty, right?"

Rob nodded.

"It's quality shit?"

Rob nodded, then said, "Sample da product. Make sure ya satisfied."

"No need, baby," Sean replied, shaking his head. "Ya word's good."

"Man, dis nigga's police!" Boogie blurted out suddenly. He quickly scanned the parking lot looking for any sign of more cops. None of the vehicles seemed out of place. No one looked suspicious. Everything appeared normal.

"Yo, Boogie, relax. He's straight," Rob growled, nudging Boogie in the side. "We've done business before."

Boogie screwed up his face and his eyes dotted back over to Sean.

His cold stare was met right back by Sean's livid glare. He locked eyes with Boogie a second, then turned his attention back to Rob.

"Yo, ya man's too fuckin' paranoid," he snapped. "If ya'll don't want this paper, I'll go elsewhere." He unzipped the duffle bag clutched in his palm, flashing the cash at them.

"Nah, nah, everything's tight." Rob was transfixed on the bundle of greenbacks. "Just take a little hit so my man feels betta."

"Fuck ya man!" Sean shouted still eyeing Boogie down the whole time.

"I'm tellin' ya," Boogie insisted. "Dis nigga's police."

Rob's eyes dotted to Boogie, then back to Sean, "Come on, baby, just take a hit."

"Fuck this, I'm out," Sean snapped, snatching open the car door to hop in. "When ya lose this bitch nigga, holla at me."

Suddenly Boogie whipped out a chrome .380 from his jacket.

"Da cash stays wit' us, nigga," Boogie yelled.

Sean turned to see the gun leveled at his chest. Moments like this, a man really needed to have his vest on. Unfortunately in undercover work, sometimes it just wasn't an option.

"Fuck ya doin'?" Rob asked, all wide-eyed.

"I got dis," Boogie barked at Rob, then turned his attention back to Sean. "Now, give up da fuckin' paper!"

"You don't wanna do this," Sean said, trying to reason with the dangerous criminal.

Boogie quickly advanced on Sean, sticking the barrel to his ribs. "Keep runnin' ya mouth, I'ma leave ya six feet."

"Okay, okay. Take it."

Suddenly, screeching tires squealed from every direction. Jay and Warren hopped out the Cherokee as the rest of the backup team raced from their vehicles. All guns were trained on Boogie and Rob.

While Boogie was distracted by the sudden appearance of the cops, Sean took advantage, and shoved the barrel away from his kidney, catching him off guard.

Boogie pulled the trigger; the .380 exploded to life. The bullet grazed Sean's arm and shattered the rear passenger window of the Infiniti. They struggled for the gun as Rob pulled his own and fired at the other cops. The team ducked for cover behind their vehicles. Warren rapidly squeezed off five rounds.

Several bullets chewed through Rob's broad chest. He flew back against the Audi, sliding to the ground.

Sean continued to tussle for dear life as Boogie fired the gun wildly. Bullets ricocheted off the ground. One of the slugs ripped through Boogie's foot and he cried out in pain.

Sean slammed his knee into Boogie's ribs. The boy crumbled to his knees, gasping for air. Sean followed with an explosive knee to Boogie's face. Boogie flew back, slamming into the pavement. Jay ran up and cuffed him.

"Thanks," Sean said to Jay, trying to catch his breath.

"That's what partners are for," Jay replied, glancing at his winded partner. "You alright?"

Sean took a moment to check the wound. "Yeah. . . it's just a scratch."

Jay turned his attention back to Boogie shoving his face into the pavement. "Oops, now get up, dickhead!" Jay said pulling the semi-conscience Boogie back to his feet. Blood trickled from his forehead.

***

At Sean's apartment, he was sound asleep with his injured arm bandaged. Lisa was cuddled up next to him, watching a steamy love scene on TV. Getting hot and wet, she gently shook him awake. "Sean, Sean."

"What?"

"Fuck me," she purred seductively.

Sean glanced over at the alarm clock. It was 1:13 am. "See how late it is, I'm exhausted," he said, then rolled over. "On top of that my arm's killin' me."

Upset and horny as hell, Lisa got up, pulled out her pocket-rocket vibrator with the pink rubber stimulator from the dresser and climbed back in bed. Sean felt the vibrations in the bed but was too tired to say a word.

CHAPTER 15

Two weeks later, a cherry red Benz, with its hazard lights flashing, sat double-parked in front of the Mill Brook Houses, a 16-story project building on Cypress Avenue & 136th Street. A group of roughnecks held court right outside of the entrance engaged in a dice game. Singles, fives and tens were sprawled at their feet.

Kaseem, brown-skinned, rolled the dice and hit. "Pay up!" he gloated, as reached down to scoop up the pot of cash. "Dis mine now, nigga."

Further up the block, the Cherokee turned onto Cypress with Warren behind the wheel. Jay rode shotgun while Sean sat in the back. Warren spotted the man.

"Isn't that Kaseem?" he asked, pointing at him.

Jay and Sean both looked at the same time.

"In the flesh," Jay replied dryly. Kaseem had been ducking them lately, missing payments.

The Cherokee pulled up to the building. Warren, Sean and Jay hopped out. Noticing the jeep, the thugs stopped their game, eyeing the approaching trio. Left holding the dice, Kaseem sucked his teeth as they closed in on him.

"Doesn't gamblin' violate ya parole?" Jay asked, standing directly in front of the well-dressed man.

"Just havin' sum' fun." Kaseem shrugged. "Stayin' out of trouble and all."

"You like disappearin' on a nigga, huh?"

Kaseem eyed him a moment. Without turning, he whipped out a nickel-plated gun and fired. Before Jay had a chance to react, the bullet caught him square in the chest, chewing through his clothes. The blast sent him stumbling backwards.

All the cats posted in front of the building scattered, running off in different directions as Kaseem quickly made his getaway, dipping right past Sean and Warren.

Caught totally off guard, they both reacted, drawing their weapons. Sean quickly checked Jay's wound. Barely catching his breath, Jay ripped open his shirt revealing a bulletproof vest underneath. The bullet lodged right over the place his heart was.

Warren fired repeatedly at Kaseem as he dashed to the CLK.

Sean helped Jay to his feet and they gave chase.

Kaseem hopped in the CLK and peeled away just as a bullet shattered his passenger window. Warren, Jay and Sean hopped in the Cherokee and charged off, hot on his bumper.

The CLK flew through an intersection and busted a sharp right, barely missing a collision with a garbage truck. The truck swerved, smashing into a parked VW BUG, destroying it. With the damaged vehicles blocking the street, the Cherokee swung around them, roaring ahead.

The CLK sped up the entrance ramp leading to the Deegan Expressway. Charging forward at top speed, the Cherokee moved faster on the CLK.

Kaseem popped his gun out the window, firing rapidly behind him as he drove. A bullet ripped through the Cherokee's windshield, barely missing the trio.

Jay leaned out the window and returned fire. The rear window of the CLK shattered from a slug. The CLK swung over cutting across two lanes before abruptly exiting at 138th Street.

Three cars waited at a red light on the exit ramp as traffic flowed pass on 138th Street. The CLK swerved to avoid slamming into the rear of the vehicles, jumped the curb and crashed into a light pole. The front-end crumbled on impact. Smoke poured from the hood.

The air bag exploded, hitting Kaseem in the chest. He struggled for air. Regaining his composure, Kaseem hopped out, firing away at the approaching Cherokee.

The Cherokee skidded to a stop as Kaseem dashed across the street, dodging traffic. Trucks and cars screeched to a sudden halt to avoid hitting the fleeing felon. Jay and Sean leaped from the Cherokee in hot pursuit. Sirens blaring, Warren pounded on the horn, demanding the vehicles holding him up to get out of the way.

Kaseem dashed into the subway station as Jay and Sean ran across the street with firearms in hand.

In the subway station, Kaseem hopped the turnstile, tripped and fell. Hitting the pavement, the gun slid across the floor. He scrambled back to his feet and dashed down the stairs leading to the platform.

Entering the station, Jay and Sean sprinted down the stairs. "Open da fuckin' gate!" Jay yelled to the station attendant, flashing his badge. The attendant buzzed the gate as Sean pushed through with Jay following on his heels.

Kaseem ran along the platform toward the subway tunnel. He bumped into a young woman headed in the opposite direction, almost knocking her over. Jay and Sean were now hot on his tail.

"Stop or die, motherfucker!" Jay yelled at Kaseem.

Kaseem continued running, never breaking stride. Stopping dead in his tracks, Jay lifted his .40, took aim at him and rapidly squeezed off five rounds.

Instantly, commuters screamed as Kaseem stumbled and collapsed on the platform. Commuters reacted, dashing for cover as braver ones strained to see what happened.

Jay and Sean jogged over to Kaseem. Sprawled out, face down, coughing up blood, Kaseem gasped for air. Noticing the curious onlookers, Jay quickly took action.

"This is a police matter!" Jay yelled. "Everyone clear this fuckin' platform immediately!" He held up his badge. "Let's go!"

Reluctantly following his orders, the commuters made their way to the closest exits.

"We're fucked, he's unarmed," Sean griped, a slow panic setting in. "The media's gonna jump all over this."

"Calm da fuck down," Jay demanded scanning the area. "Get his gun."

Sean froze, watching as the fire drained from Kaseem's dark brown eyes as his life slipped into nothingness.

"Get da fuckin' gun, Sean!"

Sean hesitated a moment before heading off to retrieve the weapon. The loud rumbling sound of a train rolling into the other side of the station echoed through the platform. Once the doors opened, people rushed to get on and off.

Moments later, Jay and Warren stood around Kaseem's corpse.

"I hope he doesn't crack," Warren said, eyeing Jay. He was worried. The musky stale air mixed with a rotten stench made the situation that much more unpleasant.

"He won't," Jay replied reassuringly. "I'll handle it."

Finally Sean returned with Kaseem's gun and handed it to Jay. Jay kneeled down over Kaseem's body, placed the .25 in his palm and adjusted his finger on the trigger.

Jay glanced up at Sean and noticed he was looking nervous as hell. Sweat dripped from Sean's forehead and his leg shook.

"Relax, young blood," Jay said smoothly as he stood, closing the distance between them. "We don't have to give a statement for forty-eight hours. Ya hear me, Sean?"

Still staring at Kaseem's lifeless body, Sean took a moment to answer. "Yeah. No statement right now."

Ten minutes later, numerous blue-and-white police cars and unmarked Chevy Impalas, along with yellow tape surrounded the subway station as plainclothes and uniformed officers tried to look busy as if they were actually investigating Kaseem's death. Some cruisers still had their top lights flashing. News trucks idled nearby with their satellite dishes stretching high into the dark sky. A few reporters moseyed about, waiting to get the latest updates while the others lounged in their warm vehicles. Sean and Jay emerged from the subway. Jay paused to light a cigarette as Sean waited.

Sean pulled out his cell phone and dialed Lisa's cell number.

Her voicemail picked up, "Hey you've reached Lisa. Please leave a message and I'll get back."

"Call me," Sean said, watching Jay head toward the curb. He hung up and caught up to Jay. "This shit doesn't affect you?" he asked, running a hand over his short wavy hair.

Jay stared off at a motorcycle zapping by. "What?"

"The killin'."

"Don't ever get it confused," Jay replied, blowing the smoke through his nostrils. "It's us or them out here. Slip up once, motherfuckers leave ya brains on ya lap. They're like Piranhas waitin' to rip the flesh off ya bones."

Warren approached them.   "You ready, Kid?" he asked Sean.   Sean nodded and followed Warren to the Cherokee.   They climbed in and pulled off.

Jay flicked his cigarette butt in the cruddy gutter and headed back into the subway.   Simultaneously, two men emerged carrying a black vinyl body bag. They crossed to an awaiting coroner van parked by the curb.

Minutes later the Cherokee pulled up to the curb outside of Sean's brownstone.   Warren looked over at Sean. "Listen, Sean, I know you're scared.   Believe me, I've been in your shoes.   Just stick to the story and everything'll be fine. He wasn't shit but a two-bit dealer anyway.   Nobody downtown gives a fuck."

Lost in another world, Sean looked over at Warren and just nodded.

****

Thirty minutes later, Sean was slumped on the couch, downing his frothy beer.   The bottles already littered the coffee table along with his glock.   The television was on, but the sound was muted as he dwelled on the conversation him and Jay had earlier.

He wondered if Jay was ever bothered by the images of the people he had killed.   It was something Sean couldn't shake from his troubled mind.

The telephone rang, jarring Sean back to reality.   He checked the caller ID before answering. Jay Robinson's name popped across the screen. He definitely didn't want to speak with him, so he just ignored the phone until it stopped ringing. Suddenly, he grabbed the glock and hurled it across the room. It crashed to the floor and fired.   Sean jumped back, shocked by the loud gunshot echo through the living room. He just stared at the fresh bullet hole in the wall right over their fish tank.

Just then the apartment door slammed shut and footsteps followed.   Lisa entered the living room with Bloomingdale's shopping bags in both hands.

"Hey, you're home early," she said as she wrinkled her nose. "It smells funny in here." The scent of gunpowder filtered through the air like weed smoke.

Sean stared at her but didn't respond. Looking around, she noticed the empty beer bottles.

"What's wrong?" Lisa inquired, raising her thinly arched eyebrows. She hadn't seen him drinking like this since they got back together.

"Nothin'." Sean shrugged. "You're home late."

"I went shopping with Ebony." She picked up two bottles and held them in front of her like weapons. "Why are you drinking?"

Sean grabbed another beer and replied, "If I wanna drink, I'ma drink. That's all to it." He cracked it open and took a swig.

"Fine," Lisa said, rolling her eyes. "I was just asking."

"Well don't ask."

She turned on her heels and went to the bedroom. Finishing the rest of his beer, Sean stood and stumbled slightly as he went after her.

In the bedroom, Lisa was pulling off her top as Sean staggered in. A brand new outfit lay on the bed.

"Where you goin'?" he asked, approaching Lisa.

"I don't wanna argue."

"Answer the question," he demanded, through clenched teeth.

He got up in her face, and Lisa backed away. "Stop treatin' me like this, Sean."

"So answer the fuckin' question."

"Ebony's taking me to Two Eyes, that club over on 14th Street."

Right then, Sean exploded, "I'm stressed out, and all you care about is partyin' wit' that ho."

"You won't talk to me, Sean," Lisa replied, turning on her heels to leave. "What am I supposed to do?"

He spun her back around to face him. "Try stayin' home for once."

"When I do, you ignore me," she shot back.

The phone began to ring. Taking a moment to pull herself together, Lisa picked up the receiver. "Hello."

She listened for a moment, then smiled and said, "You so crazy, Ebony." Sean stormed out of the room

Sean had never liked Ebony. She lived across town, in her small Afro-centric decorated studio apartment. At one time she dated a fellow police officer and spending time, as a foursome was a common thing. She was a normal, around the way girl. A little on the chubby side but it wasn't anything that couldn't be overlooked after a few drinks. Besides she had a cute face and that had to count for something.

"Yeah, something is bothering me," Lisa replied, glancing out of the window. After a brief pause, "No, he only hit me that one time. He hasn't touched me since. You know he even took that anger management class." She walked over to the dresser. "It's just. . . he's so distant now. It's getting to the point where we don't even fuck anymore."

Ebony laughed, then said, "I feel fa ya, girl. I know you need yours. Did you tell him how you feel?"

"Yep, I've talked to him, but it goes in one ear, out the other." Searching through the second drawer for something, Lisa listened a few moments, "You know, I was just getting on with my life, trying to see a new man."

Standing in the hallway at the doorway listening in on Lisa's conversation, Sean inhaled sharply.

"Whatever, girl, just have ya bony ass ready when I get there," Lisa shot back with a laugh that trickled to a halt as she saw Sean's scowling face in the dresser mirror.

****

Night rapidly turned to day over the Bronx.

Sean stood at the counter in his boxers, snacking on cereal and milk in the kitchen. The huge plastic mixing bowl he had clutched against his chest with one arm was filled to the rim.

Lisa strutted in and perused the refrigerator without looking at him or saying a word.

Deep down, Sean knew he deserved the chilly treatment. He was wrong for taking out his anger on Lisa last night.

"Looks like you enjoyed yourself last night," Sean said, munching on a spoonful of Corn Pops.

Lisa nodded, and grabbed a bowl from the dish rack. "Pass the cereal."

Sean handed her the bright yellow box, which Kellogg's stated was the best part of every day. Sean could eat the sweet corn morsels all day long and still not feel an ounce of that "goodness" the company promised.

Lisa poured herself some cereal. Sean quietly watched her pour milk over the sugar coated morsels.

"I'm sorry 'bout last night," Sean said softly.

Lisa turned around to acknowledge him with an "I'm listening" glance.

"I—I wasn't myself. I don't know who that jealous asshole was." He flashed Lisa his sad puppy eyes. "You forgive me?" He extended his arms, waiting.

Moments passed by like minutes.

"Yep," Lisa responded, walking into his awaiting arms. He squeezed her tight so she could hardly breathe.

"What's happening to us, Sean?"

"I don't know, Lisa," he responded. Planting a kiss on her forehead, he added, "All I know is I can't live wit' out you." He released her and grabbed the newspaper from the counter, glancing at the front page.

The Daily News cover story—"COPS KILLED MY SON." Underneath was a picture of a clearly distraught older woman holding up Kaseem's photograph. A queasy feeling rose in his stomach as the image of Jay killing Kaseem quickly flooded back. He tossed the paper back onto the counter.

"I'm goin' for a run," Sean said. "Gotta clear my head." He scrambled out of the kitchen. As he quickly glanced behind him, he saw Lisa pick up the newspaper.

Damn, Sean thought, grimacing, *I should have taken it with me.*

On Valentine Avenue, a block over from the Grand Concourse in the North Bronx, Sean's Acura pulled up to the curb in front of a huge church with exquisite architecture. He killed the engine and stepped out in a light gray Champion jogging suit and running sneakers. Even though he had told Lisa he was going jogging, he decided to head to church instead. The way he felt, he realized he was heading to hell on a jet plane and he needed to make a change, fast.

Taking a deep breath, Sean eyed the old historical building with the expensive stain glass windows with various depictions of Jesus and his apostles etched into it. It had been a long time since he actually been inside of a church. He was scared he might get struck by lightning as he entered the deserted cathedral. It took a moment for his eyes to adjust to the dimly lit interior. Along the back wall, two racks holding an array of religious candles were burning. Throughout the day, people from different walks of life usually stopped in to light a candle in order to atone for their sins.

From the looks of it, Sean had the place to himself. He noticed a large crucifix of Jesus hanging over the center of the altar. Walking down the center aisle, he saw a dirty-clothed vagrant, sound asleep, stretched out on one of the long wooden pews with his head propped on a garbage bag. Sean caught a strong stench of urine and funk coming from the bum's direction. It was normal to find the homeless using the church as temporary shelter from the cold. He stopped midway up the aisle and sat in one of the empty pews. He dropped his face into his palms and began to pray his heart out.

"God, please give me the strength to endure this pain and confusion I'm going through. I don't see any way out. I feel like I'm beginning to lose it. Everyday I wake up, I'm living a lie. I look in the mirror and I don't even know who I am anymore. I don't know how long I can hold on. I realize this case is important, but it's costing me my sanity along with my marriage. It's tearing me apart. I don't wanna lose my wife again."

Just as Sean finished praying, a priest walked over and placed his pale hand on Sean's shoulder. "Son, do you need to make a confession?"

"That's okay, father," Sean replied politely, glancing up at the balding older white man in the black suit and white collar. He didn't believe in confessing his sins or taking his problems to a man made of flesh and blood when he could take his troubles directly to God through prayer. Nowadays he didn't know if the priest was molesting a little kid or sleeping with hookers.

****

That evening, in a small low key non-descriptive bar in downtown Manhattan, Sean sat on a stool at the shellacked bar, nursing a beer trying to drink away the pain while the few other patrons in the place did the same. The jukebox belted out an old seventies hit from Marvin Gaye, but nobody was actually there to dance.

Fitz entered, spotted Sean and took the empty stool next to him. "You're under arrest, dirt bag," he said.

Sean stared at Fitz like he was stupid.

"What's eating you?" Fitz asked.

Sean didn't respond as he fidgeted with the beer bottle.

"I'll take a Coke, thanks," Fitz told the approaching white bartender. She had to be about 5' 6" with boobs bigger than Pamela Anderson's practically spilling out her tight tube top. Her stringy short blond hair had reddish highlights in it.

"Sure thing," the Bartender replied happily and strutted off to retrieve the drink. Fitz eyed her somewhat flat ass as she went about her business. Sean looked depressed as he sat there sulking in deep thought.

Fitz eyed the man next to him a moment, then asked, "You okay?"

"I'm good," Sean quickly assured him.

Fitz's gaze narrowed as he asked again, "You sure nothing's bothering you?"

"What did I just say?" Sean snapped.

"Fine, suit yourself."

A few beers and a couple of cokes later, Sean and Fitz were in the midst of heated conversation. Grease from the hair gel Fitz used slowly trickled down his forehead as he clenched his jaw muscles. He grabbed a napkin from the holder on the counter and wiped the grease off.

"We gotta take him down now before he kills again," Sean said.

"Not yet."

"Not yet?" Sean repeated. This was exactly the kind of bullshit he hated about the department. Everything was hurry up and wait. "He's a fuckin' cold-blooded murderer."

"You think I don't realize that?" Fitz replied, eyeing Sean. "We still have a plan to stick to…"

"Fuck the plan," Sean spat, cutting him off. "This guy's outta control!" Momentarily losing his cool, he slammed his fist down on the wooden countertop. "Fuck this shit!"

A couple of alcohol-slinging patrons glanced over at Sean. He quickly returned their stares with a flash of pure anger in his eyes that was a usual invite to each and every one of them to a can of ass whipping. Getting the message, they immediately went back to minding their own business.

"Calm down a little, for Christ's sakes, would you?" Fitz replied, glancing around at the clock on the wall. "Soon it'll be hard cots and baloney sandwiches for those two. Their days are numbered." He turned to the bartender, who was standing nearby and ordered another Coke.

Fitz eyed Sean a moment.

"Look, you're doing a good job, Sean," he said before grabbing a book of matches off the counter, and lighting up a cigarette. "You remind me of your father."

"Stepfather," Sean corrected.

"He was the only partner I ever trusted completely," Fitz continued, exhaling a cloud of smoke through his nostrils. "He was a straight shooter. I know he'd be proud."

"Would he?" Sean laughed mostly to himself then killed the rest of his drink. "You know, as a kid, I dreamed of being a cop just like him. Lockin' up the bad guys, makin' the neighborhoods safe for kids to play. Shit, that was a joke. Come to find out the real bad asses are on the force. But I should've realized that from the Jeckyll and Hyde shit my stepfather had goin' on." With that said, Sean stood, slapped two, twenty dollar bills on the counter and walked out the bar into the hustle and bustle of the outside world.

Actually feeling sorry for the poor guy, Fitz just shook his head and watched the exit door swing shut behind Sean.

CHAPTER 16

Two nights later in the Williams Bridge section of the North Bronx, an attractive black woman in her early thirties, drove her Mazda, grooving to an R&B cut on the radio. Suddenly, police lights flashed behind her. She glanced in the rearview mirror, spotting the Cherokee. With a weary sigh, she pulled over on the isolated block lined with neatly placed single-family homes.

The Cherokee pulled up behind her, and Jay and Sean hopped out. Jay approached the driver's side with his grill set in stone and Sean took the passenger side.

As Jay reached her door, she lowered the window.

"License and registration," Jay stated in a cold tone before noticing just how attractive the younger lady was. She had juicy full lips and orphan Annie red curls that drooped down to her shoulders. Her body was trim yet thick and tight in all the right places.

"I do something wrong, officer?" she asked as she searched through her pocketbook, looking for her papers.

"You rolled through a stop sign a few blocks back," Jay informed her in a warmer tone. Actually she hadn't run a stop sign at all. That was just the excuse Jay used to justify stopping the beautiful woman.

Finally finding her license and registration card, she handed him the two items. Jay haphazardly glanced over the information and then handed it back, running the flashlight over her white blouse, her huge, firm breasts pressed against the fabric down to her partially exposed thighs.

"Since I'm in a generous mood," Jay said, grinning, "how 'bout we forget this little infraction and grab a bite when I get off later." He stepped back into a cocksure stance, eyeing her like she couldn't refuse the offer.

She blinked twice, head cocking to the side as she snapped, "I'm married" and flashed the four-carat, pear-shaped diamond engagement ring and wedding band to make sure he got the picture.

"That a yes or no?" Jay asked boldly, as though oblivious to what she had just told him. He was used to getting what he wanted one way or the other. Now wouldn't be any different.

"No, Officer. I'm a *married* woman," she reiterated firmly and loudly, making sure he heard every single word. Rolling her light gray eyes for emphasis, she shot him a quick smirk.

Jay leaned on her driver side door, eyeing her, waiting. Sean couldn't believe he really had the freaking audacity to continue with his charade. The older man was definitely tripping out.

"I can't believe this," the woman said as she began fumbling in her purse once again. "What's your badge number?"

Now the one thing street-smart people know not to do is to ask a flagrant cop for his badge number unless they want to get their heads bashed in. It clearly meant they planned on reporting him or her and that usually just angered them even more. Evidently this middle class honey hadn't gotten that news. Unfortunately, Sean had a feeling that Jay would teach her that lesson.

Upon hearing her request, Jay's mood suddenly darkened. His jaw clenched up and his eyes flashed with anger. He snatched open her car door.

"What are you doing?" she demanded, her expression somewhere between half-scared and half pissed off.

"Step out," Jay demanded harshly, grabbing her by the arm to pull her out.

She gasped, struggling in his hands. "Get your hands off me. You have no right."

"You resistin' an officer, ma'am?"

After a few tense seconds, she hesitantly stepped out onto the cold black asphalt.

"Turn around. Up against the car!" Jay demanded.

Sean struggled with himself not to say something. He didn't know how much longer he could restrain himself. Sweat trickled down the side of his caramel face even though Jack Frost was nipping at his broad nose.

She glared at him, turned on her heels, complying with his orders. Jay's gaze traveled the length of her body, taking in her tight apple bottom and slim waistline. He had to admit she was a dime piece, but he quickly shook off the thought due to the unfortunate circumstances.

Moving in, Jay slowly ran his coarse palms over the curves of her body, starting from her shoulders working his way down.

"Jay, let me holla at you for a minute."

"Not now, man."

"Jay—"

Jay whirled around to face Sean and screamed, "Shut the fuck up!" Spit sprayed from his twisted up mouth.

Glaring at Sean, he unzipped his pants, exposing his dick. He whipped a condom from his back pocket.

Standing silently off to the side, Sean stood frozen in shock, watching the scene unfold, holding his bottom lip hard with his teeth; finger twitching on his gun as his morals warred with his need to keep his cover. By the way Jay behaved so calmly, Sean could tell that the man had done this many times before though he didn't remember seeing a report on that fact.

Scanning the area once more before hiking up her floral skirt, Jay yanked her light blue thong aside, rolled on the condom and poised to enter the trembling and frightful woman. Right then Sean knew he had to make a decision.

"You can't do this," the woman said, gasping. She turned her head to the side, hazel eyes widening as she saw the hard dick in Jay's hurried hand, realizing what he had in mind. She fought even harder, but Jay had something to keep her still. He slipped his gun out and then into the canal of her pussy.

"Keep talkin'," he barked, "and I'ma lock you up for disorderly conduct." He then put the gun away and slid his hands upward, groping her butt in his monstrous mittens. He parted her cheeks in a painful grip. The woman yelped in pain.

The click of the gun roared over the sound of her whimpers. Jay's head whipped around just in time to see Sean's gun aimed for his head.

The woman's breathing quickly escalated.

Jay glared at Sean. The woman pulled at her skirt, trying to get it down and stood facing the two officers, shaking like a leaf on a branch. Jay's rough hand snaked out and cupped over her shoulder, holding her in place.

Jay stared openly at the gun, daring Sean to try him. A menacing grin slowly crawled across his chiseled face.

Sean held his ground, keeping the gun between them.

"Drug dealers are one thing, but this shit ain't right," Sean said simply. His eyes tightened and his jaw clenched up. He had no plans of backing down. This was where he drew the line. If it came down to it tonight, he would have to blow the case wide open.

Their breathing frosted the air between them as tires screeched off in the distance.

Jay released the woman, but put a defiant finger up her pussy, then patted her on the ass. "Have a nice day. You're free to go." She tensed as he leaned in, whispering, "Don't ever forget I know where you stay. So let bygones be bygones."

Jay went to the Cherokee as Sean stood, watching the woman as she inched to her car, sliding behind the wheel. She threw him a grateful glance, just before she broke down in tears. Shaking as she started the engine, she pulled the car door closed and mouthed, "Thank you." A single tear rolled past her lips, disappearing beneath her baby doll chin.

The horn blared, snapping Sean out of his trance as the woman threw the gearshift into drive and tore off, weaving down the street like a bat out of hell. He watched the Mazda's taillights disappear into the darkness of the night. Turning on his heels, he stormed back to the idling Cherokee.

As Sean approached the jeep, Jay's boisterous laughter bellowed from the driver's seat. Sean glared at him and clenched his teeth as he climbed into passenger side.

"You see her face?" Jay asked still laughing as though totally oblivious to the way Sean stared at him. Jay threw the jeep into drive and floored the gas.

"Stop the car," Sean shouted, grabbing the door handle.

"What?"

Sean swung the door open while the jeep was still moving. "Stop the fuckin' car."

The jeep came to a screeching halt. Sean jumped out and Jay followed right behind him. Without saying another word, Sean rolled up to the laughing man and smashed him to the ground with one solid blow to the face.

Jay looked up at him with a sly smile, rubbing his chin. "At least you hit harder than a bitch." He spit out a disgusting glob of blood mixed with saliva onto the black asphalt.

"Fuck's wrong wit' you? You actually got off on that sick shit you just pulled, man?" Sean snapped, unable to conceal his anger any longer. "Imagine somebody did that foul shit to ya woman. You're a perverted piece of shit. You know that?"

"Please forgive me, ya Holiness." Jay laughed, giving a low bow from his waist, evidently not giving a fuck about what Sean had just said or how he felt.

Sean punched him in the jaw again, but Jay laughed even harder, angering Sean even more. He stormed off, taking the driver's side and pulled off down the street. Pulling himself off the ground, Jay had to jog to catch up to the rolling Cherokee. Sean didn't bother to slow up as he hopped into the passenger side.

Staring out the window at a huge gray rat scurrying through the garbage filled vacant lot, Sean sat fuming beneath the surface. Mashing the gas, he gunned the jeep through the intersection as the light turned from yellow to red.

The rat disappeared beneath the burned out shell of a rusted car resting in the midst. Sean realized that rats came in two varieties. One of them walked upright like a man.

***

Later that night in the precinct locker room, a bunch of cops were getting ready for their shift while one white cop stood in front of them all smiles in the middle of telling a story. He was at least 6'4" with a round gut and shaggy salt and pepper hair and a thick goatee to match. The locker room smelled like a mixture of sweat and funk. The fact that there were no windows in the place didn't help much either.

In the middle of changing into his good clothes--the designer threads he didn't wear on the job unless he was doing a undercover to do a drug deal, Sean paused to listen in.

"...then wham!-She kicks him in the balls and he keels over sobbin' like a freakin' new born. Right, Tim?" the buffed cop asked, patting an embarrassed Tim on the shoulder affirmatively. The self-conscious cop dropped his head.

All the cops laughed except for the rail thin officer who twisted up his face into a smirk. It clearly bothered him being the butt of the joke. No matter what, his loose-lipped partner always humiliated him in front of the other guys.

"When's the last time you got kicked in ya nuts?" Tim asked, sarcastically.

"The last time I stood ya wife up," the first cop responded with a chuckle. The other cops cracked up once again. The black cop spit out his soda practically clear across the room, he was laughing so hard. One unlucky officer climbing into his uniform pants got hit by some of the mist, but he just let out a hefty snicker and wiped his pale mug off with a towel hanging in the slim metal locker.

"Very funny, asshole," Tim replied, but even he finally had to laugh at the snappy comeback. He could never stay upset with his hilarious partner long.

Two rows over, listening to the sidesplitting bunch, Jay and Sean couldn't help but laugh right along with the rest of them as they changed into civilian clothes. Their shift had just ended, and both men were anxious to get on with the rest of their night.

"I'm hittin' Jimmy's tonight. You rollin'?" Jay asked, trying to break the tension even further. He pulled his hoodie over his baldhead and hung it in the locker. A few moments passed before, Sean finally answered, "I'll pass."

Thinking back to what happened earlier made him sick to his stomach. As far as he was concerned, Jay didn't deserve to wear that badge. He hoped the woman was pissed off enough to follow up and press charges. He checked his handsome bronzed features in the small square stuck to his locker door.

"Come on, just a few drinks. Don't tell me you still sour 'bout what happened earlier?" Jay inquired as he popped his face through the collar of his blue sweatshirt and threw his arms through both sleeves. "I'm payin'."

"Fuck it. I never turn down *free*," Sean replied. He still had a job to do and he just had to suck it up and act like everything was cool. He couldn't wait to nail Jay's disgraceful ass to the wall. "But don't ever pull that bullshit wit' me again."

"Alright, alright." Jay smiled, throwing up his hands as if he was surrendering. "You bringin' Lisa?"

Sean paused, then spoke, "Let me ask you a question. What would you think if Tracy was stayin' out all night, givin' you lame excuses?"

"This 'bout Lisa?" Jay asked, eyeing Sean warily.

With his mood dampening, Sean nodded. His chest tightened slightly as he placed his police issued handcuffs into the locker.

"You hittin' it right?" Jay asked jokingly.

Sean turned, glaring at Jay, ready to rip his head off. This definitely was not the time for jokes. His mood darkened and he gritted his teeth as his eyes flashed with rage.

"I'm just fuckin' wit' ya," Jay replied quickly defusing the tension. "She probably needs some space is all."

"Maybe," Sean replied and drifted off into deep thought. "Maybe."

****

Across town in the South Bronx, José's mineral gray BMW pulled up in front of Forest projects on 163rd Street and Trinity Avenue, with Chico at the wheel, double-parking next to an old beat up station wagon. With the chrome rims shining, José stepped out.

"Be back in twenty minutes," he said, surveying the busy block. People from the neighborhood shuffled up and down the sidewalk headed to various destinations. The folks, who knew who José was, tossed him respectful nods as they continued on their way.

Desmon, a young stocky black kid from the block, ran up to José as he reached the sidewalk.

"When you gonna put me on?" he asked.

"I keep telling you, you're too young," José replied. "Come see me in three years when you turn eighteen."

"Ahh, man," Desmon said in a disappointed tone.

José whipped out a wad of big faced greenbacks. "Ahh, man, nothing," he said, then stuck a hundred dollar bill into the kid's anxious palm.

Desmon's eyes quickly brightened. "Gee, thanks José!" he squealed, still staring at the picture of Benjamin Franklin that was staring right back at him. He ran over to the run down grocery store on the corner. A few hoodlums were drinking forty-ounces in front of the bodega as Desmon shot past them into the store. One Hispanic cat rocking a red bandana nodded José's way.

José ignored him and made a call on his black Nextel as he strolled up to the deserted 14-story building.

"I'm downstairs," he said. "Let me in."

The lobby entrance buzzed to life and José yanked open the heavy metal door and stepped inside.

A few minutes later, José emerged from the cramped elevator, spotting Kathy, a sexy Dominican in her early forties standing in her doorway in a revealing lounge dress. He strutted over to the smiling woman with the butter brown complexion and they shared a quick tongue dance.

Kathy pulled away. "My kids are still up, but we can talk in the staircase."

"Talk?" José replied, knowing he didn't have any plans on conversing.

She planted a wet kiss on his pouting lips. "Yep, don't you want to fuck me?" With a seductive grin, she corrected herself. "I mean talk to me."

José just smiled, his eyes shining bright with anticipation. Pulling her apartment door closed, Kathy grabbed his thick hairy arm and led the way to the staircase. Inside the stairwell, José pinned Kathy up against the wall groping her as they tongue kissed. She shoved him back and walked over to the steps leading upstairs and sat down on the third step. With a finger she motioned José over. He strutted over and stood directly in front of her as she unzipped his stonewashed jeans, pulling out his fat stubby dick.

José closed his eyes as he felt her hot wet mouth welcome his mushroom head inside with a twirl of her slippery tongue. Opening his eyes, he watched her swallow his whole shaft like a professional porno star. If he had to rate her performance on a scale of one to ten, she'd get a twenty. Her head game was just that good.

Kathy dribbled a gob of saliva onto the head of his dick and she turned around, pulling up her dress. Getting on her knees, she arched her back and spread open her plump ass, exposing her pussy and asshole. Her fat butt looked like two basketballs glued together.

Grabbing both her butt cheeks, José spread her ass open. He positioned the head on her wrinkled brown eye and pushed slowly. Her asshole seemed to open up and welcome him right in.

"Oh shit daddy!" she squealed in a mixture of pain and pleasure. "Fuck my ass."

After digging her out for a little of over ten minutes, José finally exploded then pulled out. He adjusted his jeans and shirt while Kathy dusted off her dirty knees. All smiles, she reached out to fix José's wrinkled collar.

Suddenly José's mood darkened and he turned serious

"On the flip side of things," he said, "you gonna tell me what the fuck really happened to my paper?" His eyes became flooded with rage.

Kathy's pearly whites quickly disappeared as her face fell solemn. "I already told you, somebody ripped me off." Her skin was turning pale.

"Oh," José replied. "That's not what a little birdie told me."

Kathy tried to run out of the staircase, but José was too quick for her. He grabbed her by the hair and threw her into a headlock and covered her mouth as she tried to scream.

"Nobody steals from me," With that said, José snapped her fragile neck, dragged her lifeless body over to the steps and left her slumped over in the staircase. He straightened his clothes and disappeared down the stairs.

****

Later that night, Jimmy's Café was practically empty except for one or two friends, families and couples scattered around the huge, open air dining area. Sean, Lisa, Jay and his main woman friend, Tracy, an attractive woman, in her late forties, were seated at the bar, drinking and conversing. She had met Jay a few months back at the strip club where she danced. R&B music played softly in the background.

A few couples and families were grubbing in the dining section two steps down from the bar area. A slim Puerto Rican waitress was busy taking a young couple's order.

Jay stood and headed for the bathroom that was located down the steps on the other side of the dining area.

"'Nother round, ladies?" Sean asked the two women as he polished off the rest of his drink.

"Sure," Tracy responded with a friendly smile.

Lisa shook her head and continued sipping her drink. Sean motioned to the bartender.

"What can I get you?" the sexy middle-aged woman asked him in a friendly tone.

"A cosmo and. . . amaretto stone sour, " Sean replied, flashing her a bright smile.

The bartender went off to prepare their drinks just as Lisa got up to leave. Sean grabbed her by the arm and asked, "Where you goin'?" His jealous nature was getting the best of him.

"Ladies' room. That okay?" she snapped shaking his hand off. She maneuvered around him, and went straight toward the back of the restaurant.

Jay exited the men's room just as Lisa approached. Her gaze swept over him in a way that only lovers should share and then she entered the bathroom without saying so much as a word.

Seconds later, Jay slipped inside the women's room, catching her by surprise. Lisa stood in front of a wall length mirror applying a second coat of lipstick to her luscious lips. They were all alone. The black tiled floor and burgundy walls blended perfectly with the black stalls that lined the other side of the bathroom.

Spotting Jay coming toward her through the mirror, Lisa gasped and quickly spun around, her eyes widened with fright. "You can't be in—a"

With a quick jerk of his hand, she was in his arms. Jay shoved his tongue down her throat. Gripping her hips, he pulled her even closer to him as his erection poked dangerously forward, ready for action. Her sweat scent was driving him wild. After a moment, she relaxed and couldn't resist kissing him back.

Coming back to her senses, Lisa suddenly pulled away. "What about Sean?"

"What about him?" It wasn't as if they hadn't been sleeping together for the past three months. Well actually, she had been avoiding him for the past week after telling him she couldn't see him anymore. She told him that the guilt was eating her alive. She really wanted to end things. In her mind, the sex, no matter how good, wasn't worth losing Sean. But, right now, she was just worried about Sean being close by. Even Jay was a little worried that Tracy could walk in at any moment.

"If you can honestly tell me he's makin' you happy now, I'll walk away," Jay responded, meaning every word or at least trying to sound like he did. Looking deep into her brown eyes, he waited for her reply. What Sean had taken for a genuine invitation, was actually Jay's cooked-up scheme to get to Lisa since he hadn't been able to reach her by phone all week. At that moment it seemed the only thing truly genuine about Jay was his love of self, money and women. Sean's woman was at the top of the list. The thought of losing Lisa made his heart pause. He didn't like that feeling, so until he was done and could figure things out, he wanted to keep her with him.

The total silence that fell over Lisa made it clearly obvious she wasn't happy. Knowing he was right, Jay pulled her into the closest stall. The steel door swung shut behind them. He pressed her up against the wall and started licking behind her ear. Seconds later, he slid his wet tongue down the soft curves of her exposed neck.

"Mmmm," she moaned as his hot tongue traced a path down her shoulder blade.

Her nipples hardened, poking through the sheer fabric of her blouse. A single hand reached out, cupping her breasts.

"Wait, wait. What if they catch us?" Lisa pleaded, glancing toward the closed door.

Jay held his finger up to his lips, whispering, "Shhhh."

He then began kissing her so passionately she gave in completely. She gave his hot slithering tongue a few quick sucks as though it was the throbbing head of his dick. It started getting hot and heavy as Jay gave way to the fire building up deep inside him. He could tell she felt like being a nasty girl tonight.

Dropping to her knees in the cramped booth, she unzipped him and pulled his long, dark hard shaft out of his jeans. She gave his round plump head a wet kiss, then suddenly swallowed it whole, right down to his balls. *Damn*, was all Jay could think, instantly engulfed in the pleasures of her hungry wet mouth, a talented mouth that rightfully belonged to someone else.

****

The next evening, the idling Cherokee sat parked on a run down block near 135th and Exterior Street. Jay flipped open the Daily newspaper as Sean stared out the window daydreaming. The strong wind whipping through the block shook the jeep as it blew over the exterior of the vehicle. Sean's mind was so far gone he didn't even notice the homeless woman that passed by pushing a raggedy shopping cart filled with plastic bottles and tin cans.

Jay's cell rang. Flipping it open, he said, "Talk to me," then paused before saying, "Okay. Where at?" He sat up, running a hand over his baldhead. "I'll be there." He hung up, tossed the paper on the back seat and started the engine. "Let's ride."

The Cherokee glided along Exterior Street headed toward the 138th Street Bridge. Across the East River, a panoramic view of Harlem unfolded in front of them. The lights coming from the various buildings broke through the darkness slowly starting to settle over Manhattan.

About thirty minutes later, across town in the co-op city section of the Bronx, in the parking lot behind JC Penny's, a black-on-black Mercedes Benz with black powder coated 22-inch rims sat idling. The grayish white exhaust escaping out of the tailpipe disseminated into the cool night air as the engine hummed quietly.

Inside the Benz, a shady looking light-skinned black male talked on a cell phone, keeping an eye out for someone. The plush leather seat he was slumped in was laid back so far it practically touched the back seat. He was decked out in a smooth coco-butter dyed leather with a crisp pair of blue denim jeans. His matching coco-butter skully cap was pulled low over one eye. An overwhelming amount of diamonds glistened in his Jacob watch.

"He's here. I'll holla back." Shady announced to the person on the other end, then hung up. Seconds later, the passenger door swung open and Jay stepped inside.

"What's new, high roller?" Jay snickered as his eyes locked on the iced-out timepiece Shady wore. With every movement of his arm, the expensive watch sparkled, practically blinding Jay.

"Same shit, different day." Shady pulled out two cigars from the compartment under the armrest. "You smoke these?"

"Nah," Jay responded with a shake of the head as he pulled out a cigarette and asked, "How can I be of assistance?" Lighting up the cancer stick, he slumped back in the plush seat even further, eyeing Shady.

"I need you to haul a few packages to Jersey, tonight."

"I look like a fuckin' movin' company?" Jay snapped, clearly pissed off. His ice-cold eyes stay locked on Shady. If looks could kill, Shady would've been one dead motherfucker.

Unfazed and never taking no for an answer, Shady continued his pitch, "Da price is right, playa."

"I'm listenin'," Jay replied coldly, blowing the smoke through his nostrils. Once the prospect of making money was mentioned, he became all ears. Greed had a way of calming him down. His anger slipped away almost instantly.

Shady knew he had him by the balls now, so he decided to squeeze. "Six G's."

"Ten's better," Jay shot back sharply. He never settled for the first offer. Never. He truly believed in negotiating and it always ended up in his favor. He made sure of that. Or so he thought.

"Ten it is," Shady quickly agreed with a sly grin and stuck out his palm to seal the deal.

Jay just stared at him, then gave a quick glance down at the offensive hand, then back up to the man's face. "Make sure you have the cash when I pick up the packages."

Shady retracted his hand. "Will do." He was really laughing on the inside because he had been prepared to pay fifteen if necessary. Shit. The package he was having transported to Jersey was going to net him a hundred and fifty grand in one shot. So all and all, he was coming out on top as far as he was concerned. *Fuck him*, he thought as he eyed Jay. *Da jokes on you.*

****

Later that night, traffic flowed along the top and lower spans of the George Washington Bridge as the New Jersey shoreline loomed in the distance. The Cherokee glided across the upper span over the Hudson River toward the Jersey side. Jay drove while Sean rode shotgun, puffing on half a cigarette.

"If he payin' us five grand, how much you figure he's really seein'?" Sean asked, turning to look at Jay.

"Who knows," Jay shrugged as he pondered the question further. After a moment of silence, he added, "From now on, we uppin' his fuckin' tax."

"You got my vote, " Sean said, glancing out of the passenger window, then turning back to Jay and added, "I see that rule one went out the window."

According to Jay, they never touched the product.

Jay glanced over at Sean, cracked a sly smile and said, "This is different. We just deliverin' merchandise."

"Oh, I see, it's just *merchandise*." Sean replied with a wink and a smile. "I got ya."

"Right, right. Come on, baby, it's easy money," Jay replied with a quick laugh. "Fuck it. I'll do anything for the right price. Money talks, bullshit walks."

On a quiet block, not too far from the GWB, expensive homes with well-kept lawns lined the quiet suburban street. The Cherokee pulled into the driveway of an expensive split-level home and parked next to a light-blue

Jaguar. The lights were on inside the residence. Jay killed the headlights and beeped the horn once.

After a few seconds, the garage door rolled open revealing Fitz standing inside dressed in a highly flamboyant bright pink, silk buttoned down shirt tucked into some tight gap jeans. He motioned them in. Jay pulled inside. The garage door rolled down behind them.

As Jay and Sean exited the jeep, Fitz gazed them over from head to toe with lustful eyes, greeting them in a high-pitched voice, "Aaaaay...he sent me two cuties. You guys wanna drink or something?" Sean nearly gaped at Fitz's boisterous act. The man was straighter than a white girl's ass, but he was taking to the gay undercover role as though he'd been born to it.

"Let's stick to matter at hand," Jay responded coldly not even trying to hide his disgust as he moved to the rear of the Cherokee.

Sean knew from one of their previous conversations that Jay hated faggots with a passion ever since his high school teacher tried to make a pass on him in the tenth grade. A sly smirk snuck across his lips as he remembered what Jay had told him about the incident. He knew this was one of Fitz's practical jokes.

"Feisty. I like that," Fitz replied, eyeing both of them with a grin. "So, where's my stuff?"

"Damn, he's a little to good at this," Sean murmured, making a mental note to tease Fitz about this later.

Jay opened the hatch, revealing three small plain cardboard boxes in the back. He shoved one of the boxes to Sean and then grabbed the other two.

"Where you want this?" Sean asked Fitz.

"Drop it right there," Fitz replied, pointing to a spot in the corner of the garage. Sean placed the box in the far left-hand corner next to an old wooden crate of expensive wine. Jay followed right behind him with the other two boxes.

"Thanks so much," Fitz said, with his hands on his hips. "You sure, you guys aren't thirsty? I have ice-cold lemonade."

Sean covered his mouth with one hand, holding in a laugh as he eyed Fitz.

"No thanks. I have a lady friend waitin' for me," Jay replied, his voice an octave or two deeper than normal, making sure Fitz knew every bone in his body was straight.

He climbed back into the Cherokee and tore out of the driveway.

****

Much later that same night in the parking lot of a nearby fuck motel, a burgundy Nissan Maxima pulled in and parked in the first empty spot available. The motel was located in the North Bronx near Interstate-95 and Conner Avenue. Lisa stepped out the car and headed for the motel lobby. Her silky hair bounced against her smooth chocolate skin with every step she took.

Just then, a horn blew loudly. She turned, spotting Jay exiting the Cherokee. She stopped, waiting for him to approach. He shot her a quick wink as he crossed over to her. They shared a quick kiss, then Jay placed an arm around her shoulder. "What's up?"

"Hopefully you are," Lisa snickered seductively, giving his crotch a slight rub. "Mmm," she murmured, feeling his semi-hard cock harden even more as she stroked it.

"Keep touchin' me like that and I will be," Jay whispered in her ear. She shivered with every touch. Lisa shot him a provocative glance and they locked eyes. He planned on working her pussy out tonight. She had no idea what the hell she was in for.

Minutes later, the television gave off the only light in the cheap room. Jay was spread out, on his back, across the bed watching the tube in his boxers.

Light crept through the cracks of the closed bathroom door. Jay could hear the shower running faintly in the bathroom as Lisa hummed the tune of a song. His cell phone vibrated on the wooden nightstand. He grabbed it, flipped it open, stealing a quick glance toward the bathroom as he said, "Talk to me." A moment later, he grinned. "What's up, young blood?"

Lisa emerged from the bathroom wrapped in nothing but a wet towel. Her long, wet locks were twisted up into a bun. Pressing a finger to his lips, Jay signaled her to stay quiet. She nodded, then crossed over to the edge of the bed dancing provocatively in front of him. Jay just watched her.

Her towel dropped, exposing voluptuous curves, her nice perky nipples, her tight washboard stomach and her tight round juicy ass. She had cute lickable toes and diamond shaped calves that led up to a pair of thick, juicy thighs.

"Stop worryin', she's probably out wit' some friends." Jay smirked as Sean rambled on and on. Lisa turned around and bent over giving him a clear view of her moist vagina. The lips spread apart slightly as she shook her ass from side to side.

His dick throbbed with every movement.

"Listen," Jay said into the phone, "I'm kinda tied up now. . . I'll hit you tomorrow." He ended the call and tossed the phone on the bed.

"Who was that?" Lisa asked, knowing good and well she knew exactly who it was.

"Ya husband," Jay replied. His dick hardened as he glanced over her nude, voluptuous body, which reminded him of Beyoncé. Unable to contain himself any longer, he grabbed her by the arms and pulled her down on top of him.

He parted her lips with a hard, passionate kiss. Rolling her over onto the bed, Jay climbed on top and licked his way down her neck to her breasts, down to her belly button, and headed past her neatly trimmed public hairs straight to her hidden clit. Gently he pulled back the fold of soft honey-colored skin that hid her swollen clit and began slowly working his wet tongue back and forth over and around it in circles, only stopping to give it a few quick forceful sucks every now and then. Each time he did, she grabbed the back of his head, squealing with satisfaction.

Jay inserted two fingers deep into her soaking wet pussy, treating her G-spot to intense thrusts as he circled the tip of her clit. Damn, this was some good pussy. Jay worked both spots simultaneously, hoping to send continuous shockwaves of pleasure flowing through her body.

"Mmm. Shit. Damn!" She moaned over and over, squeezing her juicy thighs together with each thrust of her hips. Finally, she locked his baldhead in place forcing him to keep licking and sucking as she started to cum.

"Yeahhhhh, right there, baby," she squealed, tossing her wet hair back into the pillows.

After she climaxed, Jay gripped her hips, flipping her over onto her knees. She arched her back until her juicy ass spread wide open. He slowly worked his tongue around the ridges of her wrinkled donut as she feverishly rubbed her clit. Two hands palmed both her soft, fluffy cheeks. Lisa shivered from the pleasure.

Jay's hungry tongue traveled along the ridge, leading from her ass to her pussy. He sucked on her swollen clit, rotating between hard and soft suction while shoving two fingers deep into her vagina to rub her g-spot again.

Within moments, Jay was knee-deep in her tight, hot pussy pumping away with her juicy thighs thrown over his heaving shoulders. He slid one of his fingers into her tight ass as he continued stroking her. And Lisa was cumming all over his rock hard pipe as her toes curled and she snatched the sheets halfway off the bed. Her juices ran down past her asshole onto the wrinkled linen.

A half hour later, Jay sat down on the edge of the bed, grabbing a cigarette and a lighter off the end table. He quickly lit it up and took a pull. His back was to Lisa who as he stared off at a huge roach scurrying across the wall.

A television could be heard blaring all the way in the next room.

"We can't do this anymore," Lisa's soft voice broke into his thoughts.

Jay turned to her with a proud grin. "Wore ya out, huh?" His ego soared, knowing he had banged that kitty just right. Multiple orgasms were definitely a plus as he explored all three of her tight holes. And she could really take it in the ass. If only Sean knew. Poor guy.

"I mean us," she replied, her voice cracking out of frustration and confusion. Tears welled up in her brown eyes. "This. We can't do *this*."

So *now* after he had given her the dick, her emotions were running wild. On one hand, she was strung out on his dick, and on the other hand maybe she truly loved Sean. But

Jay would be damned if he'd let her go. There was something about her that kept him coming back. The thought of being without her . . .well, he didn't want to think about it.

Glancing at her naked body, Jay's mind drifted back to the first time they slept together. The whole thing started out innocently. She had been crying on his shoulder about Sean walking out on her. At first, Jay was just lending a caring ear, but something about the way he cradled Lisa in his arms and up against his chest did things to him. Her womanly scent turned him on. Just thinking about it had gotten him hard. Instead of ignoring the sexual urge, he planted a sensual kiss on her juicy lips. She didn't try to fight or resist. There was something about the excitement of having sex with a person for the first time that made it all the better. Jay shook off the thought and returned back to the present.

Jay was honestly taken back by what Lisa had told him. He shoved her back onto the bed, slipping his hungry tongue into her mouth. Her tongue fought his for only a moment. He reached down, cupping the small nestle of dark curls at the center of her thighs. He slipped one finger in, then the next. Her hot walls were already throbbing again. She had an itch deep inside that needed scratching. Fuck what she was talking about. The moisture on his fingers told Jay she wanted him. Bodies just don't lie. Positioning his mushroom head on her lips, he rammed his dick into her, forcing her back on the pillows.

"You want to end this?" Jay stroked again, angered by the hurt that he felt. Lisa shook her head. "So where the fuck is this comin' from?" He was pissed off by Lisa's mind games. He was usually the one to end things. And that's the way he wanted to keep it.

"I—I don't know," she said, stammering with every thrust of his body into hers. "I don't know." She placed her hands against his chest, pushing to move him away. "We just can't." She turned her head, crying as he rammed into her again and again. Her body jerked in response. The wetness surrounding his dick and the distraught look in her eyes only fueled him on.

"You think I wanted this?" He reached a single hand to her face, forcing her eyes to meet his. He froze mid-stroke. "You think I wanted to fall in love with my partner's wife?"

Sometimes, he honestly regretted the fact he had started sleeping with Lisa. He had slept with a lot of married woman and usually, he didn't give a fuck. But this time he actually had mixed feelings. Maybe he actually did have a heart after all. And that angered him even more. Giving your heart to woman only got you living alone in a bachelor's pad that wasn't fit for a bum. Having a heart got half your paycheck paid out in alimony and the other half in child support. A broken heart could have you separated from your only son for two years. Fuck having a heart.

"Love. Wait. . . This is too much," Lisa said as tears trickled down her flushed cheeks. "Jay, I. . . I really care about you, but I…I still love Sean," she whimpered, wiping her face with the back of a delicate hand.

"So why are you here?" Jay stared at her, waiting for a much needed answer. She didn't answer. He pulled out with his feelings genuinely hurt. Deep down he almost felt like crying but he would never let a woman see him shed a tear nor any man.

Lisa stared off as though the ceiling held an answer. Suddenly Lisa's cell phone rang, breaking the long silence. She reached over to the nightstand, rumbled through her purse and lifted out the little silver phone. She glanced at the display. Her head lowered as her entire body became racked with heart wrenching sobs.

CHAPTER 17

The quiet, but cool night turned into a less-than-productive morning, which soon gave way to the hustle and bustle of the evening drug grind.

José's new ride, a black 4.6 Range Rover, eased quietly onto the corner as he scanned the block through the black tinted windows. Slumped in the passenger seat, he was running his mouth on the phone. A sexy Puerto Rican chick with curly reddish-brown hair hopped out the driver's side, crossing to the other side of the street. She disappeared into the pharmacy on the corner.

Up and down Fish Avenue, rows of weathered six-story, low-income, brick tenements lined both sides of the street. A light mixture of residents and fiends shuffled through the drug block. On the corner of Fish Ave. and Boston Road, one "ride or die" young thug in training, posted up against the mailbox as a lookout, watched all the traffic come up and down the block. It was the perfect vantage point for spotting NYPD.

In the middle of the block, two tough looking drug-dealers, Soldier and Dozen, hustled in front of one of the tenements. The lookout steered customers to Soldier, the seasoned hustler on the block, who collected their cash while taking their orders like a drive-through. He would then relay the junkie's drugs of choice to Dozen with the coded hand signals that only their crew could understand.

Jumping into action, Dozen would immediately slide customers their goods and send them on their way.

Tucked in the shadows, KP leaned against a parked car further up the block, studying his two workers and the block he ran for José's operation through half-closed bloodshot eyes. Weed happened to be his favorite pass time. A large celluloid scar ran from KP's left ear to his jawbone stopping just short of his neck—the only blemish on his otherwise smooth coco-brown skin. As the block's main overseer, he kept shit running smooth from shift changes to money drops, and he answered directly to José.

Dozen was a hotheaded hand-to-hand worker in his late teens. Cockiness oozed from him as he leaned back against the brick wall with one leg cocked up on it and his crotch in his palm. He ran the other hand over his long corn rolls as he scanned the block.

A late model Buick Regal sputtered up and the driver motioned to them. Unwilling to give up his comfortable position, Dozen glanced over at Soldier and didn't move. This shit happened all the time. Soldier's lazy ass never budged to lend a helping hand.

Soldier eyed him right back.

"Fuck you eyein' me for? Handle dat, nigga," Soldier snapped as he glared at Dozen and folded his muscular arms across his chest.

Dozen twisted up his lips, bopped over to the idling Buick and mumbled to the driver, "What'cha need?"

Inside the warm luxury jeep, José continued watching his workers handle his business.

* * *

The Cherokee roared down Boston Road with Sean behind the wheel, humming along to Al Green's "Love and Happiness" knocking on the radio. Sean was truly lost in the moment. Jay inhaled a cigarette, observing the area. The shops and bodegas were open for business as people navigated the busy block, some shopping and some just passing through.

Slumped in the back seat, Warren nodded off with a half smoked, unlit cigarette stuck between his flaking lips. Sean reached back, grabbing the cancer stick. He plucked it out the window.

Jay eyed Sean as he continued humming away without a care in the world and said, "I need summa that shit you on."

"Two for five, old man," Sean replied with a chuckle, giving Jay a quick glance. "Two for five."

"Old?" Jay asked, puffing out his chest like the wrestler Macho Man Randy Savage. "Shit, this old man'll give you a run for ya money, young blood."

Spotting the Cherokee rolling toward him on Boston road, the young lookout tensed up and stopped yakking on his cell phone long enough to holler a succession of "birdcall" warnings to the crew.

Hopping right into defensive mode, Dozen and the rest of the workers hurriedly stashed the drugs deep into the short stubby bushes surrounding the building, then slid off further down the block out of range of a possession charge. Soldier tucked a thick billfold deep into his baggy jeans, adjusting them so the knot wouldn't show.

KP didn't even attempt to move from his relaxing spot on the car. He was in a prime position to watch everything that unfolded without being easily spotted.

Slowing down near the corner of Fish Avenue, the Cherokee turned onto the block. Stopping in front of the two dealers, Jay hopped out the jeep followed quickly by Sean with firearms in hand.

"Palms to the wall, fellas!" Jay demanded pointing the gun at them. Knowing the drill, Soldier sighed and quickly complied, trying to avoid a steel-toe boot up his ass.

Dozen stood his ground, folded his arms with a sinister ice-grill, trying to act tough and asked, "Why you fuckin' wit' us?"

No sooner had the words left his mouth, Jay grabbed Dozen by his Adam's apple, slamming his back to the brick wall. "I advise you to shut the fuck up, Dickhead!" Jay barked with spit flying into the boy's twisted up face. "Turn around and spread ya fuckin' legs."

Jay released his grip and Dozen quickly did as he was told.

Jay holstered his gun and started frisking Dozen while Sean loomed in the background, standing guard with the weapon palmed at his side.

Inside the Range, José quietly fumed as the thick vein on the side of his temple throbbed. Seeing the two cops had instantly brought back all the pain of Bobby's death. With his blood boiling, he reached for the gun that would normally be under his seat only to realize he had forgot to stash it in the new ride. Feeling like an idiot all he could do now was wait to catch them another day. If he could kick himself in the ass he would have.

The strong stench of urine hung in the air as rap music blared from an apartment off in the distance. Jay pulled a wad of cash out of Dozen's pocket, eyed it and said, "Consider this confiscated."

Dozen pushed off the wall, trying to spin around. Jay lunged forward, slamming him back against the wall.

"You ain't takin' my fuckin' paper." Dozen's face was pressed to the concrete bricks by Jay's massive hand as he increased the pressure to the back of the boy's skull.

"Says who, huh?" Jay asked, now pressing the barrel to the back of Dozen's head. Practically shitting in his pants, Dozen didn't say another word. "When's the last time you seen ya boss?"

"I don't have a boss," Dozen replied with a smirk. "I freelance."

"You freelance? Bullshit," Jay said with a slick laugh. "José would run ya punk ass off the block."

"Fuck you," Dozen snapped back.

Jay delivered a swift, crushing right hook to the side of his face, then said, "No, fuck *you.*"

"Ah shit!" Dozen yelled, cupping his face.

Jay turned his attention to Soldier. "Hopefully, we won't have these same complications," he stated harshly, frisking the quiet man. He ran both hands over the shoulders and down the sleeves, then searched his baggy jeans and found a fat wad of cash.

Jay and Sean crossed to the Cherokee. Sean climbed in the driver's seat, waiting as Jay stopped, turned back to face the two dealers and said, "Tell José I'll be seein' him." He cracked a half smile, climbed in and the Cherokee sped away.

Back in the middle of the block, Soldier, KP and Dozen watched the Cherokee disappear around a corner about two blocks up.

Inside the Range, José was seeing nothing but red. Though he was angry at losing the money, he was hurting more than anything else. He had spotted the cops two minutes before the lookout did. All it took was a few seconds to stash the cash somewhere. These niggers were slipping. He had no problem given the right reason to pull these fools off the block, but he wanted to get onto the more serious task of taking those renegade cops down.

José decided not to even make his presence known but cracked the window slightly to hear the rest of his crew's conversation. Now he waited to hear what kind of bullshit lie they would come up with or if they would be straight up with him.

"I don't believe these fuckin' pigs jacked us!" Soldier shouted venting his anger.

"And we can't even do shit about it," Dozen replied, using his hand to try to slow up the flow of blood from his wound.

"Whatever, nigga. José's gonna hit the fuckin' roof when he finds out the same cops that iced Bobby just robbed us," Soldier said. "Nobody robs José. *Nobody.*"

"Now I gotta be the one to break the news to José," KP interjected, strutting over with a worried expression on his face. "Why the hell did this have to go down on my shift?"

Big Dee emerged from the lobby of the building, interrupting the both of them as he yelled, "Y'all niggas look light in da pockets."

His huge form was practically bent over as he laughed.

"Dat shit funny, nigga?" KP growled, watching Big Dee approach.

José knew that if it had been any other cat besides Big Dee, he would've been laid out right there. But Big Dee was KP's main man so he just sucked it up.

"Hell yeah." Big Dee smiled at the KP's gruff expression. "I don't give a fuck if you're pissed off." Lighting up a Newport. "When da shit happened to me, you thought it was hilarious."

Dozen pulled out half of a smoked blunt. "They got you, too?"

"What I just say?" Big Dee snapped looking at him as if he had grown two heads.

"Next time they roll through, they leavin' dis mufucka in caskets," KP stated plainly and he was dead real. Even if he didn't want to, he knew José would have it no other way or it was his ass.

"José's gonna kill us for lettin' them snatch his cake," Dozen said.

Secretly, José agreed with them, but because he had seen everything go down the only reason he'd kill them now was if they crossed him by lying.

KP stood there clenching his fists, like he was ready to knock Dozen's head off, but he maintained and just snapped, "You don't think I fuckin' know that."

Neither of them saw the Rover start up and creep into the night. José planned on clearing up matters right away. He punched a number into his cell and waited a few moments for the person to answer. "Meet me at the spot now."

****

Minutes later in a cramped project apartment, José, KP, Big D and Dozen sat around a medium sized wooden table, smoking a blunt. A Mac-10 and two boxes of bullets rested on the table along with an overloaded ashtray. The small kitchen needed a good spring-cleaning. Used pots and pans were stacked on the stove and in the sink filled with dirty brown water. A thin layer of old caked up cooking grease coated the tile behind the stove. Rap music blasted from a boom box in another room.

Chico stood guard in the kitchen doorway. His gun was bulging underneath his shirt.

"Since, ya'll let dem motherfuckers jack my paper," José stated through clenched teeth, "ya'll gotta gut those fucking pigs or I'ma gut you." He slapped the extended clip into the Mac-10. He racked the slide back, automatically loading a slug into the chamber. With a quick flick of his thick writs, he aimed the barrel at KP. Seconds ticked by like hours. KP held his breath. After a tense moment, José turned the gun on Dozen. The stunned man gasped, his chest heaved upward, and eyes closed as he let out a long breath and opened them again. Then the metal piece inched away, focusing on Big Dee who cocked his head, eyes glaring into the face of death.

José's thick lips broke into a deadly smile as he said with a quick glance to all three, "You fuck this up, it's ya ass." José then passed the gun to KP. "Now handle ya business 'fore it handles you."

KP nodded, finally taking in a breath of air.

José glanced around the kitchen, menacing eyes focusing on the stack of dirty dishes sitting in the sink. "Yo Dozen, you need to wash ya fucking plates, you nasty motherfucker," José snapped. "Hire a bitch or something. I know I pay ya ass better than that."

A peal of laughter echoed through the entire room, easing the tension and moving the foursome back to business.

CHAPTER 18

As the Cherokee pulled out of the Mobile gas station, Jay finished counting the wad of cash he had took off the two dealers. His mood darkened more than it already was.

"Shit there was only eight hundred dollars between them," he said in frustration.

"Hey, if you don't want the money, I'll gladly take it," Sean replied with a grin.

"I'm tried of this nickel and dime shit. At this rate it'll take me another two years before I have enough paper to call it quits. It's time to step the game up."

"And how you plan on doin' that?"

"We gon' make a little withdrawal from a bank."

"You mean hit up some dealer's bank account?"

"Nah, it's a little more complicated than that."

"How so?" Sean asked, definitely wanting to hear more.

"We gonna rob the motherfucker."

Totally caught off guard, Sean slammed on the brakes in the middle of the street. A Hyundai had to swerve hard to avoid slamming into the rear of the Cherokee. The driver of the small hatchback drove by cursing at the two cops.

"You crazy, we're cops," Sean said. "We can't rob a bank."

"Says who, young blood? It's been done before."

"So you tellin' me, you've already hit a bank?"

Jay just nodded as a sly grin crept across his aging grill. "Who better to do it than cops? We know the response times, the evidence gathering procedures and we have police radios to monitor what cruisers are in the area."

A car horn bought Sean back to the realization that he was still holding up traffic. He stepped on the gas and the engine roared back to life as the Cherokee charged up the block.

Jay started filling him in on the first bank robbery he and Warren had pulled off a few months prior to Sean being transferred into the narcotics division.

Instead of just walking into a bank and announcing a hold up, the two men had decided to break into a bank at night while it was closed and steal the money out of the vault. Jay was the actual brain behind the whole operation. As luck would have it, the bank happened to be located right next to a mom and pop hardware store on a quiet commercial strip.

They broke into the hardware store through the roof during the middle of the night and drilled through the brick wall that led to the bank. When they finally got through the thick-layered wall of the bank, they headed straight for the vault. The only problem was the power drill didn't make even a slight dent in the solid metal door of the vault.

Instead of panicking and admitting defeat, Jay came up with an even better idea. Since they were already inside the bank, the two of them would wait until morning and catch the bank manager off guard when he opened up the bank. They would force him to open the vault at gunpoint and then steal the money. After hiding out in the bank all night, when the manager finally arrived the next morning the two men sprung into action. Their new plan went off like clockwork and the two dirty cops made off with the cash.

Finished rehashing the story, Jay sat there grinning at Sean like a proud father after his son just made his first basket from the three-point line.

"But this time we're gonna do things different," Jay said. "We gonna walk in, hit'em fast and hard and get out in a hurry. Breakin' through walls takes too much fuckin' time." He took in Sean's reaction. "So you in or what, young blood?"

"Fuck it, I'm in," Sean managed to say but deep down inside he didn't want any part of the crooked scheme.

"Good...good," Jay replied.

"So how much did y'all get?" Sean asked, glancing at Jay.

"Now that I can't tell you," Jay replied with a devilish grin. "Don't take it personal, but I just don't feel comfortable discussin' numbers if you weren't involved with it," Jay finished before growing quiet.

"I feel you," Sean said though he really didn't; he found it hard to relate with the dirty cop.

A few seconds passed before Jay suddenly announced, "It's time to pay one of José's buddies a visit." He placed a call on his cell and waited for someone to pick up. "Yo, Warren, meet us on Burnside Ave. and Jerome in ten minutes."

By Jay's ominous tone, Sean was sure someone would end up in a painful situation.

****

Chico strutted up Burnside Avenue with his black sterling leather jacket fully open as though the freezing cold couldn't touch him. He entered a Spanish restaurant specializing in Dominican food. He bobbed through the front door like he owned the place.

Two patrons were in the midst of eating and talking about yesterday's news.

"It's really a shame how they have these poor kids crammed thirty to forty per classroom," a cute Puerto Rican honey said, taking a bite of her steak. She was thick and voluptuous with a body like Jill Scott.

Her slender friend with coco butter skin and a Halle Berry hair-do cocked her head. "It's not like that in the suburbs." Taking the straw in her mouth, she sipped on a can of Coke.

"Shit, girl, it's not like that in the school I teach in. Or anywhere else in the so-called well-to-do areas."

"This weather is so crazy."

"I know right."

A Dominican waitress with wrinkles etched in her forehead worked behind the long narrow counter taking orders and handling the register while white haired old man whisked a broom across the wooden floor. The waitress walked with an arthritic limp.

Chico strutted over to the busy waitress, planting a kiss on her weathered cheek.

"Your father's upstairs," she told him softly, rubbing him on his back.

"Okay, Ma."

Up the block from the restaurant, Jay exited the Cherokee as the unmarked Impala pulled up with Warren behind the wheel. "You can wait here, me and Warren gonna handle this." Jay said, slamming the door behind him.

Sean just nodded and continued reading his newspaper. Glancing up, he watched the two cops walk up the block and disappear into the restaurant.

Jay and Warren entered. Their eyes locked on Chico as he looked over and spotted the cops. They headed straight for him. Jay tossed a nod to the waitress, then turned his attention to Chico. "I hear ya got the best food in town."

Chico just nodded as his mother slithered away behind the counter and to the safety of the backroom.

"Okay, okay. Give me an order of arroz con pollo," Jay said, his intimidating glare locking on Chico. "Yeah, chicken should hit the spot . . . and, ahhh. . . two .45's."

Chico eyed him right back showing no signs of fear. "You got the wrong spot for that," he replied, glancing at his expensive leather band watch. "We no do that here."

Jay whipped out his gun, shoving the barrel under Chico's chin. "Take me to the stash."

Moments later, down in the cellar of the restaurant, slabs of beef and pork rested next to two big sharp butcher's knives on top of a metal cutting table.

Chico, under the pressure of Jay's construction boot, lay face down on the hard concrete next to the table. Jay stood directly over him with the gun still in his palm, applying even more weight; Chico winced in pain.

Nearby sat a huge walk-in freezer. Warren walked over, opened the huge metal door, and stood at the entrance, eyeing the contents in its belly and said, "Looks like you're up shit's creek, kid."

Inside the freezer, next to the slabs of ribs, numerous automatic weapons and assault rifles stuffed in crates and boxes littered the floor.

Just for the hell of it, Jay removed his steel-toed boot from Chico's head and then kicked him in the ribs. "Stand up!"

Chico winced before slowly getting to his feet. He gasped for air. Jay grabbed one of the big knives and forced Chico to spread his right hand out on the butcher's table.

"Nice ring," Jay said as he spotted the sparkling 3-carat pinky ring. "Now for every lie, you lose a little piggy. Understand me?" Jay asked staring into Chico's defiant eyes.

Chico nodded, his eyes closing slowly before they popped back open.

"Where's José?"

Chico tensed, eyeing his spread fingers before he returned Jay's angry glare. Big mistake.

In one fluid motion, the knife whipped through the air, glistening in the dim light, landing on the metal table with a loud thud. The tip of Chico's index finger rolled over the side and landed on the floor.

Screams pierced the air, carrying into the upper floor of the restaurant as blood splattered everywhere.

"Where's José?"

Chico whimpered, biting into his lip to ward of the pain, but he held his ground. He was a man of principles and under no circumstances would he rat out his boss.

The knife lifted again . . .

****

A half hour later near the precinct on Randall's Island, the three cops stood at the edge of the water drinking two cases of beer in the midst of conversation. The Island of Manhattan sat across the river like a prosperous city of lights just waiting to be plundered.

"I can't believe y'all actually had the balls to hit a bank," Sean said, glancing from Jay to Warren.

"Shit, we were tired of fucking around with chump change." Warren laughed. "Did you tell him about the armored truck we jacked?"

"You just did," Jay replied with a smirk. He tried to light up a smoke but a sudden gust of wind blew out the match's flame.

"Wait...wait, you guys hit an armored truck, too?" Sean asked, shaking his head in disbelief.

Jay just nodded.

Sean forced a fake smile and said, "You gotta tell me more."

Warren took the drunken opportunity to fill Sean in even further.

"So that was you guys? I heard about that heist on the news," Sean said, faking amazement as he struggled to hide his disgust. He couldn't believe he was sitting face to face with the same cold-hearted bastards that had killed an innocent father of two little girls just trying to do his job as an armored truck guard. Who would have thought it was a pair of dirty cops that had pulled off the violent robbery.

"Make sure you're ready for this, Sean," Jay said. "If not, sit this one out. This ain't dealers we're rippin' off. If we get caught, we goin' to jail for a long time." He glared at Sean. "And for me that ain't really an option."

Eyeing him for a moment, Sean replied, "That's one risk I'm willin' to take." He glanced at his watch. "Time to head home. I'll catch y'all tomorrow."

As soon as Sean was out of ear shot, Warren spoke, "You sure the kid can handle something this strenuous?"

"He won't fold. He holds up well under pressure," Jay replied, not the slightest bit worried. "Just make sure you're ready, baby."

"Oh yeah, it's already payday as far as I'm concerned." Warren grinned from ear to ear. The two men excitedly knocked fists, ready to pull off another brazen heist.

****

In a swank Italian restaurant located in Midtown Manhattan, Fitz was having a quiet dinner with his lovely wife, Rosie. A slim red head with a butter pecan complexion, she had a serious uptight demeanor. Neither one of them said a word to each other as they ate.

Fitz's cell phone went off and he answered it on the second ring, "Fitz, who's speaking?"

"It's me," Sean replied. "We need to talk and we need to talk now."

"What's wrong?" Fitz asked with a smirk.

"We need to talk in person," Sean demanded.

"Okay...okay, meet me at the spot in half an hour."

"I'll be there."

Sean hung up without saying another word. Fitz stared at his cell phone a moment, realizing whatever it was Sean had to tell him was extremely important. He looked at his wife. "I'm sorry, honey, we're gonna have to cut our meal short."

She glared at him, twisting up her face. "What else is new?"

****

About forty-five minutes later, Fitz walked through the door of the dimly lit bar he and Sean always met up at in lower Manhattan. He spotted Sean seated in a rear booth in the midst of killing a shot of Hennessy. Two empty shot glasses were already sitting on the table in front of him. Exhaling deeply, Fitz headed over to the Sean.

"The way you tossing back that liquor, this must be important," he said.

"Remember that armored truck robbery where the guard was shot execution style?" Sean asked, then continued on before Fitz could actually answer the question. "Well, it was them."

"What are you talking about?"

"It was Jay and Warren. They pulled off the job."

"Get the hell outta here."

"I'm dead serious," Sean said, leaning across the table. "They robbed a fuckin' bank too. Now they plannin' on hitting another one. We gotta end this now."

Fitz sat back in the booth without saying a word. It was obvious that he was running the whole thing through his mind. Finally he spoke, "Let it happen."

"Let it happen?" Sean asked stunned.

Fitz nodded, "Just go along with it."

"How the fuck we gonna let'em hit a bank and not stop'em?" Sean asked. "What if they kill someone? What then?"

"We'll cross that bridge if we come to it," Fitz replied nonchalantly. "Until then do your job 'til I tell you other wise."

"I can't believe this shit. You're more concerned with buildin' the biggest case possible than saving lives," Sean practically shouted, causing a few nosey customers to stop drinking for a moment and glance their way.

"You might wanna keep your voice down," Fitz said, scanning the bar.

"Screw you," Sean snapped even louder. "So I'm just supposed to go along with it?"

"Exactly, just like you been doing."

Sean slid out the booth and jumped to his feet. "Pick up the tab." He stormed out of the bar into the busy night. The sound of traffic flowing through the street outside traveled through the bar. The sexy waitress approaching the booth eyed the door as it slammed shut then turned to Fitz.

"He needs anger management," Fitz joked with a shrug. "I'll take a coke."

*****

Two days later as the first week of March rolled in, Jay called a meeting letting the other two cops know he was ready to proceed with planning bank heist. From listening to Jay, Sean knew the older cop's greed for cash was only growing stronger with each day that passed. He recruited his right hand man Warren as the getaway driver and of course he was perfect for the job. Sean was going into the bank with Jay. That way he would have just as much dirt on his hands as Jay and Warren already did.

The next day, the Caddy rolled down Bartow Avenue crossing under the New England overpass headed toward Co-Op City. Jay was behind the wheel with Warren in the passenger seat and Sean in the back. Jay made a left hand turn onto Alcott Place and immediately pulled over to the curb.

"This is it right here," Jay announced, staring at the bank sitting across the street. Customers were filing in and out of the branch. "We'll do surveillance for like two weeks and shit before hittin'." As usual Jay had taken the lead in planning the daring bank heist. He had already began strategically plotting what would hopefully be their biggest payday yet, making sure to dot the I's and cross the T's.

"Sounds good to me," Warren replied with greed in his heart, rubbing his sweaty palms together.

Sean quickly scanned the surrounding area, noticing the fire station sitting about two feet away from the bank's parking lot entrance. They also took notice of the McDonalds that was located behind them on the other side of Bartow Avenue before Jay pulled off.

During the next week, Jay and Sean each took turns nonchalantly casing the bank acting like actual customers waiting to be helped so no one became suspicious. Since Warren was the driver, Jay let him sit out this stage of planning. They looked like businessmen decked out in suits as they carried briefcases. The two men took full advantage of the bank being so busy. They were able to blend in with the crowd of regular bankers. They would patiently sit and watch taking advantage of the bank's long wait during peak hours.

Seated with his face buried in the New York Times newspaper, Jay was actually observing the bank's day-to-day operations and keeping a constant eye on the clock, which was located directly in front of him. He also noticed that an employee would wheel a dolly stacked with brown canvas sacks full of money from the vault in the rear of the bank over to the bulletproof glass door that gave access to the teller counter. The long counter was blocked off to the customers by a huge bulletproof glass partition that ran the whole length of the countertop and stretched up to the ceiling.

During Sean's shift casing the bank, he made sure to time the white branch manager's movements since they would need her keys to enter the vault. The overworked older woman with short-cropped red hair with lighter red streaks never realized she was being watched.

Mostly every morning, there would be a long line of people waiting for the bank to open. Therefore, a morning hit would be out of the question. Jay didn't like the idea of having to control the movements of too many people. The bank remained busy throughout the day except closing time and by then most of the employees weren't as alert; tired from a full day's work, they were just waiting to clock out.

Jay decided they would hit the bank a few minutes before closing time. His plan was to strike on Wednesday right before the weekend rolled in. It happened to be the day when the bank received their biggest cash shipments in order to handle payrolls for the following Thursday and Friday customer rush.

After about a week and a half worth of planning, they were finally ready to put the plan into action. The Tuesday night before they were to hit the bank, Sean didn't get an ounce of sleep. By the time the sun finally came up Wednesday morning, he was a total wreck. He knew he had to pull it together before meeting up with Jay and Warren later on. Glancing over at the alarm clock, he noticed it was 8:23 am and Lisa had already left for work. He had up until three o'clock to get his mind right. Climbing out of bed, he headed for the bathroom and jumped into the shower.

Standing under the cold water in deep thought, Sean was still upset that Fitz was actually allowing Jay and Warren to go through with the bank robbery instead of stopping it beforehand. But it wasn't Sean's call, so he had to roll with the punches whether he agreed with the lieutenant or not. But if the shit hit the fan, he was determined not to take the fall.

At three o'clock, Sean met up with Jay and Warren at a rundown but cozy greasy diner in Hunts Point as planned. The place was practically empty except for the three cops, an older Spanish couple and the staff. Stuffed into a tight booth in the back, none of the men ate any food. They sipped on coffee as they quietly going over the plan once more before heading out on their mission. Once Jay was satisfied each man had everything down pat, it was time to roll.

Exiting the diner, the three men headed for the stolen champagne colored Acura RL, Jay had secured as the getaway car because of its horsepower and handling. They climbed into the car and headed for the bank.

Pulling off at the New England Throughway, Jay made a left at the light onto Baychester Avenue and a right onto Bartow Avenue. He made a left onto Alcott Place and drove into the bank's parking lot. Driving around back, he pulled into an empty spot, facing a chain link fence that separated the parking lot from the gas station.

"Put your ski mask on, but don't pull it down all the way until we're about to enter," Jay said, putting on the ski mask. Sean pulled the ski mask over the top of his head, leaving his face exposed.

Before they made their way into the bank, Jay cleverly set his plan to disable the bank's cameras and dye pack-activating sensors into action. Fishing around in his coat pocket, he retrieved some kind of detonator the size of a TV remote and looked at it with a sinister grin creeping across his lips.

"What's that?" Sean asked leaning forward to get a better look.

"Just watch," Jay replied, then pressed the button, looking up toward the sky.

Suddenly the men heard a quick pop. Quickly glancing up at the thick wooden utility pole a few feet away from the car, Sean and Warren spotted sparks flying from the blown generator attached high up. They were amazed once they realized what Jay had just done. The exposed electrical cable wires leading from the generator ran to the rear of the bank.

"I just cut the power to the bank," Jay exclaimed, glancing from Warren to Sean. "Let's rock, young blood!"

Now the bank employees could not activate the alarm or even use the telephones since the digital phone system was powered by electricity. Jay had really done his homework.

Jay and Sean hopped out, tucking their guns under their trench coats so they wouldn't draw any unwanted attention. Throwing two huge satchels over his shoulder, Jay paused and looked back at Warren, "Hit me on the cell if anything happens."

As both men rushed around towards the front entrance of the bank, Warren quickly slid over to the driver's seat, lighting up a cigarette while he waited.

As they entered the first set of doors, both of them pulled the ski masks down over their faces. The first one through the second set of doors, Jay fired a shot into the ceiling to get everyone's attention, then aimed the .45 at the weaponless security guard. "On the ground now! They don't pay you enough to be a hero!"

The shook up guard did exactly as he was told.

Entering right behind Jay, Sean stood guard at the door with gun in hand, so no one inside would try to escape. He was on pins and needles. His nerves were working in overdrive as watched his partner kick into high gear.

"This is a bank robbery. Everybody hit the floor!" Jay yelled as the surprised customers screamed in fright. Moving toward the customer service side of the bank, he aimed the gun at the startled white manager standing by her desk trying to make a phone call. "Tell the tellers to open the door before I leave ya brains all over ya nice shirt!"

The scared manager nodded her head but still stood there frozen with the receiver in her hand.

"Move now!" Jay yelled, clutching the gun even tighter.

Snapping into action, she dropped the phone and headed for the bulletproof glass door.

"Open the door," she yelled to one of the female tellers cowering behind the counter. Jay was right on her heels. The frightened black teller let them in.

"Fill the bag," Jay shouted at the teller who had just opened the door. He tossed her one of the satchels. "Hurry it up! The rest of you step away from the counter!" The terrified tellers quickly did as they were told.

After she filled up the satchel with all the money from the cash drawers, Jay hustled all the tellers into the back room. "You open the vault!" he shouted to the manager. "Everyone else down on the ground. Don't move." He slammed the door shut behind him as he followed the petrified manager to the bank vault.

Not moving fast enough for Jay's liking, the manager was shoved toward the vault in the back. With shaky hands, the manager struggled to find the key for the vault. After a few nerve-racking moments, she found the right key and opened the vault.

"Fill the bag with money!" Jay demanded tossing the other satchel at her.

After she filled up the bag and handed it back to Jay, he pushed her to the floor. "Don't move!" he shouted, turning on his heels. Heading for the exit, he noticed a white boy—wanna be thug—on the ground eyeing him as he approached.

"Hey Eminen," he said, "wanna lose your fuckin' skull? Eyes on the ground!"

Every ounce of toughness quickly fled his pale face as he quickly lowered his head.

With their ski masks still on, Jay and Sean quickly exited the bank with the biggest score of their careers.

The getaway car was already idling right out front of the entrance with Warren anxiously waiting to put the pedal to the metal. The two men calmly strutted over to car and hopped in. Before Sean had a chance to shut the car door, Warren peeled away from the curb just as police sirens could be heard drawing near. Warren was about to make a right onto Bartow Avenue when the three men spotted two police cruisers speeding toward them. With his eyes almost bulging out of his sockets, Warren quickly busted a hard u-turn on Alcott Place and floored the gas. They were now in a high-speed chase heading through the streets of Co-Op City.

"What the fuck?" Jay swore to himself, turning around to look at the police cruiser with flashing lights in the near distance. They didn't realize that a woman sitting behind the wheel of her car parked across the street had observed them enter the bank and had already called the police. If Warren hadn't forgotten to turn on the police walkie-talkie resting on the seat beside him, he would have heard the emergency call go out over the airwaves.

Sweating up a storm, Sean pulled off the ski mask. Lowering the passenger window, Jay started firing at the pursuing police cars.

"What the fuck you doin', they're cops?" Sean yelled, glaring at his trigger-happy partner. At that moment, he knew Jay was beyond heartless. The man was down right insane.

Jay just continued shooting like he hadn't heard a word Sean said. The police in the first car returned fire as Warren weaved around a slow moving station wagon driven by an old lady. Luckily for them, the afternoon traffic was real light. A slug shattered the rear window of the car, raining glass all over Sean who was busy ducking bullets in the backseat.

Warren made a sharp right onto Asch Loop with Jay still firing. The fleeing car and both the pursuing police vehicles exchanged fire the entire length of the extra long block. The few pedestrians walking through the area ducked for cover. One man jumped over the hood of his car just in the nick of time to avoid being run over by the Acura as it flew by at top speed, clipping his side view mirror heading toward the intersection ahead. At the intersection, upfront vehicles could only make a left or right turn.

The speeding Acura blew through the red light making a hard left onto Co-Op City Boulevard, barely missing an Audi as the frightened driver inside slammed on his brakes. The police car right behind them wasn't as fortunate. It slammed right into the driver's side of the stopped Audi. The other police car swerved around the wreckage still in hot pursuit of the fleeing Acura.

Finally emptying his clip, Jay turned to Sean and yelled, "Pass me the M4!"

"Are you fuckin' crazy? Those are cops you're shooting at," Sean shouted. "Or did you forget we're cops, too?"

"Pass me the motherfucking gun," Jay yelled, straining to reach the fully automatic Colt M4 carbine assault weapon lying on the floor of the backseat near Sean's feet. Jay had brought it along as backup for just this type of situation.

Reluctantly, Sean grabbed the weapon and handed it to Jay. Snatching it out of Sean's hand, Jay racked the weapon, stuck it out of the window and let loose with a burst of gunfire. The hail of slugs chewed up the headlights, bumper, grill, hood, windshield, and cherry top lights of the police car as the driver swerved to avoid the shots. The police car clipped the rear end of a parked Pontiac Grand Prix and went airborne. It flipped over in the air and crash-landed on its roof, skidding along the asphalt until it came to a stop.

"Yeah," Jay shouted in excitement as he glanced back at the wreckage. Relief flashed across Sean's tense face as Jay pulled the gun back inside the car. With the police no longer in pursuit, the shooting was finally over. Warren made a right onto Peartree Avenue, which turned into Conner Street. The speeding Acura made a left onto Tillotson Avenue and jumped onto the New England Throughway heading east towards New Rochelle.

Crossing into New Rochelle, the Acura hopped off at the first exit and made a left onto Main Street.

"Make a right here," Jay said, pointing to Cleveland Avenue just ahead. The Acura headed up Cleveland Avenue and made another left onto Flower Street.

"Pull in right here," Jay said, pointing to the driveway of a single-family house that had a for sale sign stuck in the lawn. The Acura pulled into the open garage. Jay quickly hopped out and pulled down the garage door.

"Woo, you are the motherfucking man," Warren shouted with a wide grin as he exited the car. The two men bear hugged each other in excitement.

Stepping out of the back seat with a smirk on his grill, Sean was the only one upset about what went down. Bits of glass fell from his clothes onto the pavement.

"Why the long face?" Jay asked jokingly before turning his attention back to Warren. "We just made one of the biggest scores of our life and this guy's poutin'."

"Hey kid, if it'll make you feel better I'll take your share," Warren said toying with Sean.

Breathing hard and fuming beneath the surface, Sean just eyed both of them without saying a word.

Ignoring their uptight partner, Jay and Warren continued praising one another as Jay popped open the trunk and retrieved the satchels filled with their ill-gotten windfall.

Entering the vacant house through the entrance in the garage, the three men divvied up the cash equally in the empty, dimly lit kitchen. There were more than enough greenbacks to go around. They had managed to get away with over six hundred grand and live to tell about it. The three cops made a pact not to tell anyone else about the heist and to never talk about it amongst themselves after that day.

As soon as the trio parted ways, Sean was on the phone with Fitz only to be told the department still wasn't ready to make the bust yet. When it came to wrapping up a case, Internal Affairs moved at a snail's pace. So Sean had no choice but to continue on with his undercover work as if the bank robbery never took place. Fitz told Sean to hold on to his share of the money just in case Jay wanted to see it. Sean definitely would have to hide it from Lisa so she wouldn't start asking all sorts of questions he didn't want to have to answer. He ended up stashing the money at his mother's house until he had to turn it over to the department, then he headed home, cleaned up and went to bed.

CHAPTER 19

Cigarette smoke clouded the air of the Internal Affairs office as Black puffed on a cancer stick. He kicked back in a chair across the table from Fitz.

The expensive slick suit-wearing lieutenant, sipped on a hot cup of coffee, filling out a stack of police forms. Mike leaned against the bars of the box-sized window, bringing Black up to speed on things. His blood-red eyes followed Mike's fluttering hands. Black found the constant arm movement extremely distracting.

"We have a man inside already," Mike stated before lighting up his own cigarette. "Now, we just need you to hammer the nail in the coffin," he finished, blowing a ring of smoke out of his tar stained mouth.

Black watched the smoke dissolve into the stale air, then asked, "What if they suspect somethin'?"

Mike eyed him a moment, then replied, "Just be real convincing so they don't." Grabbing the can of soda sitting on the windowsill, the big Irish guy took a big gulp as Fitz filled Black in on the things they needed him to do.

****

Later that evening, back in the South Bronx, three stacks of cash wrapped in rubber bands rested on the glass coffee table in Black's living room. Jay and Black talked on the couch as Warren listened from his comfortable spot on the love seat.

Sean peered past the draped curtains gazing out of the window. Below, steady traffic flowed through the street as a few tenants made their way through the concrete courtyard. Children played in a thin layer of snow.

"You been off radar lately," Jay said, eyeing the dark man warily.

"I was handlin' sum business outta town," Black replied smoothly.

Sean turned his head to look at Black. The man's eyebrow twitched. He was lying with a straight face, all-cool like. Evidently, Black was familiar with looking cops in the eye and lying right to their grills.

Jay just glared at him, not saying a word. But Black didn't break a sweat as he tried to deflect Jay's thoughts back to the pile of cash sitting on the table.

"Everything I owe is there," Black said, nodding toward the stacks of bills.

Jay quickly eyed the cash, then scooped it all up counting the first stack.

"You don't trust me?" Black asked, trying to break the ice as he sat back and crossed his long legs. He glanced over and noticed Sean staring at him. His dark brown eyes quickly dotted back to Jay.

Jay didn't find the question funny and snapped, "Should I?" From the tone in his voice, Sean knew Jay's patience was wearing thin. Hopefully, Black knew not to press the issue.

Warren watched as Jay finally finished counting the cash.

Jay tucked the three stacks into the inside pocket of his coat and said, "Make this the last time I ever wait for my cash." His eyes scanned Black's, waiting for a response.

"You da boss," Black replied with a slight bow of the head for emphasis, playing to Jay's ego. Sean almost laughed.

Satisfied they had an understanding, Jay stood to leave. Sean followed with Warren right on his heels. Black hopped up right behind them and said, "I'm just da middleman. Da money y'all makin' off me ain't shit. There's a way we can all get paid and I'm talkin' high six figures."

Jay stopped dead in his tracks and turned around, eyeing the slim, tall man a moment before asking, "And how's that?"

Black's thick lips spread into a sly grin. The trio entered the apartment once again.

****

A few minutes later, Jay was behind the wheel of the Cherokee flying up Boston Road. Warren rode shotgun as Sean chilled in the back, puffing on a cigarette.

"You think José's holding as much cash as Black claims?" Warren inquired still thinking about Black's proposal to rip-off one of José's biggest stash houses.

"If anybody should know, it's Black. That chick of his is José's sister," Jay responded.

"Yeah," Warren said with a grin. "I almost got some head from that bitch."

Both men turned to him.

Warren shrugged. "But money came first."

"Yeah right, motherfucker," Jay snapped. All three men shared a quick laugh.

Meanwhile on the rooftop of one of the six-story tenements on Fish Avenue, KP smoked a blunt with Dozen. Nearby Big Dee was posted up at the ledge, looking over at the empty street below.

"Shorty was givin' me brain right here the other night," Dozen bragged, then took a long pull of the burning blunt. He couldn't hide his trademarked wide ass cheese grin.

"Yeah right, ya lyin' ass nigga," KP spat, looking at him for the liar that he was. Everybody who knew Dozen, knew that cat lied about any and everything under the sun. He lied so much his lies became true at least in his own head.

Just then, Big Dee spun around interrupting them. "Yo, I think it's them."

KP and Dozen dashed over to the edge and glanced over. The Cherokee crept slowly through the street below.

"Hell, yeah. Dat's definitely them," Dozen yelled with excitement.

KP pulled the Mac-10 from the book bag strapped over his shoulder, snapped back the slide and passed it to Dozen's outstretched hand. He immediately swung the Mac over the ledge, firing rapidly at the unsuspecting target below.

A hail of bullets simultaneously chewed up the roof, trunk and hood of the Cherokee. Slugs shattered the front windshield. Jay, Warren and Sean were completely caught off guard as even more slugs rained down on them lodging into the floorboards.

"What the fuck?" Jay yelled, slamming on the gas.

"Drive, drive!" Sean yelled at Jay just as a slug ripped through the roof lining and chewed through Warren's pants leg.

Warren's skin quickly turned a pale pink as he clutched his wounded thigh. Blood gushed through the bullet hole.

"Fuck! I'm hit!"

Jay swerved to avoid the continuous shots. The Cherokee sideswiped a parked Camry, crashing into the left front half of a Jetta parked behind it.

From the rooftop, the three men surveyed the damage. They eyed the wrecked Cherokee with smoke rising from the engine. They couldn't tell if the occupants were still alive inside.

"Oh shit, son," Dozen yelled, waving the Mac-10 through the air.

"We out," KP barked as he took off running across the rooftop. As KP made his getaway, Big Dee and Dozen were right on his heels.

Hopping over the ledge of the building, KP leaped through the air, landing one flight below on the rooftop of the next building over, and continued running. Dozen landed right after him. Big Dee followed with a loud thud.

Back on the street, Jay was already out of the Cherokee and drawing his gun, yelling, "It's comin' from the fuckin' roof!" He dashed over to the building where the shots had just come from.

He tried to yank open the front door, which shimmied on the hinges, but it wouldn't open. Stepping back, he aimed at the lock and fired a slug, destroying it completely. He ripped open the door and dipped into the lobby.

Jay dashed up the stairs, flight after flight, until finally reaching the top landing. He kicked open the exit door leading to the roof.

Charging through the exit, Jay raised his gun eye-level to firing position. He quickly panned the rooftop, making a complete three-sixty turn, ready to blast anything that moved. Not a soul was in sight.

The shooters were long gone.

"Fuck!" Jay yelled then squeezed off three rounds into the air out of pure frustration.

A few hours later, Sean, Warren and Jay emerged from the crowded emergency room of Our Lady of Mercy on East 233rd Street into the cold night air. Warren limped along with a cane as they crossed the parking lot heading to their new ride, a dark gray Cadillac Deville.

"You lucky it missed major arteries," Sean said, opening the front passenger door for Warren.

"Try telling my leg that shit," Warren growled, in a bit of pain as he slowly climbed into the car.

"They did give you some pain pills for that shit, right?"

Warren nodded. He was still half doped up from the first dose of tranquilizers.

The Caddy rolled off with Sean behind the wheel. Jay sat in the back quietly fuming. His continually clenched his jaws as he rubbed his stubby haired chin. He broke from his heavy thought process. "You reap what you sow. And now it's time for harvest. We gonna pluck them motherfuckers off one by one."

Later that night out on Long Island in a darkened bathroom, Warren coughed a few times, slumped back in an empty bathtub with his wounded leg resting on the rim. There was a visible patch of dried up blood that had seeped through a small area of the cotton bandages wrapping his thigh. Holding a dirty glass crack pipe to his ashy lips, Warren flicked the lighter on under it and took a deep pull. *The purple hills never looked so bright*, Warren thought to himself, as he turned glassy-eyed. The high had his mind blown.

****

Back in the North Bronx, Sean entered his dark residence, turning on the hallway light. He was surprised the smell of a hot home cooked meal didn't greet him at the door after a hard day's work, but then again Lisa hadn't cooked a nice meal for him since their anniversary. It was obvious from the quietness and the rest of the dark apartment Lisa wasn't home. Since she was a schoolteacher, he knew she definitely wasn't at work this time of night. He headed to the bedroom and hit the light switch. The lights popped on as he crossed to the answering machine and checked to see if she had left him a message. The digital display was blank.

Heading to the kitchen, Sean grabbed a cold beer out of the refrigerator, cracked it open and took a long gulp. He walked over to the kitchen window and glanced up and down the quiet shadowy tree-lined street. Not a soul was visible on the block except for an old man taking out the trash next door. There was no sign of Lisa or her white Maxima anywhere on the block.

Meanwhile over on Bronx River Boulevard, the Caddy was parked curbside in the shadows with Lisa's white Maxima sitting behind it. All the windows were steamed up. Inside the idling car, Lisa's unzipped jeans were down around her ankles exposing her juicy ass with her pink silk thong lost deep in the crack. On her knees in the passenger seat with her head in Jay's lap, she was giving him a serious blowjob as her hand worked the shaft of his penis up and down. Jay's eyes were shut and his head was pressed back against the headrest as he enjoyed every moment. With the heat they were generating, Jay could have cut off the sweltering heat shooting out the air vents.

Back at Sean's apartment, he sat on the bed, making a phone call. The line rung a few moments before Lisa's voicemail picked up. "This is Lisa. Please leave a message and I'll get back to you as soon as possible."

"This is the second time I'm leaving a message," Sean said, rubbing his forehead. "Call me back as soon as you get this." He slammed the cordless back down on the base and grabbed the cold beer that was resting on the nightstand, gulping the rest of it down. He lay across the bed and stared at the ceiling. This definitely wasn't the Lisa he knew. She never went anywhere without telling him or calling him. Now she hardly ever answered her cell phone. In the need of fresh air, Sean decided to hit a club. What's good for the goose was good for the gander.

****

At the same time, across town in a condom and trash peppered alleyway behind the Right Look clothing store, José paced back and forth as KP, Big Dee and Dozen looked on. Standing on the sidelines near the chain-linked fence, Chico had on his standard mean mug with his severed finger bandaged, watching José's back. A huge Rottweiler with a monstrous head, sat quietly at Chico's feet as he held on to the heavy-duty leash attached to the leather collar strapped to the dog's muscular neck.

"Shootin' off da roof," José barked and stopped directly in front of KP. "Off da fuckin' roof? Ya'll niggas *snipers* now?" He stood eye to eye with the embarrassed man. "'Cause I sure as hell can't tell." His gaze scanned the three faces. "Da only thing you amateur pricks hit was da fuckin' jeep! And y'all should know better. Real killers get up close and personal." José formed his hand into a mock gun and pressed two fingers, representing a barrel, to KP's temple.

"I'ma real nigga," Dozen blurted out.

José spun around, back smacking Dozen across the lips with brutal force. "Don't you ever interrupt me, stupid motherfucker!"

Dazed and shocked, Dozen nodded as he wiped blood from his mouth. His tongue ran across his teeth, finding one a little loose.

"Now, get the fuck outta my sight," José demanded, glaring at each one of them.

"So we don't get our paper?" Big Dee churned in, knowing he was pressing his luck.

"Not a fuckin' cent," José snapped and pulled out a .44 bulldog. "Unless you plan on takin' it in blood." His face screwed into a sinister snarl as he glared at Big Dee hoping he would try him.

Big Dee wasn't that fucking foolish. José wouldn't hesitate to drop a nigger with the hands or the guns. If Big Dee stepped out of line tonight, some lucky funeral home would be pumping embalming fluid through his system by tomorrow.

"Ya got it. Ya got it," Big Dee replied immediately copping a plea. A quick glance down showed his knees knocking from shaking so badly.

"Nigga, I been had it," José snapped. "Now get da fuck up outta here, ya, fat fuck!" He finished with a wave of the gun. The three men quickly made their way exit out of the alleyway and out of José's menacing glare.

"Listen, José, I know this might be a bad time to bring this up, but the connect called. He wants his cash."

"Shit, that nigga gotta wait," José replied not bothering to look at Chico.

"He's been waiting for two weeks."

José shot him an evil eye that would have frightened the devil himself, "Who the fuck you work for, him or me?"

"You, boss."

"That's what the fuck I thought," José snapped. "Let me worry 'bout who gets paid 'fore I stop paying ya stupid ass."

Chico knew when to shut up and now was the perfect time.

José pulled out his cell and punched in a telephone number.

****

It was midday and hot and sticky in La Pintada, Panama. Amongst the lush green slopes, gaunt looking Panamanian workers, mostly all men, were picking coca leaves and tucking them into huge cloth sacks hanging from their strained shoulders. Their emaciated faces were riddled with crow's feet and sweat as the sun relentlessly beat down on them.

Manuel stood at the top of the hill, surveying his thriving kingdom. His 5'6' slender frame was draped in an eggshell colored linen suit that fluttered in the warm breeze whipping across the fertile plain. A straw cowboy hat crowned his salt and pepper hair and a pair of dark shades hid his eyes. This was the man that José answered to. An overgrown bodyguard walked over and handed Manuel a cell phone. "It's José."

"Hey amigo, I'm hoping you bringing me good news."

"There's been a slight set back," José informed him.

"*Que*?" The flawless six-carat pinkie ring on the older man's right hand sparkled every time a sunray hit it, shooting a streak of light across his aged but clear buttermilk colored face every now and then.

"The swine been real active lately," José replied. "But it ain't nothing I can't fix."

"Let's hope not," Manuel chose his words carefully. "You've always been a man of your word. Don't disappoint me."

An old beat up pickup truck carrying huge bales covered by a black tarp sped along a narrow dirt road kicking up dust leading to a huge clearing about seven-feet behind Manuel.

"You have my word, Manuel."

"If not, I'll have your balls."

In the clearing, the bundles were undone by the men in the group. The women separated the coca leaves. A band of underweight workers carried armload after armload of the harvest to an enormous cannibal pot, which rested on top of a raging wood log fire and dumped them inside. As the coca leaves were being boiled down, a huge plume of thick black smoke streaked the almost cloudless blue sky. The workers braved the heat, stirring the boiling hot solution.

"Always remember even though I'm thousands of miles away," Manuel said, "I have eyes everywhere and right now a few of them are on you."

"It won't have to come to that."

"Let's hope not."

To the right of the lush valley is where the jungle started to take hold. Tucked into the edge of the thick bush was a primitive but enormous makeshift lab, which contained all the drug making equipment. The lab was camouflaged extremely well so drug enforcement planes couldn't spot it from the sky. Evil eyed enforcers smoked cigarettes and sported automatic weapons at every point of entry.

The coca was now turning into a white paste.

In the makeshift laboratory, a line of workers stood over long metal tables packing brick after brick of pure cocaine. The bricks were then saran wrapped, tied up, weighed, and stamped with "Sin" before being tossed into black duffel bags.

A medium-sized diesel-engine box truck sat parked on the hillside with a bunch of sweaty overworked workers loading dozens of coke filled duffel bags into the rear.

****

Back in the U.S. on a dark block in lower Manhattan outside of Club Vine, partygoers waited in line as three muscular bouncers maintained control at the front entrance. Luxury vehicles lined the block.

Inside, the club was jumping full force. The dance floor was packed with sweaty couples and singles dancing their hearts out. People lined the purple nylon trimmed black bar, drinking and conversing. Sean occupied the second to last bar stool, sipping a beer in deep thought. A sexy chocolate colored honey with the body of an African goddess sat down on the empty stool next to him. She looked him over from head to toe, but he didn't even notice.

She motioned to the bartender. "A shot of tequila, please."

The black bartender nodded and started to pour her drink. She glanced over at Sean. He still wasn't paying her any mind.

"So what's your name?"

Snapping back to reality, Sean locked eyes with her. "Me?"

Unable to contain her flirtatious grin, she nodded.

"Uh, Sean."

"I'm Vivian," she said, extending her hand. "Nice to meet you."

Sean shook her soft manicured hand and replied, "Same here."

The bartender returned with Vivian's shot. She licked the salt off the rim of the glass then downed the tequila as Sean watched. Following it up with a slice of lime, she sensually sucked on the juices.

"I take it you're not from New York." Sean said, trying to make friendly conversation.

"How could you tell?"

"Your accent."

"I'm from Atlanta," Vivian looked around. "You here alone?"

Sean just nodded.

"Me too, I'm in town on business," Vivian said. "So what brings you to a club all by your lonesome?"

"Honestly, stress. I needed to get out," Sean replied with a hint of sadness showing through.

"Stress is never good," Vivian said, leaning in closer. "Whenever I'm feeling all stressed out, toe curling sex usually releases the tension."

Sean practically spit out all of his beer across the counter.

"Excuse me," he said, feeling slightly embarrassed.

Vivian giggled then asked, "You wanna go back to my hotel room? It's only a few blocks away."

Sean thought about it for a moment then said, "Why not?" He finished the rest of his beer and left the empty bottle on the counter.

****

As soon as they entered the dark hotel room, Vivian was all over him like a dog in heat not even bothering to turn on the lights. She licked his ears, his neck, and his face while grabbing his crotch. Lost in the heat of the moment, Sean enjoyed the much-needed attention.

After a few tense seconds, he pulled away. "I'm sorry, I...I can't do this."

"Why?" Vivian practically pleaded. "I have condoms."

"It's not that. I'm married," Sean informed her, raising his hand to show her his wedding band.

"I know, I peeped it in the club. I don't care. I just wanna feel you inside me."

Damn, Sean thought. The head on his shoulders was telling him not to do it, but the head in his jeans was screaming to hit that pussy. Since he took his marriage seriously, he was determined to do the right thing.

"I can't. I'm sorry. I love my wife."

Vivian's mood saddened. "Hey I understand," she said, trying to play it off. Still unable to hide the disappointment in her voice, she added, "My body doesn't but I do."

CHAPTER 20

A week later on Boston Road near the corner of Fish Avenue, Soldier stepped out of the beat up Chinese storefront into the brisk April night air. Pausing a moment, he caught the scent of someone smoking some potent weed nearby. Glancing at the corner, Soldier spotted a tall older Jamaican dread pulling on a marijuana filled backwood. His long thick locks fell pass his broad shoulders.

Soldier tossed him a shout, "Yo, Yo!"

The Dread nodded, with a half grin revealing one gold tooth along his top row.

Stepping off the sidewalk, Soldier's beady eyes dotted both ways making sure no traffic was coming. About two blocks up the hill on Boston Road, he spotted a pair of headlights slowly approaching but what he didn't see was Caddy parked halfway up the block behind a Honda Passport. He quickly strutted across the deserted street.

The speeding Caddy quickly bore down on Soldier. Hearing the roar of a revving engine, he spun around, spotting the charging car. He took off running, swinging his right arm under his left armpit; he fired a few rounds at the pursuing car without even looking back.

Bullets ricocheted off the pavement and a slug pierced the swerving car's grill. Hot steam shot out of the hole in the engine. The bullet did nothing to slow the vehicle down.

Warren's firearm popped out of the passenger's window, returning fire. Jay fired from the back window. Sean was in the passenger seat clutching his gun.

Suddenly a horn blared, and Warren turned his head just in time to see a navy blue Lincoln town car used as a bootleg cab heading straight for them.

The cab slammed into the backdoor of the driver's side of the Caddy speeding through the intersection, and sent it spinning a few feet before it came to a halt. Unfazed, Jay and Sean hopped out in hot pursuit, still firing at Soldier through the quiet tree-lined block.

Warren stayed behind with the car. The scruffy white cab driver got out rubbing his red bruised forehead. The cracked front windshield had a head imprint on the driver's side from the impact of the cab driver hitting the window.

Soldier hopped fence after fence until he came to a one-way street. He dashed into the middle of the street as a late model Toyota pulled up. The woman in side quickly slammed on the brakes and the car slid to a stop. He pulled on his gun and carjacked the frightened older lady, pulling her from the car. Hopping in, he peeled off.

Jay released a burst from his .40 caliber. It blew out the back window of the fleeing car and the right taillight.

Inside the Toyota, Soldier ducked the shot and floored it.

Out of breath and gasping for air, Sean and Jay watched as the car hightailed it around a corner out of sight. Warren pulled up in the Caddy just in time. Jay and Sean hopped in. The idling car peeled off after Soldier.

The uninterrupted gunfire being exchanged from the car chase left the smell of gun smoke and burnt rubber hanging in the air.

The Toyota flew through an intersection, barely colliding with a northbound tow truck. The truck swerved and smashed into a VW Bug, totaling it. With the damaged vehicles blocking the street, the Caddy swung around them.

The Toyota flew pass an alley followed quickly by the Caddy, which was about five seconds off the fleeing car's bumper. Sparks flew as the Toyota's hanging tail pipe scraped the asphalt.

The Caddy shot forward, slamming into the rear of the Toyota. The speeding car swerved a moment before regaining control. The Caddy slammed into the rear again.

Soldier's eyes shifted to the rearview mirror as he gauged the Caddy's distance. The Toyota swung a hard left around a corner onto Bronxwood Avenue. The street was under construction. A huge section of the road was fenced off. A 9-by-12 foot hole, about seven-feet deep had been dug in the middle of the street. A Cubicle Con-Ed maintenance truck sat parked across the street from the construction. One of the Con Ed workers was sipping a soda on the sidewalk as his partner climbed out of the truck.

Hearing the screeching tires, the two men glanced up and saw a Toyota heading for the ditch they had dug.

Caught off guard, Soldier panicked and lost control. The Toyota slammed through the metal chain linked fence and dropped halfway into the deep pit front first. Knocked completely unconscious, Soldier was trapped inside. The car's undercarriage was left exposed.

The Caddy pulled up to the corner of the block. The three men surveyed the damage. Slowly, Jay lifted his .40 Cal, took aim at the gas tank and pulled the trigger. As soon as the bullet pierced the metal tank, the car exploded with Soldier still trapped inside. The whole car went up in flames.

A smirk crept across Warren's lips as he looked over at Jay. Jay watched as the hot flames engulfed the car. Warren glanced in the rearview mirror at Sean.

Sean nodded his approval and Warren pulled off.

****

Two days later on a nippy night in the Bronx, the Caddy sat parked in the middle of Fish Avenue. Sean was behind the wheel with Warren in the passenger seat reading "Slut" magazine and Jay slouched low in the back seat, staring out the window. From his position, Jay could see anyone entering the block from Boston Road.

"There he goes," Jay announced, sitting up in the seat.

With his Yankees fitted cocked up on his fuzzy corn rolls, Dozen bopped right pass the car without noticing the watching trio. Three caddy doors swung open and Jay, Sean and Warren hopped out, charging for the unsuspecting thug.

Hearing the commotion behind him, Dozen glanced back and his eyes popped out of his sockets as he spotted the three angry narcs rushing toward him. He took off running as if his life depended on getting away because it did. His crisp navy blue cap fell to the wet concrete and five seconds later Sean's foot crushed it to the earth.

They pursued him like bloodhounds on the scent of a raccoon. An older black man stepped back to get out of the path of the cops.

Dozen dashed into one of the tenement buildings midway up the block and slammed the door close. He lunged up the first two steps, but by the time his sneaker hit the fourth step Jay had already smashed through the door. He leaped up the first pair of steps and grabbed Dozen by his zipped up bubble jacket and snatched him back down the staircase. Dozen bounced off the wall right into Warren's open arms. The angry cop shoved him down the six steps leading to the basement.

Tumbling down the stairs, Dozen landed hard on his left side. The three cops heard some bones crack as his head hit the concrete floor with a solid thud. His wind was knocked out instantly. He struggled for air.

"You like shooting cops, huh?" Warren shouted, charging down the steps to the cramped basement level. Jay paused midway down the steps and watched the scene unfold. The delicious smell of someone in the building frying chicken hit his flaring nostrils.

Finally catching his breath Dozen pleaded, "I ain't shoot no cop. I swear."

Warren kicked him in the rib cage. His cuffed up boot connected with a sickening crack.

Dozen screamed.

Watching from the entrance level, Sean winced like he was the one in pain.

"I wanna know where the fuck José is!" Warren yelled, kicking him some more. He was totally out of control.

Balled up in the fetal position, Dozen "I don't know."

"Wrong answer," Warren said, pulling out his revolver.

"No please," Dozen pleaded as fear flashed in his eyes.

Aiming the gun at Dozen's head, Warren replied, "Then tell me what the fuck I need to know."

"Okay, okay. He has a clothing store called the Right Look on Simpson Ave'."

Without saying another, Warren shot him execution style in the forehead.

****

Later on that night the "2" train rumbled along the elevated tracks into the Simpson Avenue train station above. People shuffled across the street below, window shopping and heading for home. One block away, a U-Haul van sat parked mid-way up the block. Sean slouched behind the wheel, keeping an eye out. Next to him, Jay stared out the window, waiting.

The cargo area in the back was empty except for Warren using a milk crate as a makeshift seat, the cane propped next to his leg. He fidgeted with the batteries in his metal flashlight in the midst of telling a story.

"So, she's laying there, legs spread wide and my freaking cock won't get hard," Warren ended with a chuckle.

Sean glanced over his shoulder and said, "Try ginseng. It'll have ya dick like wood." He made a jerking motion with his hand for emphasis.

Sudden movement caught Jay's attention. He sat up, keeping his eyes locked on their target up the street.

Someone moved inside the Right Look clothing store a couple stores down. The lights shut off and three shadowy figures head for the front door.

"Time to roll," Jay announced and Sean started the engine.

José and two employees emerged from the dark store a few seconds later. They said their good byes to José and the employees walked off, leaving the big man behind to lock up.

Glancing over at the double-parked BMW, José spotted Chico's lazy ass sound asleep in the driver's seat. Normally Chico would already be out of the car, waiting to pull down the security gate for José. José shook his head as he glared at Chico.

Clutching the bottom of the rippled steel gate, José yanked it down with all his might. The gate slammed to the concrete with a loud rattling thud. A sudden turn of the key locked it in place. For a second he stared at the black crud stuck under his fingernails, then spat on the snow-covered sidewalk.

José strutted to the car and tapped on the driver's window trying to wake up Chico. Frustrated, José yanked open the door and yelled, "Wake ya lazy ass da fuck up, nigga! I ain't payin' ya to—"

Chico's head fell back. Blood was everywhere, running from just above his Adam's apple down to his crisp blue jeans. His throat had been slashed practically from ear to ear. José's eyes popped wide. He stood in a panic hold at the window. José staggered back, horrified by the gory sight.

The U-Haul silently crept up beside a stunned José. The side door flew open and, Jay and Warren quickly grabbed José and snatched him inside. The van immediately sped off, turning the corner with José's legs still dangling wildly out of it.

Inside the van, José threw the first of a series of wild punches with Jay and Warren on the receiving end. Sean kept glancing at the tussling trio through the rearview mirror as Jay and Warren fought to subdue the three hundred pound man. All he saw was flying fists.

"You fuckin' pigs killed my brother!" José yelled as he continued swinging wildly.

Tired of catching José's harsh blows with his face, Jay pulled his gun and pressed the barrel to José's eye.

"One more move and you's a dead motherfucker!" he growled, spitting the blood that had collected in his mouth onto the metal floor. The cold steel poking José's eyeball calmed him down instantly.

"On ya stomach, *now*!" Jay demanded.

Slowly, José rolled over, his nose pressed against the cold, exposed sheet metal. Warren grabbed a pair of plastic cuffs and zip-tied the massive hands and feet tightly.

"You definitely pack a helluva punch, I'll give ya that," Jay said, rubbing the sore spot on his chin where José had landed two lucky shots.

"Y'all fuckin' faggots killed Bobby!" José blurted out.

"Nah," Jay replied with a snicker and a shake of his head. "Ya dope did that."

"Fuck you! Ya fuckin' pig!" José yelled struggling against the cuffs. Suddenly José's horrific screams replaced the cursing as Jay rammed his boot between José's partly spread thighs, crushing his testicles against the hard metal floor of the van.

His cries fell on deaf ears as Jay turned to Warren and asked, "You believe this shithead had the balls to stick a price on me?"

"On us," Warren reminded him.

Minutes later in Manhattan, the van lurched to a quick stop at the end of a deserted pier staring out at the Hudson River. The side door quickly rolled ajar as Jay and Warren dragged a struggling José out the rear, flinging him into a heap on the cold slab of concrete. Winston cigarette butts littered the ground. The bitter cold wind cut through the pier on its way down the river.

Twisting around to get a better view, Sean stayed planted in his seat observing the scene unfolding in front of him. He knew what was about to go down but couldn't risk blowing his cover trying to stop it.

Jay handed Warren a beat-up throwaway pistol—what the cops called a firearm, which they've confiscated off some thug in the streets and kept hidden in their police cars in case of emergencies. Shooting an unarmed black male, then planting the weapon on his corpse to cover things up—was one of those emergencies.

Warren clutched the rusty gun tightly, training it toward José's knees with a smug smile.

"Which one, tough guy?" he asked.

José eyeballed him back, showing no sign of fear and snapped, "Betta kill me, motherfucker!" right before hacking a wad of spit at Warren's scuffed up, no-frill, sneakers.

"Soon enough, but not just yet," Warren replied as he squeezed the trigger. A bullet exploded through José's left kneecap, then another one followed shattering his right knee.

José's raspy screams pierced the quiet night.

"You hurtin'?" Jay asked taunting the man, whose eyes were surprisingly dry. He motioned for Warren to pass the revolver back.

"Fuck you, pig!" José managed to yell through clenched teeth, a shudder ripping through his body.

Warren held the gun out to Jay. He grabbed it and replied, "No, fuck you," and then he put a bullet through the window of José's soul. Blood gushed from his now eyeless socket.

Struggling somewhat, Jay and Warren scooped up José's lifeless body, carried him to the edge of the pier and dumped him in the river. The corpse hit the water with a huge splash and disappeared beneath the choppy currents.

Physically exhausted, Jay and Warren looked at each other. Both of them were out of breath and practically gasping for air.

"Damn, that fat fuck was heavy," Jay joked with a smile that broke the chilling moment.

"Who you telling?" Warren replied with a frown, rubbing his lower back like an old man. "What the fuck's your problem, rookie? Why you stay in the car?"

"Ain't no rookie," Sean snapped back. "Just smart. You do realize that by killin' José, you've just dried up half the money and dope in the entire area, right?"

Jay and Warren froze, looked each other and groaned.

Sean glanced over to the pier, then back to Warren. "Is that true y'all killed his little brother?"

"I just injected him," Jay replied nonchalantly. "José's dope did the rest."

Every inch of Sean wanted to tear Jay a new asshole but what good would it do. He felt like he was fighting a losing battle. Sean really felt sorry for José's brother Bobby; he was the innocent one in all of this.

CHAPTER 21

Early the next morning, completely wrapped under a thick quilt, Sean and Lisa were sound asleep as the phone started ringing.

After the third annoyingly loud ring, Sean grabbed blindly for the cordless phone sitting on the nightstand.

"Hello," he answered in a raspy voice.

"We're on tonight," Jay announced on the other end of the line. "See ya at work." He hung up before Sean had a chance to even respond.

Placing the receiver back on the base, Sean glanced over at the alarm clock. It was 9:45 am on a Tuesday. He groaned inwardly as he tossed the covers back and stood. He stretched, then headed to the bathroom.

Sean flipped on the light, crossed to the sink and splashed cold water on his face. He took a long hard look at himself in the mirror.

A sudden movement from the corner of his eyes, showed Lisa standing quietly in the doorway. She watched Sean stare at his own reflection a moment.

"What's going on Sean?"

"Nothin'," Sean replied, turning around to look at her. "Go back to sleep."

As Sean stood there staring at Lisa in her cotton cartoon pajama pants and one of his white Hanes T-shirts, he couldn't help but think about how much he actually loved this woman. They had been together so long, through thick and thin.

"As soon as this case is over," he said, "I'll take some time off."

Her jaw dropped as her loving eyes danced with excitement.

"Maybe a cruise or a trip to Miami would be nice." Sean continued.

He reached out for her. She flowed easily into his arms.

"It'll be just the two of us, like old times," he assured her.

She leaned her head on his shoulder. He breathed in the soft lavender scent of her hair. He could feel his manhood slowly awakening, the blood rushing into his shaft sent it skyward at maximum speed. They started to kiss slow and passionate like old times. He ran his hands along the curves of her silky smooth thighs causing goose bumps to pop up on her soft skin. She closed her eyes, enjoying the sensations vibrating through her entire body. Her cinnamon colored nipples stood like twin towers.

Savoring the moment, Sean led Lisa to the bed and there, he took his time licking every inch of her tasty frame from head to toe. Sucking on her pretty toes, he ran his tongue across the bottom of her foot and gently bit on the heel. It felt like he was touching and stroking her everywhere at once. Actually that's because he was.

Biting down on one of her fingers, she shivered with every touch and stroke of his manly hands. She inhaled his masculine scent, licking on his salty neck as he made his way up to her luscious lips. His hungry tongue invaded her inviting mouth. Her tongue fought his back.

Unable to hold out any longer, Sean entered her, taking his time so that she enjoyed every inch stretching out her tight walls. He loved the way the slippery heat felt as his throbbing manhood slid deeper into her pulsating love box. He loved the why she held him close to her breast. He could actually feel her heart beat. They fell into a smooth deep rhythm. The sweat soaked sheets were everywhere but on the mattress. The musky smell of sex only served to turn them on even more. The exhausted lovers practically collapsed after exploding in unison. They drifted off to sleep wrapped in each other's sweaty arms. The love making session was definitely a reawakening.

****

Around three that same day, Sean pulled into a parking spot of The Old Ridge Motel, somewhere on the north side of Yonkers. He exited the Acura, crossed to motel room number ten on the ground floor and knocked on the nondescript door.

After waiting a few moments, the door creaked opened.

Fitz batted his eyelids and in his sweetest, feminine voice said, "I'm all yours, cutie." He snickered.

"In ya dreams," Sean replied, squeezing past Fitz as he stepped inside. The small room was cheaply furnished and had cigarette burns scattered throughout the worn-out commercial rug. It happened to be the perfect place for hookers and their tricks. The room smelled like mildew and stale cigarette smoke.

"Where's Scottie?" Sean asked glancing around the shoddy room as he pulled a chair from the wooden table and sat down.

"At the store," Fitz replied.

An empty rumpled KFC box sat on the table with chicken bones and a half eaten biscuit inside.

"You didn't save me any?" Sean asked jokingly, but his stomach grumbled at the thought of food. Lisa had hit him off with a hearty breakfast—scrambled eggs, toast, bacon and his favorite: grits and butter. He glanced at the muted TV; Emeril was cooking up one of his delicious meals that only made Sean's gut protest even more.

"Listen, Sean," Fitz cut in, turning extremely serious. "I gotta hip you to some disturbing shit."

Sean eyed him, waiting to hear what he had to say. Surprisingly Fitz clammed up.

After a few seconds of odd silence, Sean snapped, "What?" His curiosity got the best of him.

Fitz hesitated for a moment, his coco skin flushing with color before he said, "First, you've gotta promise me you'll keep a cool head."

"What the fuck is it?" Sean asked, rising from his rickety seat.

"Scottie thinks, we shouldn't tell you yet," Fitz replied, then dropped his head into his palms. "But since we came up through the ranks together, I really think it's only fair for you to know."

"Fuck what Scottie thinks," Sean practically yelled, getting more and more pissed off by the second. "Spill it."

Fitz grabbed a large manila envelope resting beside him on the bed and handed it to Sean.

Sean eyed the plain package a moment, a slow burn hitting his gut. He stared at Fitz, waiting. His forced his hands to remain steady as he opened the flap. Photographs slipped out of the other end, landing on the table.

Sean tried to look at the photos, but anger blurred his vision. Breakfast almost made a furious return. The blood immediately drained from his stunned face and he turned pale. He couldn't believe what he was seeing. Slumping down in the seat, he stared at the glossy pictures. He sat there in complete and utter shock.

The first frame showed Lisa getting into the Caddy as Jay waited in the driver's seat on a dark city block. Her white Maxima was parked directly behind the other car. The second showed Lisa and Jay tongue kissing passionately. The third showed Lisa in the backseat of the Caddy with her top off and lacy bra on, riding Jay like he was a mechanical bull. The fourth was Lisa giving Jay a kiss on the lips in the motel parking lot as he held her in a bear hug. The fifth was Lisa and Jay entering the motel room.

With anger totally consuming him, Sean dropped the photos, slamming his fists down on the table. He hopped up, practically knocking over the table and bolted for the door.

Fitz sprang into action, quickly blocking Sean's path.

Sean jerked left, trying to make a beeline around him.

Fitz stepped right back in his way continuing to block him.

"Get the fuck outta my way!" Sean yelled as he tried to sidestep Fitz again.

Still blocking his path, Fitz calmly tried to reason. "Whoa. . . whoa. Calm down, Sean, I know you're upset but you still have a job to do."

"Fuck the job!" Sean snapped, trying to shove past Fitz.

"Listen to me, Sean," Fitz demanded, throwing his entire body against the door so Sean couldn't leave. "You gotta cool down. You're a cop first, husband second."

Sean glared at him, wanting to rip his head off. Deep down inside, he knew Fitz was right.

"This isn't the way. Okay." Fitz put a bracing hand on his shoulder. "Trust me. It's not."

Sean took a deep breath and stood there, eyeing him a moment.

"Now, throw some water on your face," Fitz said, sighing softly.

Sean stood for a moment before storming into the bathroom. Relieved, Fitz moved away from the wooden door and sat back down on the bed. He lit up a cigarette and took a deep pull. The men heard a vehicle pull up out front. The engine died and a door slammed shut.

Seconds later, Scottie walked through the door, carrying a brown paper bag into the smoke filled room. Jay and Sean had transported drugs for him—as *Shady*—just last week. And just like Sean, he was an undercover agent with Internal Affairs.

When the door swung open, Sean peered out from the crack in the bathroom door.

"He here?" Scottie asked glancing around the gloomy looking room.

Fitz nodded.

"You tell him?" Scottie asked, closing the door.

Fitz nodded again.

"How'd he take it?"

"Same way you would," Fitz replied flatly, blowing a billow of smoke into the air.

Just then, Sean emerged from the bathroom, drying his wet face with one of the hard motel towels.

Scottie stole a glance at Sean. "You okay, man?"

"Been better," Sean replied half-heartedly as he sat down at the table.

Scottie grabbed a cold beer from the bag. "I figured you'd need this," he said, tossing the can to Sean.

Sean caught the beer, cracked it open and took a huge gulp, literally trying to drink away his pain. Scottie crossed over to the bed and sat down next to Fitz.

"Look, I know how you're feeling," Scottie said flatly.

"Do you?" Sean retorted not wanting to hear the bullshit. "Cause that's not your wife in the fuckin' pictures!"

"Okay. . . okay." Scottie held up a free hand. "You're right, but you have to stay focused. Jay will get his. Tonight the tables turn."

"Just wait 'til he realizes you're Internal Affairs," Fitz interjected.

"I'd feel better puttin' a bullet in his ass," Sean stated coldly, imagining himself pulling the trigger as Jay begged for his life.

Fitz and Scottie gave each other the eye. Fitz looked at the blank television screen. Scottie stared openly at Sean, knowing good and well Sean meant what he said.

"Sean, you have to handle this right," Fitz replied, turning back to look at the anger filled, heart broken young man.

"We need you in the right mind frame," Scottie said, eyeing Sean. "Can you handle this?"

Sean stared at the floor, taking another gulp of brew.

"Sean," Scottie said, raising his voice, "can you handle this?"

After a moment, Sean looked up. He nodded slowly before his eyes stared out at the crumbling stretch of wallpaper before him.

"Good. I'll drink to that," Scottie said and turned the beer up to his lips.

****

Later that night around 8:30 PM in the diner in Hunts Point, waiters and waitresses took people's orders while other customers were engrossed with food and conversation. The smell of food cooking on the grill engulfed the tiny place.

In a tight booth at the rear of the diner, Jay and Warren were in the midst of eating and talking. Sitting in total silence, Sean hadn't touched his burger and fries. His mind was a thousand miles away.

"I say we cut Black completely out the picture. We can split the cash three ways," Jay suggested as he gulfed down his grilled chicken sandwich.

"I second the motion," Warren replied, sopping up the rest of his New England clam chowder with a large crust of French bread.

They both looked over at Sean for his approval. He had remained painfully silent since they left from the precinct earlier. With his jaw tightly clenched, he stared out the window at the light rain that was turning into puddles as soon as it hit the ground. An eighteen-wheeler rolled through the block with its diesel engine growling.

"You usually gulpin' down everythin' on the menu," Jay said, eyeing Sean's full plate. The food continued to get colder. His eyes traveled up to Sean's mug.

"My stomach's upset," Sean replied flatly, glaring at the man. He tried his hardest to maintain his composure, eyeing Jay with a slight hint of anger in his eyes.

Jay returned the stare. At that exact moment, Sean wanted to leap across the table and choke the shit out of Jay, following it up with a bullet to the forehead. Instead he just sat there looking at Jay. The weird exchange made Jay shift in the seat a brief moment before Warren finally broke the silence.

"It's about time I bought that Harley I been eyeing," he chimed in.

Jay turned his focus back to Warren, "Shit. . . papa needs a new pair of kicks, gator at that."

They both laughed.

Sean didn't.

At the sound of their laugher, Sean pushed back the urge to put a bullet in both of their skulls and call it a night. Instead, he just sat there grim-faced and seething beneath the surface. His heart was bleeding with pain.

They left the restaurant, hitting the sidewalk as traffic flowed along all six lanes of the elevated Bruckner Expressway. The men walked over to the Caddy parked three cars down from the entrance and climbed in. The engine roared to life and the highlights popped on.

The Caddy barreled along Southern Boulevard toward 141st Street, making a sharp right turn onto 141st Street traveling up Cypress Avenue.

A group of older thugs from the block held down the corner of 141st Street and Cypress talking shit under the metal awning in front of a bodega as the car approached.

Spotting the cops, most of the cats posted up on the sidewalk eyeballed the passing Caddy with suspicion.

Sean and Warren stared right back at the cocksure roughnecks as the gray vehicle continued down the block. The rain finally stopped, leaving nothing but wetness in its wake.

Pulling up in front of a brick six-story tenement building, a young Spanish couple walked by smiling and holding hands, sending a wave of sudden pain to Sean's heart, followed by a quick burst of anger.

Exiting the car, Jay, Sean and Warren strolled to the entrance.

Scanning the surrounding area, Jay spotted a black van parked up the block.

"Hold up, fellas," Jay announced, stopping dead in his tracks. His eyes were still glued to the van.

Warren and Sean paused.

"What's wrong?" Warren asked, his white skin flushed pink from the cold air.

Covering his lips with a single hand, Jay replied, "Don't be obvious but check out the black van up the block, across the street. Looks like surveillance."

They both glanced at the van through the corner of their eyes trying not to make it noticeable.

Knowing all too well that Jay was right; Sean had to think real fast.

"You're bein' too paranoid," he said flatly.

"Shit don't feel right. Let's save it for another day," Jay insisted before doing a three-eighty and strolling back to the car parked at the curb.

"Another *day*?" Sean snapped, remaining right where he stood. "Get ya fuckin' mind right. We here now, let's get this fuckin' money!" He thumbed in the direction of the car. "Stop lettin' your bullshit paranoia fuck wit' you."

Eyeing Sean, Jay just stood there, upset and caught off guard. "You picked the wrong time to grow some balls, young blood."

"What you think?" Sean asked Warren.

"I'm with the kid on this," Warren replied evenly, shifting the weight of his body onto his good leg. He was fiending to get his clammy hands on some cash so he could lay up with a hooker and get high after their shift ended.

"My fuckin' gut's tellin' me Black set us up," Jay snapped, glaring at both men.

Inside the stuffy van, Mike, Fitz and Scottie were glued to cameras and video monitors set up in the rear, focused on the arguing trio up the street. Everyone was on pins and needles. The police radio crackled… "What should we do?" A female voice asked over the airwaves.

"Just sit tight, nobody moves unless I say so," Fitz said into his walkie-talkie.

Their eyes were still stuck to the monitors as Jay crossed over to the driver's side and climbed in. Warren hoped in the passenger seat right beside him. Still lingering on the sidewalk, Sean lit up a cigarette before slowly strolling back to the car.

"Ah fuck, they're getting back in the car. What the fuck?" Fitz groaned in frustration, crushing the empty foam coffee cup in his palm.

"Looks like he got cold feet," Scottie injected, showing hardly any emotion.

Mike shook his head in disbelief. "This can't be happening." He quickly lit up a Salem.

"Well, it is," Scottie piped in.

They all watched the video monitor as the Caddy made a quick u-turn before speeding into the dark night.
****

Roaring up the block in the Caddy, Jay, Warren and Sean rode in an awkward uncomfortable silence, each man deep in his own troubled thoughts.

Jay worried their long run of extortions and rip-offs might be coming to an end. But then again, even if it was a departmental sting they had nothing on the three of them 'cause they hadn't gone through with the deal. Feeling somewhat relieved, Jay slowly started to calm down a little. He decided it was time to pay Black a visit.

Warren was pissed because now he wouldn't have any cash to spend for the night. He would have to pawn his

TV later just to get a fucking hit. His whole paycheck was already completely shot.

On the outside, Sean looked cool. On the inside, he was going totally ape shit. Everything was fucked up. The set-up failed so they couldn't make the bust yet. This bullshit had set IA back cause they wanted to catch Jay and Warren with their hands in the cookie jar, which if they were smart they would have done during the bank robbery a few weeks back.

Across town posted up in front of a corner bodega, Black sipped on a forty ounce as he talked to his man, Mel.

Mel took a tote of a skinny blunt. "How'd you get out on bail facin' murder, anyway?"

"What you 20/20 nigga?" Black snapped, looking the nosey man up and down.

"Just curious."

"Curiosity killed da fuckin' cat. Remember dat," Black barked, clenching his fist like he was ready to take a swing.

"A'ight...chill," Mel replied tossing his palms up as he copped a plea.

Suddenly a hot, thick chocolate-coated cutie with a mean apple bottom exited the store heading for the crosswalk. She had a serious switch in her strut, which made her ass jiggle like jelly.

Her plump juicy ass was all Black saw. "Hey sexy," he bellowed, trying to holler at her.

She ignored him and kept right on walking across the street.

"Fuck you, bitch!" Black yelled after her. "I was doin' you a favor!"

She flipped him the finger over her shoulder without even glancing or breaking her seductive stride. Mel was practically bent over, howling with laughter.

"Fuck you laughin' at," Black barked. "I look like Dave Chappelle, nigga?"

Mel slapped his hand against the wall, still laughing.

Out the corner of his eye, Black saw the speeding Caddy approach. He took off running up the block. The beer slipped from his grasp, shattering on the wet pavement as he splashed through a puddle.

The Caddy ripped around the corner in hot pursuit.

Jay quickly swerved barely missing Black's double-parked Yukon with its hazard lights flashing as it zipped up the block.

Running at top speed, Black dipped into a narrow alley behind a row of tenement buildings littered with trash and dog shit. He stumbled, tripping over a garbage bag. His clothes wet and dirty from the fall, he hopped back to his feet and kept moving.

Behind Black, tires squealed as the Caddy skidded to a stop. The trio bolted out, hot on his heels. Sean bumped into a young boy, knocking him to the ground. The bushy haired kid stared up at him with a blank stare. Thinking fast, Sean quickly snatched the stunned boy up and pushed him out of harm's way.

Black swung around, firing a hail of slugs at them, still sprinting at full stride. They ducked behind a trash bin as bullets flew past. The foul smelling garbage inside didn't help the situation any. A few slugs chewed through the metal dumpster. Jay, Sean and Warren returned fire.

A few feet up the block an older woman screamed as she ran for cover with her five-year old daughter.

A wall of slugs barely missed Black as he dashed around the corner of the last building, into the connecting alleyway, running along the rear of the tenement.

Rounding the corner, Jay fired at Black but missed as he zigzagged to avoid the shot in the narrow alley. Sean and Warren were right on Jay's heels. All three men were breathing hard. Falling behind, Warren stopped, pale as a ghost, looking like he would pass out any minute.

Black suddenly made a beeline, slipping through a hole in the fence. He dipped across a vacant lot into the back of an abandoned building.

Cutting through the garbage-filled lot, Jay and Sean continued chasing after him. Lagging short ways behind, Warren took a slow jog through the vacant lot.

"Split up," Jay yelled, heading in the same direction as Black. Sean and Warren broke off in different paths along side the decrepit building.

CHAPTER 22

Jay entered the dark, abandoned building that was littered with debris.   Light from the street lamps crept in through gaping holes in the walls. Moving deeper into the building's belly, Jay searched cautiously for Black.   Dirty water dripped from the exposed floorboards poking out from the second floor through the huge jagged holes in various spots along the ceiling. The strong stench of urine hit Jay's nostrils like a ton of bricks.

Hiding behind a wall, Black nervously clutched his gun tightly as Jay approached. A line of sweat trickled down his dark cheek. Black gripped his steel even tighter as he started psyching himself, rocking back and forth, calming his thoughts. Suddenly he lunged out, firing wildly at Jay, only to watch every single slug miss its mark.

Jay returned fire with his own barrage of bullets. Black wasn't as lucky.

One shell apiece ripped through Black's stomach and arm. He staggered forward slightly, then collapsed. His gun slid across the floor, landing in front of an old beat up and rusted refrigerator.

Bleeding profusely from his wound, Black tried to squirm away, leaving a trail of blood in his wake. Jay waltzed over to Black.   His boot landed with a loud crack against Black's ribs.

Black screamed.

Jay squatted. "Did ya dumb ass really think you could fuckin' set me up? You know who the fuck I am?

"I—I had to," Black whimpered, coughing up blood.

"Just like I gotta finish what I started," Jay stated harshly, pressing the gun to his head.

A shot fired. Jay looked at the gun he held, knowing he hadn't pulled the trigger. A slug slammed into Jay's chest. Staggering backward, he looked up. Sean stood a few feet in the distance with the barrel of the glock still smoking.

The heat from the burning shell deep inside Jay's collapsed lung quickly brought him to the reality that his partner had just actually shot him. The slug severed his spine as it chewed through his back. It was the kind of wound a man hardly ever survived and if he lived, he'd definitely end up paralyzed.

With every ounce of strength slowly leaving his body, Jay dropped to the dirty wet ground, landing on his back, sprawled out practically side-by-side with Black. As fate would have it, both men now lay bleeding to death.

Sean rushed over to him and stood, glaring down at Jay with pure hatred in his dark brown eyes. Jay stared up at him trying to catch his fleeting breath. His eyes searched Sean's as he gasped for breath.

Kneeling down over Jay, Sean shouted, "How long you been fuckin' Lisa, huh, motherfucker?" He didn't give a fuck about the life and death struggle his partner Jay was currently enduring.

"I—I . . . I wouldn't do that," Jay murmured, gasping for much needed air—one battle Sean definitely wanted him to lose.

"Don't lie to me. Don't you fuckin' lie to me!" Sean barked, clutching the hot steel in his palms. "You fuckin' back stabbin' bastard, I saw the fuckin' pictures!"

"You talkin' crazy. We partners, young blood." Jay wheezed through coughs. "This me and you."

Sean shoved a crumpled up photo in the man's face. It was a shot of Jay and Lisa fucking in the Cherokee. Right then Jay's eyes fluttered closed as he sighed. They flashed open as he tried to explain, "We didn't mean for it to—"

Sean leveled the barrel at Jay's head. "Save that bullshit."

"So you gonna kill me over a bitch?" Jay asked.

"That bitch is my wife!" Sean shouted, holding his emotions in check. "You of all people know how much I love her. She's the only reason I'm still doin' this fuckin' job!"

Realizing that being nice wasn't getting him anywhere, Jay refused to beg for mercy like some coward.

"Save the fuckin' sob story," he mustered the strength to say. "If you satisfied her, I wouldn't have to."

"Fuck you!" Sean yelled completely infuriated; pressing the barrel to Jay's sweat-soaked forehead.

"You finally growin' balls, huh?" Jay half-laughed, coughing up more blood.

"After all the young lives you've viciously snuffed out, it's finally your turn to reap what you so coldly sowed."

Determined to die like a man, he locked eyes with Sean, showing no fear.

"Certain lines in life you never cross. Fuckin' my wife was one," Sean stately coldly and then squeezed the trigger. Exploding out of the barrel, the bullet disappeared into the center of Jay's skull leaving a gaping entry wound.

Jay was dead before he knew what hit him.

Warren quickly ducked back behind a wall, knocking over some debris. His mind could not register what he had just witnessed. He remained motionless as his thinker raced a mile a minute. For a moment, he thought it was actually the drugs fucking with him until he realized he hadn't gotten high yet.

Startled by the loud noise, Sean scanned the perimeter but didn't spot anyone. He turned his attention to Black and put him out of his misery with a single shot to the head.

"You might as well come out, Warren," Sean shouted when he finished.

After a few seconds, Warren slowly stepped into view with his gun trained on Sean. His gun arm shook like a twig in strong winds as all his hairs stood on end.

"What the fuck just happened, Sean?" Warren demanded, sounding hysterical as he approached Sean cautiously.

"You gonna shoot me now?" Sean asked boldly without actual concern for his own life.

"Tell me what the hell just happened," Warren demanded, still keeping Sean locked in his gun's sights. He stopped about six feet away from Sean.

"Did you know he was fuckin' Lisa?" Sean yelled at him.

"Drop the fucking gun, Sean," Warren ordered.

Completely ignoring his command, Sean slowly raised his glock, aiming at Warren.

"No, drop yours! What you gonna do, turn me in? We're both dirty. Don't forget that fuckin' kid you killed!" Sean quickly reminded him.

"You just killed Jay...he's our freaking *partner* for Christ's sakes! He's one of us...drop the gun, Sean, now!" Warren demanded, tears in his blue eyes for his dead friend.

"I go down, you go down," Sean stated just as calm as ever. "So you better kill me." At this point in his screwed up life, he didn't mind dying.

"Don't make me fucking do this," Warren practically pleaded. Sean didn't budge an inch.

"He was fuckin' Lisa! What if it was your ex-wife, huh?" Sean asked, holding the gun steady on Warren's chest. "What if he screwed the woman you loved?"

After a few tense moments, Warren finally lowered his gun. He understood where Sean was coming from cause truthfully he would've done the same thing if it had been him.

"What the fuck we gonna do now?" Warren asked, glancing down at Jay's lifeless body. It hurt his heart to see his partner's life snatched away like that, but he didn't want to risk going to jail. Tears fell from his eyes as he quickly focused on Sean.

Sean looked down at Black's corpse and said solemnly, "It's fucked up how Black got the drop on Jay."

Warren just stared at Sean, nodding. He knew what had to be done.

CHAPTER 23

Minutes later, marked and unmarked police cars, ambulances and news vans littered the taped off area surrounding the abandoned building. The only thing keeping most of the sad and depressed looking officers busy was the different conversations they were having amongst themselves huddled in their separate little cliques.

Sean and Warren exited the bare shell of the building and stood in the midst of it all as Captain Hardy approached them. News reporters jockeyed into position for interviews behind the yellow police tape.

"You guys had a long night, go home and get some rest, " the Captain ordered. His eyes were blood shot from shedding tears a few moments prior to his arrival at the scene over the loss of one of his best detective.

****

Later that same night in Valley Stream Long Island on a quiet middle-class block lined with one-family homes, a new canary yellow Mustang with Warren behind the wheel pulled into the driveway of a brick split two-level home. He exited and crossed to the front door, sticking the key in the lock.

"Excuse me, detective, we need to have a little talk."

Warren immediately turned and found himself face to face with Mike and Fitz.

"First of all, who the hell are you?" Warren snapped, tapping on the thirty-eight tucked under his armpit as he glared at the two unfamiliar men. By the suits and ties, he figured they had to be some form of law enforcement.

"Internal Affairs," Mike replied calmly, displaying his badge.

Warren's facial expression changed immediately from one of anger to that of concern.

"What's this about?" Warren inquired, stepping away from his door.

Fitz eyed the shiny Mustang and asked, "How can you afford such an expensive piece of machinery on a cop's

salary?" He locked eyes with Warren. "I know I sure can't."
He winked.

Warren bristled with anger, but remained silent.
Shifting all his weight onto his left leg, he tried to keep his
composure.

Mike looked at Warren. "We'd like you to come
downtown and answer some questions."

"For what?" Warren snapped.

"I think you know," Mike replied calmly, his dark gray
eyes still glued to Warren.

At that moment all of the blood drained from his pale
face and a knot tightened in the pit of his stomach.

"Now, do us all a favor and do this peacefully," Mike
stated sharply.

A few minutes later in the unmarked sedan, Fitz drove
while Mike rode shotgun and Warren sat quietly in the back
seat, staring out the window.

Mike turned to Warren, "So, how long you guys been
shaking down dealers?"

Warren just stared at him, then turned back toward the
window and continued staring out at the passing cars and
SUVs speeding by on the highway.

"Not real talkative, huh?" Mike asked sarcastically,
still staring at Warren. "You guys are brazen. I give you that."

In a small plain room in the center of Internal Affairs
office, Warren sat at a small metal table viewing numerous
photos. Sipping on a hot cup of coffee, Fitz stood nearby
watching him.

Photo one: Jay, Sean, and Warren heading into
Black's building. Photo two: Jay, Sean, and Warren
emerging from Black's building. Photo three: Jay, Sean, and
Warren divvying up the cash on a dead-end street. Photo
four: Warren waiting in the getaway car as Jay and Sean
emerged from the bank.

Fitz crossed to the entrance of the room leaving as
quietly as he had come in. Warren could tell the clean cut
older man had on an expensive suit.

As soon as the door swung shut, Warren dropped his
head into his sweaty palms. He had to sort shit out before
Fitz came back. He was determined not to break. Being a

cop, he knew everything there was to know about interrogations. All he had to do was request a lawyer and the whole process had to be stopped immediately. But then again, requesting a lawyer was the first sign of guilt for a cop and things would go downhill from there. Then again things were already headed down hill at a high rate of speed.

Moments later, Fitz entered the room holding a videocassette, "Anything you wanna tell me?"

"You have nothing," Warren replied, trying to hide the anxiety building.

Fitz popped the cassette into the VCR, pressed play and turned on the 27-inch monitor. "Have a look."

Warren eyed the tube as a picture popped up onto the screen. A grainy view of a surveillance camera—showing Jay, Sean and Warren in Black's apartment appeared before him. Jay was in the middle of counting a huge pile of money while Warren sat on the loveseat the whole time.

"Need to see more?" Fitz asked, motioning with a free hand towards the monitor. "Because that police chase was amazing. I'm surprised you guys managed to get away. You're one hell of a driver."

Warren didn't respond. His mind was racing. They had him. Fitz turned it off, crossed over to the table and sat down in the metal chair across from Warren. He stared at Warren for a long quiet moment.

Warren glared right back at him.

"Isn't the quality we get with today's technology fantastic?" Fitz asked with a smug grin on his face.

Warren remained stone face, realizing the need for a lawyer had increased with each passing movement.

"Anyway, not to bore you, I'll get straight to the point," Fitz continued, rubbing his palms together eagerly. "You've been under surveillance for some time now. We have a box full of tapes like the one you just saw."

Warren glanced down at the table, fidgeting with his sweaty hands.

Right then, Fitz knew he was starting to crack...somewhat. Plus, he still had an ace up his sleeve. "Listen, we're prepared to offer you a deal if you plead guilty. Save us the headache of going to trial."

Warren looked up, just staring at him, his wounded leg throbbing.

"I suggest you take some time to—," Fitz said, before a knock at the door interrupted him. "Come in."

A young white police officer stepped halfway in and piped, "You have a call."

"Thanks," Fitz replied, then turned back to Warren, "I'll be right back. Don't go anywhere."

Warren didn't find any humor in the stale joke.

Making it halfway out the doorway, Fitz stopped dead in his tracks and turned around.

"Oh, did I forget to mention, Sean's with us. *He's* Internal Affairs." Without saying another word, he stepped out and slammed the door shut behind him.

Warren gaped at the closed door. Sean was IA? Anger flooded his system. He couldn't believe his ears. He felt betrayed. That motherfucker had it coming to him. Now, Warren was prepared to give Fitz an earful when he came back.

****

Five hours later after being released from the exhaustingly long interrogation session, Warren emerged from the plain, discreet ten-story Internal Affairs building located on Broadway and 131st street. Taking a deep breath of fresh polluted air, he paused for a moment to light up a smoke. What he really needed was a quick hit of coke but unfortunately for him he didn't have any. His nerves were shot and his mind was fried from all the questioning.

Warren hustled up the dark lonely block, going over the only two options he had available, commit suicide or testify against Sean. They had offered to cut any time he received in half if he cooperated. The thoughts through his brain were interrupted prematurely by a woman's commanding voice.

"What up, Nigga?"

Totally taken aback by some woman calling him the "n" word, Warren turned around and met with a bright reddish-orange flash leaping from the muzzle of a black .9mm automatic. Stunned, his beady eyes widened just as the first round sent him staggering backwards. The other three slugs that quickly followed embedded themselves in the meaty flesh of his chest and stomach.

With his body sprawled halfway on the cold sidewalk and halfway in the filthy gutter, Warren squinted trying to make out the dark shapely figure approaching him.

A six-inch heel stepped into the pool of blood beginning to collect on the sidewalk near his wounded midsection. ReRe leaned in closer so he could get a better look and she could get a better shot.

His eyebrows rose as he recognized the woman towering over him. The dying man's eyes stay glued to the gun she was leveling at his head. "You…"

"Hey there, big boy, you still want me to pop your top?" ReRe asked, letting out a sinister giggle before pulling the trigger.

Blood and brain tissue sprayed the sidewalk as ReRe hopped into an idling Ford Expedition. The SUV sped off into the night as a bunch of uniformed cops and plainclothes officers rushed out of the building to find Warren's dead corpse. The crackle of thunder rumbled across the dark sky as a flash of lightning reached down from the heavens. Immediately, a heavy pour followed drenching the stunned officers hovering over Warren's lifeless body.

CHAPTER 24

The rainy night quickly turned into a clear cool morning over the island of Manhattan. The alarm clock in Sean's bedroom read 5:29 am. Six empty beer cans and an empty bottle of Jack Daniels littered the floor around the bed. An ashtray full of butts was on the nightstand. A single hand reached out. The other side of the bed was surprisingly empty. He turned over, still in a deep sleep.

A loud crash of his apartment door being kicked in jarred Sean out of his drunken slumber.

Instinctively, he reached for the glock resting on the nightstand. But before he could grab it, five cops sporting bulletproof gear rushed in with their guns trained on him.

"Touch it, you're dead!" the lead officer yelled, clutching a submachine gun for dear life. This white boy was ready to let the deadly weapon rip if necessary.

Sean knew by the tone of his voice not to test him. He dropped his hand back to his side.

"Slowly, turn on your stomach!" the lead officer demanded.

Complying with his command, Sean rolled over onto his face.

"What the hell is this?" Sean asked.

The lead officer quickly shuffled over to Sean, yelling, "Hands behind your back!"

Sean did as he was told. The lead officer quickly cuffed him roughly.

"You can't do this. I'm I. A.," Sean barked.

Just then Fitz stepped through the crowd. The expression on his face was somber and frightening.

"Just couldn't let it go, huh, Sean?" Fitz asked, moving in closer. "Had to take things into your own hands. You're under arrest for murdering a fellow police officer."

Immediately clamming up, Sean didn't say another word.

Slithering over to the closed bathroom door, a nosy cop pushed it open and gasped, instantly shocked by what he saw inside. His jaw dropped open and for a brief moment he struggled for words.

"Lieutenant, you better look at this," the cop finally mustered the strength to say.

Fitz hurried over to the bathroom, looked in and exclaimed, "Oh my God," as he rushed inside.

Sean turned his head left and looked into the bathroom.

Lisa hung, naked and unconscious, handcuffed to the shower beam. Black and blue marks covered almost every inch of her bruised and swollen body. A raveled up leather belt rested on the tiled floor. Her eyes were swollen shut and her lip was split open and caked with dried up blood.

Fitz checked her wrist and found a strong pulse.

"You're gonna be alright," he assured her. "I'm getting you some help. Call a fucking ambulance!"

He whipped out the cuff keys from his pocket and unlocked her bruised wrists. Slowly he lowered her into the bathtub. "Somebody get me a sheet!"

A few minutes later, Sean emerged from the brownstone escorted by Fitz. Shuffling down the steep set of steps, they reached the sidewalk moving past an idling Emergency Response Team Police truck to an awaiting unmarked car parked at the curb.

Fitz held the back door open and Sean stepped in. Even though it was morning time, a herd of dark clouds moved in, shutting out the sun. Lightning crackled through the rather gloomy sky and a light rain began to fall to the earth.

"This would've broken your father's heart," Fitz stated rather flatly.

"Cry me a fuckin' river," Sean replied coldly, glaring up at Fitz.

Shaking his head, Fitz slammed the door shut and climbed into the driver's seat.

****

In the federal courthouse two days later in downtown Manhattan, the proceedings were underway. The small court was packed with Sean's his mother Gail, his younger sister Michelle and a few cousins and friends. A bunch of uniform cops and detectives were there to lend their support. Fitz and

Mike lingered inconspicuously a few rows back in the midst of the crowd. Surprisingly none of Jay's family members were there.

Sporting a dark pair of designer sunglasses to hide her black eyes, Lisa was seated in the rear, trying to make eye contact with Sean who was seated behind a huge wooden rectangular table next to his tall, thin lawyer. Sean flipped a Bic pen back and forth between his sweaty fingers taking in every word the prosecutor spoke.

The prosecutor, a short, pudgy black man with thick-framed glasses and a salt and pepper Don King Afro, stood at the front of the court room facing the judge in the midst of making his point. "Due to the serious nature of the crime, the prosecution recommends that the defendant continues to be held without bail."

The judge, an older white woman, peered at the prosecutor over her wire thin glasses.

"Your recommendation has been duly noted by the court," the judge said, jotting notes down on her legal pad. "The defendant is hereby remanded to MCC until his next court date. Scheduled early June."

"Excuse me, your honor, my client as of two days ago was a cop with no priors. He should be allowed bail," Sean's lawyer injected, standing to his feet.

"Due to the seriousness of the charge, the court believes the defendant needs to be off the streets for the public's safety," the judge replied. "Appeal it at the next date."

The lawyer whispered something into Sean's ear then placed his papers into his briefcase. Sean glanced back at his crying mother and the rest of his sad family. His eyes were set in stone, revealing no emotion whatsoever. He mouthed the words, "I love you," before turning back around.

A few minutes later, out in the busy court hallway, Gail was discussing the case with Sean's lawyer as people filed out of the courtroom heading for the elevators a few feet away. Sean's sister stood off to the side watching her concerned mother.

"I don't want my child rotting in some jail," Gail said, her eyes watering. "He made a mistake."

"I know...I know.   Unfortunately, this is how the

system works," the lawyer replied. "Now it's up to us to prove it was an act of momentary insanity once we go trial. Until then, there's pretty much nothing else we can do but wait."

****

At the MCC New York Prison, a sexy black female correction officer escorted Sean down the narrow corridor as inmates whistled and hollered at the fresh meat. She stopped in front of a faintly lit cell already occupied by a huge monstrous convict, other inmates called Hulk. The dark skinned man stood 6'3" and weighed close to three hundred and fifty pounds, solid muscle. The only thing missing was the green skin and screwed up hairdo. His head was bald except for a long patch of hair that was braided into a ponytail in the back of his cranium.

Hulk stopped etching a half finished portrait of a naked woman onto the cell wall. A snake with long sharp fangs was wrapped around the length of her body as it stared the beautiful woman in the face. He eyed Sean with a menacing sneer.

She stuck the skeleton key into the lock and unlocked the cell door.

"Home sweet home," the CO said with a sly grin. "You two guys get acquainted."

Sean stepped in and scanned the cramped cell he would now call home at least until the trial was over. Hulk continued eyeing Sean, weighing him seriously. Soon as the C.O. walked away, Hulk purposely bumped into Sean almost knocking him over.

"The word's excuse me," Sean snapped, glaring up at the big man with a flash of anger. He wasn't about to back down, no matter how big the bastard was. The way he saw it, he was David and this giant of a man was going to end up like Goliath.

"Not when you're in my way," Hulk replied, inching even closer.

Sean continued staring at him, but he decided to keep a cool head and stepped aside. He didn't need the problems right before he went to trial.

Moving right back into his path, Hulk got up in his face. "You're still in my way."

"Look, if you gonna do something, do it. If not, get the fuck outta my face," Sean replied sharply, not showing an ounce of fear as he balled up both fists. He was ready to take a swing if necessary. Big man was definitely testing his patience now. His jaw was clenched together so tightly; Hulk could see the vein in his forehead throbbing. In all due reality Sean had fucked up guys almost twice this inmate's size before. If there was one thing for sure, Sean was nice with the hand skills.

Hulk glared at the angry man. Dead silent. His rugged face locked in stone. Not finding any fear in Sean's eyes, Hulk finally spoke, "You got heart, little man." He cracked a friendly smile.

"That's big man to you," Sean corrected, easing up somewhat.

Hulk's smile widened even more as he extended his huge hand. "They call me, Hulk."

"I can see why," Sean replied, looking up and down Hulk's humongous frame as he shook the big guy's hand.

And just as quickly as it started, the test was over, a test every man in the prison system had to go through at some point during his stay. Some passed while the others became punks for the hard rocks who intimidated them. Fortunately Sean was far from weak, physically or mentally.

"You get the top," Hulk informed, crossing to the bunk beds. He slid a sharpened shank from under the top mattress and handed it to Sean. "That's yours," he said, cocking an eyebrow. "You gon' need one in here."

At the same time, passing by the cell, Julius, an older con that possessed the gift of wisdom, knowledge and leadership, witnessed the weapon exchange. He made a mental note and kept moving down the tier like he hadn't seen a thing. In prison a man had to know when to mind his own business or end up getting slashed or even worst, dead. An inmate could lose his life in a flash if he wasn't careful.

Sean eyed the rusty deadly weapon closely, looking around in concern. "What about the COs?"

"I rather do six months in the hole than have six cons' run a train in my hole. Get me?"

Definitely getting the picture, Sean nodded and tucked the rusty blade under his mattress.

Falling silent, Hulk went back to finishing up his masterpiece. Sean stood there watching the big man work for a moment, then climbed up on the bunk and spread out on his back. He felt exhausted but sleep totally evaded him as his mind started to wonder back to the outside world he had left behind. He shifted onto his side, facing the wall so Hulk wouldn't see the tears flowing from his eyes.

Still eyeing the graffiti scribbled wall, Sean's mind flashed back to the day he graduated from the police academy. It was a surprising warm, sunny spring day in June. The ceremony took place in Whitman Hall at Brooklyn College in Brooklyn.

The police commissioner, sporting a chest full of commendations on his dress blues, stood at a podium addressing the 2,500-seat auditorium filled with the graduating class decked out in brand new uniforms, families and a few selected members of the press. Beside him, in an expensive black pin striped suit was the mayor.

"Once again, it's an honor to be here, standing before such a huge, diversified graduating class of 2000," the commissioner said, pausing to let the roar of applause flowing through the place die down. "In sticking with the tradition of the police department, we'd like to present the Mayor of New York City, Rudy Harrington."

Somewhere in the middle section of the massive graduating class was Sean. His eyes were fixed on the Mayor as he took over the podium to address the crowd.

Sean smiled brightly as the mayor pinned a shiny new badge onto his neatly pressed uniform and the room erupted in cheers. This was the day he had dreamed about ever since deciding he wanted to become a cop. No one shouted louder than his beautiful mother, his fiancée Lisa and his younger sister. They were so excited and proud of him. He couldn't stop smiling that whole day.

When Sean first became a cop, he loved going to work. He lived and breathed it, actually believing he could change the world. Then slowly the reality hit that no matter how many drug dealers and criminals he locked up, double that seemed to pop up the next day. It was like the streets were a breeding ground for Satan himself. Actually the streets were his breeding ground.

Still crying in total silence so Hulk wouldn't hear him, Sean eventually fell asleep.

****

In the small prison library the next day, Sean sat at a table looking through a thick law book, trying to gather legal information to help his case. There was a bulky stack of law books next to him. Julius entered the room with a black book in hand, spotting him. The older man headed straight for him.

"That's good reading but this is better, youngin'," Julius said, handing Sean a black leather bound Bible.

Taking the Bible, Sean stared at it a moment and then said, "Thanks."

Julius nodded then strutted off without saying another word.

"Hey, what's your name?" Sean asked the leaving man.

Julius stopped in his tracks and turned around. "The name's Julius, youngin'."

"I'm Sean."

Julius nodded then turned back around and walked out of the library.

Sean slouched back in his chair, staring at the good book but didn't bother to open it. It had been a long time since he read the Lord's word. He sat it down on the table and went back to gathering the info he needed.

Later on that same day at the payphone banks for inmates near the dayroom, Sean was talking on the phone at the end. Other inmates occupied the rest of the phones in the midst of conversation and making calls.

"I'm okay, Ma, really," Sean insisted, trying to reassure his worried mother. The only problem was he didn't have anyone to reassure him.

After a brief awkward pause, she asked, "You sure, baby?"

"Yes, Ma, I'm sure. Just stop worrying about me."

"I could never stop worrying. You're my son."

Sean eyed an inmate swaggering past him. "I know, but I made my bed now I gotta lay in it."

****

One month later, the trial proceedings were already underway as Fitz quietly slipped into the crowded court. The family of the defendant Sean filled the room to capacity. There was barely any standing room left in the rear of the cramped courtroom. No one on Jay's side of the family bothered to show up. All eyes were on Sean's lawyer including the sexy older judge and the black Cornell West look-alike prosecutor.

Sean's lawyer stood near the jury box, in the middle of addressing the jury. The jury happened to be surprisingly mixed with four whites, six African Americans and two Puerto Ricans paying full attention to every word rolling off the frail lawyer's thin lips.

"I ask you to place yourself in my client's shoes. He was an undercover cop dealing with the enormous amount of pressure it took to get up everyday and maintain his cover. This man was a witness to numerous murders and extortions that he was unable to stop due to the sensitive nature of the case. I know my client is on trial for murdering a fellow police officer, but the victim was far from innocent. Don't forget he even robbed numerous banks and as you well know he was sleeping with my client's wife. That alone could send any God fearing man over the edge." The lawyer moved to the other side of the jury box, never losing eye contact with the jurors.

The lawyer continued on with the rest of his closing statement, "Now he's being persecuted for one moment of temporary insanity. I'm not trying to excuse his actions or saying taking a life is right, but under those circumstances and stress, any man or woman could snap. Ladies and gentlemen of the jury, I ask you not to take part in this state's lynching of my client. Do the right thing. Find him not guilty." He walked back to the defense table where Sean was seated. "The defense rests, your honor."

The judge nodded her approval to the lawyer as he sat back down. The lawyer quickly whispered something into Sean's ear and Sean nodded in response.

Hopping to his feet, the prosecutor made a show of the defense's closing statements before leading into his own closing arguments. "Ladies and gentlemen of the jury, as you can very well see," pointing towards Sean who was alert and paying full attention to the prosecutor, "the defendant is of sound mind and I can guarantee you, he was of sound mind when he murdered his partner in cold blood. I'm not going to stand here and bore you with the facts of this case because you all are already aware of them. But what I am going to ask you to do is send a message to the defendant and the rest of the community that it is not excusable to take a human life no matter the circumstances or reasons."

When the prosecution finally rested its case, the judge ordered the jury to try to reach a fair verdict based on the facts and evidence of the case not on any media hype or hearsay. She then dismissed the jury so they could deliberate.

After only six hours, the jury had reached a decision. Notifying the judge and the attorneys, they returned to the courtroom and took their places in the jury box.

"Has the jury reached a verdict?" the judge asked.

The jury foreman stood and answered, "Yes, your honor."

"Please continue."

Sean bowed his head in silent prayer as the jury foreman read the verdict, "We, the jury, find the defendant guilty of murder in the third degree."

Gasps ran through the quiet courtroom, but Sean showed no emotion as the verdict was read. His mother let out a pain filled wail as her tears started to flow. Michelle collapsed to the floor in tears as other family members reacted to the devastating news. Court officers rushed to maintain control of the courtroom, quickly ushering Sean out of the court before things could get out of hand.

Even though Warren was dead, his handwritten confession still helped to convict Sean. Plus the fact that Sean had used his own service weapon to commit the murder didn't help much. Taking the circumstances into consideration, the judge ended up sentencing Sean to fifteen years behind bars instead of the life without parole he could have received. Despite the sentence, there was still a bright light at the end of the long dark tunnel ahead. At least he would have a chance to start fresh when he got released. Some people never get a second chance.

****

Two months later at Marion Federal Prison, Sean entered the packed visiting room escorted by a buffed C.O. with Elvis sideburns. The tanned officer pointed him in Lisa's direction.

Sean just stood there staring at her for a moment. Sitting in a crammed booth behind a glass partition, Lisa looked up and smiled at him as best she could considering the awkward situation. He hadn't seen her for months. All the pain and hurt along with a touch of anger quickly resurfaced. At the same time, he couldn't help but notice how beautiful she was. Her smile still had the same affect on him. Her hair was pinned up in a bun and her cherry red painted lips looked so inviting.

For only a moment, he wished he could kiss her again. Smell her sweet scent again. Hold her close again. Make love to her again. Then just like that, his mood quickly darkened as he remembered everything she had put him through. If it weren't for her, he wouldn't be locked in this hellhole. He hated himself for still feeling any affection toward her after what she had done to him. Reluctantly, he crossed to her. Pulling out the sturdy wooden chair, he sat down and just glared at her, not saying a word. He didn't know what to say.

A beat up black phone hung on the wall on each side of the thick glass for communication. Up and down the line of claustrophobically small booths, inmates and their loved ones were catching up on lost time.

Finally Lisa picked up the receiver.

Sean hesitated a moment before grabbing the phone. Slowly, he brought the receiver up to his ear and listened.

"Hey, baby," Lisa stuttered with a weary smile.

Smirking at her, Sean asked, "Why are you here, Lisa?"

"I...I don't know," Lisa replied, tears streaming down her flushed cheeks. "I just felt we needed closure."

An uncomfortable silence hung between them for what seemed like an eternity.

"How are you doing in here?" she asked, glancing around at the iron bars covering the only two windows in the place.

"Okay considering the circumstances."

Lisa's tears started flowing even heavier. "I love you so much, Sean."

"You should've thought about that before you fucked Jay."

"I'm so sorry—"

"You're sorry," With his anger getting the best of him, Sean leaned in closer to the thick glass, looking Lisa dead in the eyes. "Nah, I'm the one that's sorry for marryin' your ass. I'm filin' for divorce."

"Sean please."

"Please—what Lisa? You screwed my partner," Sean wiped his eyes, trying to fight back the tears. He didn't want her to see him cry. "And, and you expect me to feel sorry for you? I loved you, Lisa."

"Please, baby, just let me explain." Lisa pleaded. "You weren't showing me enough attention."

"Oh, so, I'm supposed to understand why you fucked another man now, huh? Cause I didn't show you any attention!" Dropping the receiver, Sean bolted out of the chair, knocking it over onto its side. He headed for the exit as a bunch of nosey eyes followed.

Lisa jumped up, pressing her face to the glass. "Sean, please don't..." She began banging on the thick partition, trying to get Sean's attention, but he kept walking like he didn't even hear her.

The C.O. guarding the exit door let him out. Sean disappeared behind the steel door as it slid close. Lisa's tears turned into heaving sobs as she just stood there shaking.

CHAPTER 25

The next afternoon, Sean lay on his metal cot with the thin mattress and stared at the ceiling in his dimly lit cell. He was a thousand miles away in deep thought, thinking back to the days when everything in his life was all good.

The echo of heavy footsteps getting closer and closer snapped Sean back to reality. After a moment or two, the footsteps stopped directly in front of Sean's cell.

"How are you Sean?"

Recognizing the voice, Sean sat up to face Fitz and replied, "Been better."

Fitz moved closer to the bars and said, "You know I never meant for you to get caught up in this."

"Shit happens," Sean replied, having already come to terms with doing the time that lay ahead of him. His stepfather had always said, "You do the crime, you do the time."

"You definitely remind me of your father."

"Stepfather," Sean snapped, having to remind him as usual.

"No matter what, he always played the hand he was dealt. No complaints. Even when he had that stroke right before he passed, he didn't complain."

Fitz was dipped in an expensive suit with a pair of square-toe alligators on his feet.

Sean stared at him a moment and then asked, "What do you really want? I know you didn't come all this way for small talk."

"Just checking on you. I promised your fath—I mean stepfather I'd look after you no matter what. I put a few dollars your commissary. I'll send you something every month."

"You don't gotta do that," Sean said. "I don't need the pity."

Fitz pulled out a cigarette. "No, I do, if it wasn't for me you wouldn't be in this mess. Consider this my debt to you." He lit the cancer stick and took a pull. "Everybody pays taxes."

"What did you just say?" Sean asked.

Fitz blew out the grayish white smoke through the corner of his mouth. "Everybody pays taxes."

Suddenly, it all hit Sean like a ton of bricks and he exclaimed, "It's you Jay was paying off."

"See, you're a natural." Fitz let out a sinister laugh, then replied, "It's in your blood."

"I can't believe this shit," Sean said, stunned, his mood quickly darkened. "You used me to set Jay up," he snapped his voice rising as he stood right in front of the iron gate separating him from Fitz's lucky ass.

"Not like he was a saint," Fitz replied with ice in his voice.

"Why?" Sean asked, having to know the answer.

Fitz shrugged, pacing before the door. "He got too cocky, too greedy and started short changing me."

"You conniving motherfucker," Sean barked barely able to contain his anger.

"Hey, I learned from the best," Fitz replied calmly, leaning in even closer. "Your stepfather taught me the rules."

Seeing nothing but red, Sean reached past the cell bars and grabbed Fitz by the collar, yanking him up against the bars. "You're lying!"

Fitz broke loose from his tight grip and said, "I'll be seeing you, Sean." With a grin, he adjusted his suit jacket and strolled off.

"Come back here you two-faced motherfucker! Come back here!" Sean yelled at Fitz's retreating back.

Fitz just kept strutting down the corridor toward the cellblock exit.

"This isn't the end," Sean shouted, sinking to the floor of his cell in total disbelief, feeling defeated. At this point, he was hell bent on getting his revenge. He started knocking the back of his skull against the cell wall in anger. Then he heard a small still voice say, "Vengeance is mine saith the Lord."

Suddenly an overwhelming feeling of peace came over Sean as he glanced up at the Bible resting on the metal shelf overhead next to three other books. Standing up, he pulled it off the dusty shelf and cracked it open to 1st John, and his eyes fell on chapter five. He began reading the passage.

This then is the message, which we have heard of him, and declare unto you, that God is light, and in him is no darkness at all.

If we say that we have fellowship with him, and walk in darkness, we lie, and do not know the truth:

But if we walk in the light, as he is in the light, we have fellowship one with another, and the blood of Jesus Christ his Son cleanseth us from all sin.

If we say that we have no sin, we deceive ourselves, and the truth is not in us.

If we confess our sins, he is faithful and just to forgive us our sins, and to cleanse us from all unrighteousness.

If we say that we have not sinned, we make him a liar, and his word is not in us.

Suddenly tears flooded Sean's brown eyes and he was overcome with conviction, realizing he had actually turned into one of the monsters he had been chasing as an undercover. Tossing the Bible on his cot, he dropped to knees and began praying for forgiveness. Tears rolled down his cheeks as he repented of all his sins. He stayed there for almost twenty minutes, pouring his heart out. When he stood back up, after finally making peace with himself, it was like a weight had been lifted off of his shoulders and right then he knew the Creator had given him a second chance at life. Redemption. He decided at that moment that he wouldn't seek revenge on Fitz. In due time karma would eventually catch up with Fitz. Like the Bible says, you reap what you sow.

Placing the Bible back on the shelf, Sean noticed the letter Lisa had wrote him. Exhaling deeply, he grabbed envelope from off the shelf, opened it and read the letter for the first time:

Dear Sean,

I don't even know where to begin. Knowing you, you probably won't want to even read this letter but I had to give it a try anyway. I love you so much. I know that I really hurt you deeply, but I need you to know I never loved Jay. I loved you from the first day I saw you. You didn't deserve to have your heart broken like that. No matter what happened between us, I had no right to cheat on you. I finally realized I have a sex addiction and I've started going to counseling for it. I just want you to know how truly sorry I am. I just hope you can find it in your heart to forgive me one day. I'll always be here for you no matter what. Please let me come visit you. I just want to see you so we can talk in person. I've never been good at writing letters.

Love you always,

Your wife, Lisa

By the time Sean finished reading her letter, he was completely in tears. He let the letter slip from his fingers onto the floor of his cell as he laid back down on the cot and stared up at the ceiling. A thousand thoughts were running through his mind at once. From everything he had been through in the past few months to his beautiful wife Lisa. He couldn't run from the truth. When it was all said and done, he stilled loved her. Unable to shake her bright smile from his thoughts, it finally hit him that maybe he could forgive Lisa after all. It was only right being the Lord had forgiven him for killing another human being and all the other sins he had committed in his life. He knew it wouldn't happen overnight, but he was definitely willing to give their marriage another shot. After all the wedding vows they took was till death due them part.

"Light's out, fellas!" A CO shouted just as all the lights in the housing area and cells cut off.

Staring into the darkness, Sean made up his mind that first thing in the morning he was finally going to write Lisa back.

THE END...

Currently Available:

Q-Boro Books Presents

ISBN: 0-9753066-4-2   Author: Kiniesha Gayle

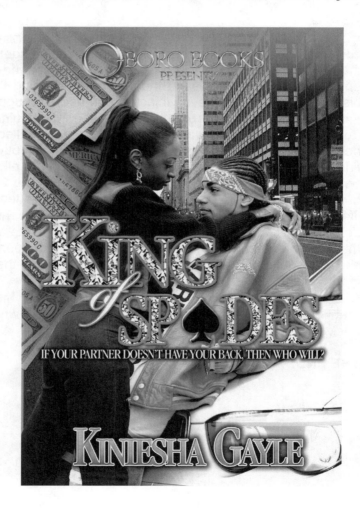

IF YOUR PARTNER DOESN'T HAVE YOUR BACK, THEN WHO WILL?

ISBN: 0-9753066-2-6   Author: Anna J.

ISBN: 0-9753066-0-X   Author: Mark Anthony

ISBN: 0-9753066-3-4   Author: Erick S. Gray

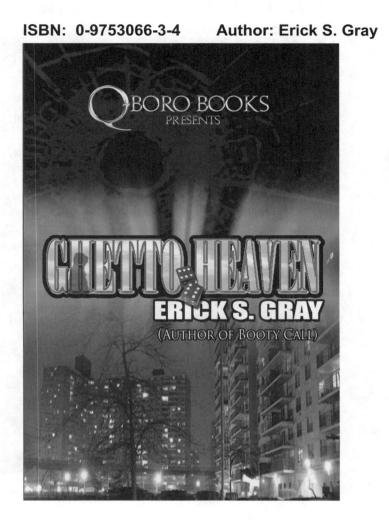

ISBN: 0-9753066-1-8   Authors: Various

ANTHONY WHYTE | MARK ANTHONY | ERICK S GRAY

{volume one}
STREETS
OF NEW YORK
an **Urbanthology**

Coming Soon:

Q-Boro Books Presents

Money Power Respect
Last Temptation
Ice Cream For Freaks
Shameless
Streets of New York, Vol.2
Streets of New York Vol. 3

Mo Shines is from the Bronx, New York. He currently resides in Ohio, where he is hard at work on his next novel while simultaneously working on several film projects.

Visit his website at: www.MoShines.com